Destroy Me

Karen Cole grew up in the Cotswolds and got a degree in psychology at Newcastle University. She spent several years teaching English around the world before settling in Cyprus with her husband and two sons, where she works as an English teacher at a local school. She recently completed the Curtis Brown writing course where she found her love of writing psychological thrillers.

Also by Karen Cole

Deliver Me
Deceive Me
Deny Me

Destroy Me

KAREN COLE

Quercus

First published in Great Britain in 2021 by

Quercus Editions Ltd
Carmelite House
50 Victoria Embankment
London EC4Y 0DZ

An Hachette UK company

A CIP catalogue record for this book is available
from the British Library

PB ISBN 978 1 52941 361 8
EB ISBN 978 1 52940 382 4

10 9 8 7 6 5 4 3

Typeset by CC Book Production
Printed and bound in Great Britain by Clays Ltd, Elcograf S.p.A.

MIX
Paper from
responsible sources
FSC® C104740

Papers used by Quercus are from well-managed forests and other responsible sources.

To Pippa and Robin

Clouds sail past my window, shape-shifting as they go, and I pass the time by trying to work out what they resemble. That one, with the hint of grey at the edge, looks like a crab claw; another is like an embryo or a mermaid – I can't decide which. I wish I could defy gravity and float up there with them. It seems blissful, the idea of resting my head on a cloud. But I know that in reality a cloud would just be damp and cold, like fog.

I notice things like clouds now. I notice a lot that I never noticed before – for example, the way the leaves on the bush outside my window shiver in the wind and the spider's web that's tangled in its branches. There's no sign of the spider, but I can see a fly caught in the deceptively delicate thread. It isn't moving but that doesn't necessarily mean that it's dead.

I know how that fly feels. I know what it feels like to be trapped – how quickly anger and frustration can turn to despair; and despair to resignation. I know that prisoners try to find ways to keep their sanity – that they jealously store memories and feed off them slowly, rationing them so there will be enough to last. And that when they run out of memories their imaginations expand to fill the void. My mind often leaves my body behind and journeys to places I've never been. It soars into the sky and it plunges to the depths of the ocean with giant squid and treasure-laden shipwrecks. On good days I can appreciate the magical power of my mind.

But on bad days – and I have to admit they are more frequent than the good days lately – my mind shrinks into bitterness and recrimination, and then I start to plot and plan and think about all I have lost and who is to blame.

One

I'm in the kitchen slicing onions for tonight's spaghetti Bolognese, when I hear Dylan yelling.

'Mummy, you're on TV! Come quickly!'

The knife slips, slicing into the tip of my forefinger and I curse under my breath as blood oozes out, dribbling on to the chopping board and staining the onion pink. Tearing off a strip of paper towel, I press it into the wound. Then I scurry into the living room where I find Dylan cross-legged on the carpet, his mouth smeared with chocolate, surrounded by the debris of his Lego castle. Delilah is lying next to him, licking the chocolate wrapper. My first instinct is to snap at him. He knows that Delilah mustn't eat chocolate – that it's bad for dogs. But I pick up the wrapper, take a deep, angry breath and bite back my annoyance. He's only five years old and he's had a tough time lately. I need to remember that.

'You're too late, Mummy,' he says reproachfully. 'You were on TV. But you're gone now.'

I rub my stinging eyes, making them smart even more, and blink at the screen. The news is on; something about a climate-change protest. People are marching and chanting, holding up banners. A grey-haired woman in a tie-dyed shirt is being interviewed, proclaiming earnestly, jabbing her finger at the reporter. Maybe Dylan saw someone that looked like me in the crowd, or perhaps he simply made it up. Lately, he'll do almost anything to get my attention. Since Theo moved in with Harper, I think he's worried that if he doesn't keep tabs on me, I'll leave too. If I'm out of his sight for more than a few minutes, he panics. And several times in the last few weeks I've woken up to find that he's crawled into bed with me, his little arm clamped on to me like a limpet. I don't make him go back to his bed. If I'm honest, I like the company – I like the feel of his warm, little body breathing next to mine.

'You don't want to watch the news, do you?' I say, switching to another channel. I don't want him to see something that will distress him. He had nightmares after an episode of *Scooby Doo*, so God only knows what trauma-inducing effect a news piece about knife crime in London or war in Syria might have.

But he's lost interest in the television anyway. He's busily ripping the heads off his Lego people and stacking them one on top of the other. 'Look what I made,' he announces proudly. 'He's got one, two, three, four . . . ten heads!'

I examine his handiwork uneasily. Theo lets him watch all kinds of stuff that is way too old for him – as if he's in a rush for him to grow up. It's one of the things we argue about. *Used to* argue about. We don't argue any more. We just exchange chilly pleasantries on the doorstep and short, practical instructions about Dylan.

'Mm, that's great, sweetie,' I say brightly, squatting beside him on the carpet and running a hand over his soft, stubbly head. I'm already regretting my decision to have his beautiful black curls cropped. I thought it would make him look tougher, less of a target for bullies at his new school. But the barber went overboard with the clippers and the overall effect – his short bristles, puny body and huge eyes – makes him look more like a victim than ever.

'Are you looking forward to your first day tomorrow?' I ask anxiously. How will he cope with being separated from me? Will he make friends, or will the other kids tease him? Will his off-the-wall humour and strange, dreamy manner set him apart? I try to ignore a rogue image of him standing all alone and lost in the playground, a group of kids pointing and chanting insults at him.

'Mm,' he says, as he picks up a plastic dinosaur. 'Look, they're fighting.' He smashes the dinosaur into the man with ten heads and the heads topple, scattering over the carpet. He doesn't want to talk about tomorrow. Of course he doesn't. He's only five. Tomorrow barely exists for him. He's living in the moment. Loving life. I could learn a lot from him.

'Make sure you tidy all those up when you finish,' I say, as I head back to the kitchen. I need to stop worrying. There's no point in spending your life worrying. What good does it do? I ought to live in the moment like Dylan. I pull the medicine box out of the cupboard and root around for a plaster. Perhaps I should go back to that mindfulness course I started a while ago. What was it the coach told us? Pay attention to everything around you. Don't judge, just be aware. I wrap the plaster around my finger, watching the way the red blood seeps through the fabric. I'm not judging, just observing. Then I stare out at the sky through the window. It stares back, grey, blank and indifferent. The garden is wet from the recent rain, the leaves dripping, the grass saturated. A sparrow hops across the lawn pecking for worms. The hedge needs trimming. Theo always used to do that. No, that's a judgement. I mustn't judge. I turn back to the cooking and tip the onions into the pan, watching them sizzle. Not judging them. I breathe deeply through my nose. Tomorrow will be okay, I tell myself. Everything will be okay.

After we've eaten and Dylan's had a bath, he clambers into bed, clutching the fluffy Komodo dragon Harper bought him at London Zoo. They went about a month ago, all three of them: Theo, Dylan and Theo's girlfriend, Harper. And Dylan came back, eyes shining, full of stories about funny monkeys and how they all laughed when Harper dropped her ice cream. That's when I knew that Harper was probably a permanent fixture in Theo's life. I hate to admit it, but there's no way he would have introduced her to Dylan if he wasn't serious about her.

'Why's your face all cross, Mummy?' Dylan asks me, running his fingers along the Komodo dragon's fur.

'Is it?' I look at my reflection in the mirror on his wardrobe door and catch a glimpse of my expression. He's right. I do look cross. I look bitter, angry and old. In this light I look much older than my age, not to mention fat. A fat, bitter old hag, I think. With an effort I wipe the frown away and smile fondly at Dylan.

'I'm just tired,' I say.

'I want to sleep in your bed, please, Mummy,' Dylan begs, hopping up and down. His face is still flushed from the bath and his eyes are glittering with fatigue and excitement.

'Big boys sleep in their own beds.' I say, kissing his cheek. It's soft and smooth and he smells of talcum powder and baby shampoo. 'Now lie down.'

I sit next to him on the bed, propped against a pillow, his head resting against my belly, and read him our favourite story, 'Naughty Nelly's New Neighbours'. It's a simple but clever story about a girl whose neighbours turn out to be monsters.

'Do you think our neighbours are monsters?' Dylan asks me, wide-eyed, when I've finished. He wriggles down under the covers and pops his thumb in his mouth. I think about Eileen, who lives next door – the way she yelled at Dylan the other day for accidentally throwing his ball into her garden and the malicious gleam in her eye when I told her about Theo leaving.

'They could be,' I say. Then, catching the alarm in his eyes, I add, 'Friendly monsters, of course.'

Once Dylan's asleep I make sure his things are packed for tomorrow and I make his lunch: cheese and Marmite sandwiches, some carrot sticks and a bag of salt and vinegar crisps. Then I take a pack and eat it myself. One won't do any harm. This is day two of my diet and I'm craving sugary and salty food. I sit down at my laptop and write. My target is a thousand words a day and the deadline is looming. I'm writing a young adult book – the second in a series about a teenage ghost.

When Theo and I first married, we lived in Bristol. He had a job at a nearby school, and I worked as a local news reporter at the *Bristol Gazette*. I loved my job, but I'd always harboured a secret ambition to write a book and I spent most of my evenings and weekends scribbling away and firing off short stories to publishers and competitions without any luck. Then, shortly after Dylan was born, Theo was offered Head of Department at a school in Cirencester and we decided to move back to the town where I grew up. It's a small place and it was hard to find a job in journalism here, so I decided to make a serious attempt at writing the book I'd always dreamed of writing. And about three years ago, when Dylan was two, I saw a competition in a magazine for young adult fiction. On a whim, I sent off the first three chapters of a ghost story called *Embers*. To my amazement, I won, and just like that was given a contract for two books.

Normally, I love delving into a fictional world where anything is possible and I'm very much in control. But tonight, the words won't come. I'm trying to write the first chapter, which picks up after the end of the last book when Molly, my heroine, discovers that she died in a car accident. But for some reason, this evening, I feel completely uninspired. Every single sentence squeezes its way on to the page, painfully. After about an hour, I give up and check my phone to see if the guy from the other night has phoned me. Of course, he hasn't. Feeling disappointed but not that surprised, I pick up my laptop and wander absent-mindedly into the kitchen where I open the packet of chocolate animal biscuits I bought for Dylan and munch my way through them while I read what I've written. The whole thing seems like garbage and it doesn't tie in with the first book at all. I sigh, and reaching for another biscuit, I realise there aren't any left. I've eaten the entire jumbo-sized packet. And I've dropped crumbs all down the front of my t-shirt. My stomach seems to have grown exponentially in the last five minutes, bulging over the top of my jeans. What would Sara at Weight Watchers say? What would Luke think if he did actually phone for another date?

Feeling frustrated and disgusted with myself, I delete the whole chapter. Then I check my messages on Facebook. I have two Facebook accounts – one for me and one for 'Ophelia Black', my alter ego. Ophelia Black is the pseudonym dreamed up by the publishing team for *Embers* because they thought that my real name, Catherine Bayntun, was too difficult to spell and not very sellable.

On my real Facebook page my friend Gaby has sent me a message asking what happened after she left the other night. Ophelia Black has two: one from some obscure magazine asking me to answer a few questions and another from someone called George Wilkinson. I open the message from George. There's no writing, just a photograph – a picture of a gravestone.

Weird.

The headstone looks relatively new, shiny and black. The inscription is obscured by a vase of pink roses; just the last letter of the name is visible. I enlarge the image, but I still can't read it. The last letter could be an R, but I am not sure.

Why would anyone send me a picture of a grave? It's slightly unnerving. Is it some kind of threat? No, it's probably just a fan trying to spark a new idea for a sequel to *Embers*, I decide. I click on George's profile. He looks like an ordinary middle-aged man from Wisconsin in the USA. In the picture, he's grinning at the camera. He's wearing a baseball cap and has a bushy moustache. He doesn't look like the kind of person who would read *Embers*. He's way too old for a start. I close the page. It's nothing, I tell myself. George Wilkinson has clearly mistaken me for another Ophelia Black. But even so, I feel a twinge of unease as I snap the laptop shut and head to the living room.

In the living room, I set up the ironing board to iron Dylan's school shirts and switch on the TV, catching the end of the evening news. After the weather forecast, the local news comes on. The newscaster is talking about a pile-up on the A417, but I'm not really listening. I'm still wondering why George from Wisconsin sent me that message.

But when I happen to glance up at the TV, I notice that the woman reading the news is looking particularly serious. She's talking about a crime that was committed on Friday night – a grisly murder, and in Cecily Hill of all places! It's just a ten minute walk from here. I put the iron down. I'm shocked. That kind of crime just doesn't happen in this sleepy Cotswold town. It's a place where people come to retire – a pretty, peaceful place where people get up in arms when someone builds an extension without planning permission or because the new pavements caused someone to break their hip. Even the news anchor looks visibly shaken as she relates the details. The police, she says, aren't sure about the exact time the victim was killed, but they have revealed that she was stabbed no fewer than four times in the chest.

Then a picture flashes up on the screen and everything else is completely wiped from my mind. I forget the ironing. I forget Wisconsin George. I even forget Dylan. I can't think of anything but the image dominating the screen. Time stops and the world around me blurs and stretches into lightning-fast shrieks of meaningless colour. It's just me and that picture in a universe which suddenly makes no sense.

'This woman was seen on Friday night near the scene of the crime,' says the news reader grimly. 'She is thought to be in her early thirties, and she was wearing a white t-shirt with blue jeans. Police are appealing for her or anyone who knows her to come forward and help the police with their enquiries.'

It's a computer-generated photofit of a woman with a plump, round face and long, brown, wavy hair. Except for the fact that her skin is a little too smooth, and her face is expressionless, making her look slightly plastic, the image is very realistic. She's got a high forehead, thick, arched eyebrows and there's even a small brown mole on her left cheek. She's an ordinary-looking woman – entirely unremarkable. She looks like the best friend in a movie – the one who inexplicably spends all her time worrying about the beautiful heroine and doesn't appear to have a life of her own. You certainly wouldn't single her out in a crowd, but nevertheless, her features make up a face that, like every face on the planet, is unique as a fingerprint.

And Dylan was right. She looks exactly like me.

Two

How is that even possible?

I was nowhere near Cecily Hill on Friday night. It must be a coincidence – a chance resemblance. They say everyone has a doppelganger, don't they? This must be mine. But a deep feeling of unease crawls into my belly. How plausible is it that someone who lives in the same town as me looks exactly like me?

I barely have time to process it all before the news anchor peers gravely into my living room and drops another bombshell. This time it's the victim: a photograph of a woman about my age, grinning at the camera, punching her hands above her head in triumph on top of a mountain. More images flash up. She's at a party, her arms linked with friends; then she's on a beach, holding up a cocktail glass. The implication: this is a woman who lived life to the full, making her murder even more despicable – her death even more poignant.

'Charlotte Holbrooke, known to her friends as Charlie, was found dead in her flat on Saturday night. She had been stabbed four times.' She continues, her eyes misting with tears. 'She was married just last month.'

We are shown a photo of Charlie in a wedding dress with her husband, a man called Adam. They're standing under a sort of arbour, gazing into each other's eyes. He is handsome, square-jawed, with floppy, blond hair and piercing blue eyes. Then they show another photo of the happy couple on their honeymoon, in front of a wintry scene of Rome, the rooftops speckled with snow. Both are pink-faced and smiling in woolly hats and scarves. They look happy and in love.

'If you were in the Cecily Hill area on Friday night or in the early hours of Saturday morning and saw anything suspicious, please get in touch,' the newsreader implores as a phone number rolls across the bottom of the screen below her. 'And if you saw this woman –' that impossible picture fills the screen again – 'or know who she might be, please contact us.'

My hand is shaking as I switch off the TV.

I don't drink much as a rule. And I certainly never drink alone. But right now, it seems like the appropriate response. The only response to such an outrageous shock. I stumble into the kitchen and pour myself a vodka – a present from Gaby last summer, from her visit to Russia – and I gulp it down. The liquid burns my throat and I wince, but I carry on until the glass is drained. This can't be a coincidence.

Because I know her. I know the victim. Charlotte Holbrooke. Charlie. She used to be Charlotte Kent before she married, but I would recognise her anywhere.

It must have been . . . what? At least seventeen years since I last saw her. But she hasn't changed. She still has that same thick head of amber-coloured hair, the same heart-shaped face and bright hazel eyes. Still *had*, I remind myself. She has changed now, of course. She's dead. Charlie is dead. You can't change much more than that.

I pour myself another vodka, this time tempering it with orange juice. I try to remember the last time I saw Charlie. It must have been just before we left for uni. We were sitting in a pub garden at a damp wooden table. I don't remember much of what we said or why we were there. All I remember is Charlie, pale and unusually serious, saying, 'This is it, Cat. We're off to start new lives. Let's keep in touch.'

I think we both knew, even then, that her words were hollow – that there was no way we would stay in contact; that our friendship was ruined for ever.

The acrid smell of burning wafts into my nostrils.

Shit.

16

I rush back into the living room. Black smoke is billowing from the iron.

Shit.

I lift it up and uncover a large black scorch mark imprinted on clean white cotton. It's burned a hole right through to the ironing board.

Shit shit shit. I only bought that shirt today. I'll have to throw it away now.

I switch off the iron, toss the shirt into the bin outside and slump down on the sofa, clinging to the armrest, digging my nails into the velvet cover. The room seems to be swaying, lurching from side to side. Fear grips my throat so that I can barely breathe, blackness curling at the edge of my mind.

This can't be happening. Charlie has been murdered. My old school friend Charlie has been murdered and the police are looking for someone who looks exactly like me.

Someone must have given the police this description. After all, that's how they make photofits, by adjusting the image until the witness is satisfied that it looks like the person they saw. But who? And why? Could it be a deliberate attempt to incriminate me? Why would anyone want to do that? I am an ordinary thirty-five-year-old woman, who lives her life trying to be kind and trying not to cause offence. I don't have any enemies.

I try to hang on to facts that make sense. *What was I doing on Friday evening?* But right now, panic floods through me, banishing rational thought. I can't remember. *What was I doing?* I dropped off Dylan at Theo's flat and then what? *I wasn't there*, I try to reassure myself. *I didn't do it. I can't be charged with something I didn't do.*

Then it comes back to me. Of course, how could I forget? After Weight Watchers, we went for a drink at the Black Bear in Tetbury, Gaby and me. And we met that guy there – Luke. He drove me home and he spent the night. The first time I've had sex with someone other than Theo for at least eight years.

I go to the kitchen and make myself a cup of tea, beginning to feel a little calmer. If the worst comes to the worst, I have a solid alibi at least. I wasn't alone for even a minute on Friday night. I'm sipping the soothing hot liquid when the phone rings loud in my little house, making my heart strike against my chest. The police have made the link already, I think, in a blind panic. They're phoning to ask me to come to the station.

But I needn't have worried. It's not the police. It's Theo.

'You wouldn't believe what I just saw on the news,' he says cheerfully.

'I saw it,' I say tersely. My heart rate slowing slightly.

'There's been a murder and the photofit . . .'

'I saw it.'

'You must have a twin,' he chuckles. 'An evil twin.'

This is just an amusing diversion for him. It's annoying, but also, in a weird way, reassuring. If he thinks it's funny, maybe I'm taking it too much to heart. Of course, no one could take this seriously. I'm a law-abiding citizen, a mother of a young child. I've never been in trouble with the police. I've never even had so much as a speeding ticket.

There's a silence on the other end of the phone.

'What do you want, Theo?' I ask, feeling suddenly weary.

'Can I speak to Dylan?' he asks. I picture Theo on the other end of the phone squashing his lower lip together between his thumb and his forefinger, the way he does when he's thinking. I know his every gesture and, for a second, I feel a longing so intense it takes my breath away. I want him here with me right now. I need him to laugh and shrug and make everything seem okay.

'He's asleep already,' I say coldly. 'He's starting school tomorrow.'

'Oh, that's right. I forgot. Oh well, wish him luck from me. Shall I pick him up on Friday?'

'Yes, I'll let his teacher know.' I don't relish the idea of explaining our domestic situation to the teacher, but I suppose it has to be done.

'Are you okay, Cat?' He sounds almost like he really cares.

'Yes, I'm fine. Bye, Theo, see you soon.'

'Goodnight.'

I hang up, trying not to picture Theo's face on the pillow

19

next to mine, his warm breath on my cheek – the way he would always say 'goodnight' and kiss me, before rolling over to his side of the bed. *At least I can spread out now*, I think. *I can sleep on whichever side I like.* When Dylan isn't in bed with me, I sleep diagonally across the bed just for the hell of it. I fold up the ironing board, telling myself that space in a bed is a good substitute for a living, breathing man.

Then I go into my bedroom and fire up the computer. Logging on to Facebook, I find Charlie's profile.

Messages have gone up on her page already. Charlotte Holbrooke. *We are heartbroken. Heaven has another angel. A beautiful soul. You were a friend I was proud to know. Have a margarita for me in heaven.*

Tears prick at the back of my eyes. It's been a long time since I saw Charlie. But she was important to me at a time in my life when feelings were raw and friendships more intense. And I suppose I loved her. Reckless, fun, crazy Charlie. I picture her curled up in my parents' armchair, smoking a spliff or balancing precariously on the school wall, laughing as Mr Baker shouted at her to get down.

But I am ambushed by another memory. Driving home from a party. Charlie leaning out of the car window like a dog, her hair flying behind her. Me shouting over the roar of the engine. 'Get in, Charlie. You're going to kill yourself!' And her just leaning further out, yelling, 'Live a little, Cat. You know what they say . . .'

I shut down the computer.

Charlie always lived dangerously. She liked to take risks and push things to their limit. But I could never have predicted that her life would have ended like this – so violently; so horribly. *What happened to you, Charlie?* I wonder as I head to bed. *Did you get yourself involved in something you shouldn't have?*

Three

A pale silver sun is nudging through the morning cloud as we walk to Dylan's new school. He hops along beside me, down the river path and past the horses swishing their tails in the field. Despite the rain yesterday, the water level in the river is low, and I can see all the rubbish that has accumulated at the bottom. A family of ducks is waddling carefully over the Coke cans and weeds, no doubt wondering where all the water has gone.

Green Park Primary School is an old stone building at the far end of town. It's changed a lot since I went there. In our day, the fence was on the road. Now it's all high walls and security. In the playground, parents are milling around. A few of them are taking photos of their children – girls in checked green and white dresses with buttoned-up cardigans and boys in grey shorts and green jumpers posing on the steps of the school. I wish I'd remembered to bring my phone to record Dylan's first day. But I was too preoccupied with other things this morning, worrying about that news report last night. Will any of the other parents recognise me? I've scraped my hair back and worn a baseball cap and sunglasses in an attempt to disguise myself. But judging by all the strange glances I'm getting it hasn't worked. I try to ignore the huddle of mothers whispering by the pagoda, and make my way straight to the classroom, head down, gripping Dylan's hand tightly.

'Ouch, Mummy, you're hurting,' he says as I climb the steps to Mrs Bailey's classroom.

'Sorry, baby,' I say, letting go of his hand.

'I'm not a baby. I'm a big boy.'

'Yes, of course you are.' I force a smile. *Please God let them not say anything to their children about me. They wouldn't, would they?* I try not to imagine Dylan surrounded by a group of kids chanting, 'Your mummy's a murderer'.

'Dylan, welcome!' exclaims Mrs Bailey with a saccharine smile. That's right. I'd forgotten he came here with Theo for the induction, so she already knows him. Dylan hesitates, his fingers digging into my hand.

Mrs Bailey stoops over so she's at his eye level. Her eyes glitter blue in a soft, faded face, her grey hair coils artfully over her neck. She has a wispy baby voice which seems incongruous in a woman of her age.

'Do you think you can you find your name on the board?' she whispers to him, as if they're sharing a secret, and Dylan smiles shyly, nods and heads to the corkboard where laminated name cards shaped like butterflies are Velcroed.

'That's right, well done!' she exclaims as he pulls one off. Then she straightens up, looks at me for the first time and does a double take.

'Have we met before?' she asks, frowning.

'No, my husband came to the induction. My ex-husband,' I correct myself.

'Oh, okay,' her eyes narrow thoughtfully. 'I could have sworn . . .'

Her voice trails off and she fiddles with the glasses on a chain around her neck. Then she turns to another parent, a hassled-looking father in jogging gear, and beams at him. How long will it take her to connect my face to the photofit she most likely saw last night? I wonder. More parents and kids are arriving. A little girl is screaming, trying to drag her mother away. I feel like screaming too. I just want to get out of here. The walls seem to be closing in and I feel exposed, as though everyone's staring at me, whispering about me. At least Dylan seems fine. He's trotting off hand in hand with the teaching assistant without so much as a backward glance.

'See you later, Dyl,' I call, but he doesn't hear me, and I duck out of the classroom while he's distracted.

I scurry out of the playground, head down, hoping no one else will recognise me. I'm staring at the concrete, trying to avoid eye contact as I turn out of the school gate and I don't notice the woman right in front of me, rushing in the other direction, clutching the hand of a little boy. We collide and her handbag drops, the contents spilling out.

'I'm so sorry!' I exclaim, helping her to scoop up the purse and lipstick and various scraps of paper and receipts.

'No, no, it's my fault,' the woman says breathlessly. 'We shouldn't have been running. We're late. You wouldn't believe the morning I've had!' She stands up and smiles at me benignly. She's tall and pretty, with bright red lipstick, sleek black hair and friendly grey eyes. I steel myself for a change in her expression, a flicker of recognition or for her features to harden into suspicion. But they don't. *She clearly hasn't seen the news*, I think, breathing with relief.

'We're looking for Butterflies classroom,' she says. 'Weird name for a class, isn't it?'

I nod and grin. 'It's over there,' I tell her, pointing to the new one-storey block. 'My son is in Butterflies too.'

'Is he really?' She seems to take more of an interest in this fact than it merits. 'What's his name?'

'Er, Dylan. Dylan Bayntun.'

'Mummee,' the little boy tugs at her arm impatiently.

'I'm sorry. I've got to go,' she laughs as she's dragged

away. 'But I'm sure we'll get to know each other later. I'm Georgia, by the way.'

Georgia seems nice, I think, as I walk back through the centre of town. It would be useful to make friends with some of the mothers at Dylan's school. It will help him make friends too . . . but how likely is it that Georgia will want to socialise with me after she sees that photofit?

Halfway home, on impulse, I stop outside Curl Up and Dye and look at the list of prices pinned on the door. It's always struck me as an amusingly bad name for a hairdresser. I mean it's not exactly encouraging, is it? Is that how you will feel after your haircut, like you want to curl up and die? But I can't feel much more like curling up and dying than I currently do. And it doesn't matter if my hair is cut well. I just want to look as different as possible from the way I look now.

The salon smells of ammonia and the radio is on, playing a jangling tune. A skinny assistant with jagged blonde hair and a nose ring sashays up to a sort of podium with an appointments book on it and gives me a chilly smile.

'Yes?' she says.

'I'd like my hair cut and dyed, please.'

She takes up a pen and sucks the end. 'When would you like to come?'

'Er, now, if possible.'

She looks around the empty salon. 'Um well . . . okay. Take a seat,' she says reluctantly and bustles away into a back room. So I sit and wait, flicking through a magazine, reading a story about a woman who had an affair with her daughter's husband. I don't get to the end of the story to learn what the daughter did when she found out, because the assistant bustles back with a stylist who introduces herself as Cheryl and ushers me to a chair in front of the mirror.

I stare at my reflection as she combs through the tangles and examines my split ends dubiously.

'So, what do you want done?' she asks.

I take a deep breath. 'I want it cut short, in a bob. About your length and blonde.'

Cheryl purses her lips. 'Are you sure? That's quite a drastic change.'

'I'm sure.' *The more dramatic the better*, I think. All I can see when I look at myself is that appalling photofit.

Cheryl shrugs and fetches me a colour chart. 'What do you like?' she asks.

I stab my finger at a shade on the lighter end of the spectrum.

'Beeline Honey?' Cheryl frowns. 'Are you sure you wouldn't like something a little darker, like Hot Toffee or Havana Brown?'

'No, I want Beeline Honey or maybe Medium Champagne,' I say firmly. 'I need a change. I'm getting a divorce.'

'Oh, I see.' She nods and smiles – a warm smile this time, and her face is transformed. 'You want a revenge haircut.'

'Something like that.'

'Well, I'll see what I can do.' The mention of my divorce has softened her and I think she feels she can relate to me now because she spends the next half an hour or so, while my hair is cooking, telling me all about her ex-boyfriend, Sam, who cheated on her.

'God, I hate Sam,' I say when she pauses for breath, and she laughs.

'Yeah, Sam and your husband, what a pair of losers,' she says, switching on the blow dryer and drowning out my answer.

'It looks lovely,' she says, holding up a mirror behind my head and admiring her handiwork when she's finished.

I swivel my head in front of the mirror and my hair swishes and falls in a sleek blonde sheet. The result is really weird. I look like a successful, professional woman. Nothing like the photofit. Nothing like me.

'Thank you,' I say, paying her. 'You've done a great job.'

There's nothing like a new haircut to boost your mood and I walk home feeling much calmer and more hopeful. Every so often, I catch a glimpse of myself in a shop window and I see a woman I don't recognise as me. I don't even look all that fat, I decide. *This is the start of a new chapter in my life,*

I think. I'm going to take care of myself. No more binge eating, no more worrying and I'm going to always be kind and patient with Dylan. Perhaps I'll even go to the gym. Now I've dyed my hair, no one will make the connection between me and that photofit. I turn into my street, my hair bouncing like a shampoo ad, my confidence soaring.

But on the corner I stop abruptly and steady myself on a garden wall, fighting the instinct to turn and run. Because way down at the other end of the street I see something that makes my heart freeze.

There's a police car parked right outside my house.

Four

At number fifteen a curtain twitches and I catch a glimpse of Eileen Robinson peering out from the gloom of her living room, her pale moon face stained with malice. For a second, our eyes meet. Then she presses her lips together and jerks the curtains closed. No prizes for guessing who recognised the photofit and called the police.

I've done nothing wrong. I've no need to worry, I tell myself as I make my way up the road. Even so, my legs buckle and my heart races when I reach my house. I walk right past the police car, my head held high, pretending I haven't noticed the two officers sitting inside. Then I open my front gate and step on to the path, but the sound of the car door slamming behind me jolts through my whole body.

'Catherine Bayntun?' says a voice and I turn, polite surprise plastered on my face.

'Yes?' I say, trying to keep my voice calm.

A middle-aged woman with short, grey–blonde hair and a careworn face is holding out her hand. Just behind her, a young, plump man with a florid complexion is smiling awkwardly.

'I'm Detective Inspector Littlewood and this is Sergeant Fisher,' says the woman. 'Can we come in and have a quick word?'

'Sure.' I fumble with the lock, hoping they haven't noticed that my hand is trembling as I push open the door.

'Lovely dog,' Sergeant Fisher says, patting Delilah on the head, taking in the Lego, still sprawled all over the floor, the crumbs on the sofa and the wilting pot plant on the windowsill.

'I like your hairdo.' DI Littlewood perches on the edge of the sofa and appraises me with shrewd blue eyes. 'Have you been to the hairdresser's recently?'

I touch the back of my head self-consciously. Was it a mistake? Does changing my appearance so drastically make me look guilty – as if I have something to hide?

'Yes, I went just this morning,' I say warily.

'Very nice.'

'Thank you.'

There's an awkward silence. They're clearly not here to chat about my hair. 'Er . . . would you like a drink? Tea, coffee?' I offer.

'No thanks, Catherine,' DI Littlewood, smiles. Her manner is genial, pally almost. But her eyes are sharp, and they seem to take in everything and cut straight through my new look to the soft, scared core of me.

'We're looking into the death of Charlotte Holbrooke,' she says. 'The woman that was murdered in her home a couple of days ago.' She pauses, watching my reaction carefully. I try to assemble my features into the correct response, though I'm not sure what that is. Shock? Surprise? 'It's just a routine enquiry,' she adds in a way that I guess is supposed to be reassuring. 'Did you know her at all?'

At this moment, if you could see inside my brain, it would look like a herd of wildebeest, stampeding in all directions.

'Er, no . . . well, that is yes. I mean I saw her on TV last night.'

DI Littlewood arches her eyebrows and exchanges a meaningful look with Sergeant Fisher.

My cheeks are burning. Why am I behaving as if I'm guilty? Why didn't I just admit I know her? The police can easily find out the truth and when they do, I'll look even more suspicious.

'Actually,' I blurt, my face hot, 'I did know her a long time ago. We went to school together. But I haven't seen her in years.'

'Oh?' DI Littlewood nods, revealing nothing. Sergeant

Fisher smiles awkwardly, sits down on a toy car, picks it up and places it on the coffee table. Delilah sits next to him, wagging her tail and watching him intently. He scratches behind her ears and clears his throat. 'Can we ask where you were last Friday night, the thirtieth of August.' he asks. 'Were you anywhere near the town centre?'

'No, of course I wasn't,' I say quickly. Too quickly.

DI Littlewood observes me with polite curiosity. 'Where were you, if you don't mind me asking?'

And if I do mind? I think. Out loud I just say: 'Um what time?'

'Why don't you tell us about your whole night. From six pm until the morning?'

'Friday?' I've had time to think, rehearse this in my head. I know what to say. 'I dropped off Dylan, that's my son, with my ex at about six o'clock. He takes him every other weekend. Then I went to Weight Watchers.'

'Weight Watchers?' DI Littlewood jots something down in her notebook. 'You don't look like you need Weight Watchers,' she adds politely.

'No, well I lost a couple of stone after my husband left. It turns out divorce is the best diet ever,' I laugh bitterly. 'I should probably write a book about it. Sod the Keto diet, try the Divorce diet.'

Sergeant Fisher rubs his round belly and chuckles.

'Divorce didn't work for me. I could probably do with going to Weight Watchers myself, though I don't know how I'd handle all that being-weighed-in-front-of-everyone stuff. Where do you meet?'

'In the Phoenix Centre.' I rummage in a drawer and hand him a flier with Sara's phone number on it. 'Sara Walters is our coach. If you speak to her, she'll confirm that I was there.' Sara knows everyone in this small, rural town and she loves to gossip, so if there's anyone that didn't already know that I'm a suspect in a murder case, they will now. But I don't really have a choice. I need this alibi.

'Did you go straight there from your ex-husband's place?' Sergeant Fisher asks, leaning forward, sucking the end of his pen.

'Yes.'

'And how long were you there? At Weight Watchers, I mean.'

'About an hour. But after that . . . I went for a drink.'

'Where?'

'At the Black Bear.'

'The Black Bear?' Littlewood frowns and purses her lips. 'I don't know it.'

'It's in Tewkesbury.'

'Tewkesbury? That's quite a long way to go for a drink . . .' The way she says this makes it sound suspicious. Then again, she manages to make everything I say sound suspicious.

'Yes, my friend wanted to see the band that was playing there.'

'Oh, so you went with a friend?'

'Yes, from Weight Watchers. Her name is Gaby. Gaby Wright.'

Littlewood puts on her glasses and jots the name down. 'Do you have a contact number for her?'

I give her Gaby's number. *Gaby will back me up*, I think. Gaby and I will have a laugh about this when it's all over. But the questions are coming hard and fast and I've no idea how a murder investigation is usually conducted, but I'm beginning to think they're being quite thorough if I'm someone they don't view as a person of interest.

'Just Gaby?' Littlewood peers at me over the top of her glasses. It makes her look like a strict schoolteacher, one who's caught you cheating on an exam.

'Yes.'

'So, what? You had a few drinks? How long were you there?'

'Until closing time and then I went home.'

'Alone?'

'Not exactly,' I admit, and I flush with embarrassment. An image flashes into my mind. A handsome face, black hair, luminous green eyes, a pale, gym-toned stomach. Luke.

'Oh?' DI Littlewood leans forward and picks up her pen.

'I met someone at the pub. His name is Luke . . .' I break

off, realising that I never asked his second name. I'm not even sure that Luke is his real name.

'And when you got home. Did you go in alone?' She catches my expression. 'I'm sorry if this seems nosy, but it could be important.'

'No, he came with me. He stayed the night.' I say. My cheeks are on fire now.

Sergeant Fisher tries to hide a smirk behind his hand and DI Littlewood stares studiously at a spot above my head. *My sex life is none of their business*, I think crossly. *I'm a grown woman. I'm single. If I want to sleep with a man I barely know, that's up to me.*

'So how did you meet . . . this . . . Luke?' she asks, stressing the name, as if she has doubts that he's real.

'Er . . . we just got chatting in the pub.' *My business*, I think firmly.

'Right. And what time did he leave?'

'He left in the morning. I'm not sure what time, but it was light.' I remember that when I woke up that morning daylight was streaming in through the gap in the blinds and Luke was already dressed in the suit he'd been wearing the night before. He must have showered and used my toothpaste because he smelled fresh and clean as he bent over me and kissed me on my bare shoulder.

'You were out for the count,' he grinned, kissing my neck

again, and I breathed in his scent, trying to keep my mouth closed, so he wouldn't smell my morning breath.

'But I didn't want to leave without saying goodbye,' he said. 'And thank you for a beautiful evening. I've got to go to work. I'll call you, okay?'

I close my eyes, trying not to think about how happy I was that morning. How excited and buoyant, like a child. Is it possible that that was just a few days ago? I feel a century has passed since then.

'He had to go to work, so I'm guessing it was about eight, eight-thirty.' As I say it, I wonder if he really had to work or if that was just an excuse to get out quickly. Of course, he never had any intention of calling me.

'Do you have a contact address or number, just so we can verify your account of the evening?' Littlewood asks.

'No,' I admit sheepishly.

She clears her throat. 'What about your ex-husband? Can you give us his address and phone number?'

'Why? What's Theo got to do with anything?' I'm getting a little impatient and nervousness is making me antsy.

'We'd just like to talk to him, that's all. Get a complete picture.'

Picture of what? Reluctantly, I scribble down Theo's address and number on the back of an envelope. I can imagine Harper will have a field day when she finds out I'm a suspect in a murder case.

'How would you describe your relationship with your ex?' Sergeant Fisher sits back, lacing his fingers over his belly.

'Um, civil. We're trying to keep it friendly for our little boy's sake.'

'Very commendable. My ex and I don't speak . . . or if we do, it's only in four-letter words.' He chuckles.

DI Littlewood throws him an icy look – clearly, he's deviating from the script.

There's a silence while DI Littlewood looks around, her sharp eyes scouring the room, and Sergeant Fisher leans back, his arm draped along the back of the sofa.

'You haven't asked us why we're asking you all these questions,' he says. 'You must be wondering.'

I nod slightly. Of course, I already know why, but I'm unsure whether it's wise to let them know that.

DI Littlewood clears her throat and hands me a printout. 'A witness provided us with this description of a woman they saw outside Charlotte's flat the night she was murdered,' she says.

The paper trembles in my hand. I take a deep breath and glance down at the picture. It's the same image I saw on TV last night. My own eyes stare mildly back at me from the page. Instinctively, I reach up and touch the mole on my cheek – the one mirrored on the photofit. I wasn't imagining the resemblance last night. If anything, on closer inspection it looks even more like me.

'Of course, now your hair is blonde you look a little different,' DI Littlewood is saying. Her voice seems to be coming from a long way away, as if I'm underwater and she's on the surface calling down to me. 'But I think you'll agree that it's uncanny.'

I try to laugh, but it comes out as a sort of frightened squeak. 'Yes, I saw it on the news. It does look like me, I know. But obviously it's not. You can't seriously think . . .'

I wait for them to laugh with me – to reassure me that it is indeed ridiculous. But DI Littlewood just gives me a small, thin smile and Fisher gazes at me thoughtfully, tapping his fingers against his thigh.

'Witness testimony is notoriously unreliable,' says DI Littlewood. 'But you have to agree it's a strange coincidence. How would you explain it?'

I breathe slowly through my nose. My heart is racing in my chest. I can't let them see how rattled I am. That will only make them suspect me more.

'I don't know,' I shrug helplessly. 'Maybe the witness mixed me up with someone else or saw me another time and got muddled about when they saw me. Who gave you the photofit?'

Littlewood exchanges a glance with Fisher. 'I'm afraid we can't reveal that information,' she says evenly.

'You can't think of anyone who would want to hurt

you? Cause trouble for you?' asks Fisher. 'Do you have any enemies?'

'No, of course not.' *Harper maybe*, I think. *But I would want to cause trouble for her more than she would for me. She's the one who wronged me, not the other way around.*

There's another long, awkward silence while they both stare at me curiously. I'm starting to think it might be a tactic. Some people can't bear silences. Perhaps they think that if they're silent long enough, I'll start talking and incriminate myself. Well, I'm not falling into their trap. I fold my arms in front of my chest and meet their gaze defiantly. Then, I look pointedly at my watch. 'I've got to go and pick up my son from school soon,' I say.

'At eleven o'clock?' Littlewood says sceptically.

'Yes, it's his first day. He's finishing early.'

'Okay, well . . .' she stands up slowly and Sergeant Fisher follows suit. 'I think that's about all for now. Thank you very much for your time, Mrs Bayntun. We'll be in touch.'

Is it my imagination or does it sound like a threat?

Five

It's started raining while we've been talking and Littlewood and Fisher dash to their car, holding their bags over their heads. After they've gone, I close the door firmly behind them, lock it and head to the kitchen where I rip off the picture of the skinny model in a bikini I have sellotaped to the fridge. I tear it up and throw it in the bin. Then I root through the fridge, cut myself a large chunk of cheese and shovel it into my mouth. After that, I open a packet of Penguin biscuits and steadily munch my way through them. I eat automatically without even tasting, and I know even as I'm doing it that it's not a good idea, that I'll regret it later, but I can't seem to control myself. The food slips down my throat. It has a welcome numbing effect on my mind.

'Food is not your friend, Cat.' I hear Theo's voice in my

head. It almost feels as if he's standing behind me. I can see his raised eyebrows, the slight amused curl of his lips.

Fuck off, Theo, I think. *You don't get to judge me any more. Not after what you've done to me.* He always said he didn't mind my generous curves, even when I piled on a couple of extra stone after Dylan was born. He always *said* all the right things – that he loved me the way I was, that it just meant there was more of me to love. Well, actions speak louder than words and his words turned out to be worthless lies. He lost the right to have anything to do with my life after he cheated on me with Harper. Harper, of all people! Waiflike Harper, who looks as if a strong gust of wind could blow her away.

The chocolate sticks to my tongue and teeth and I stare angrily out of the window at the rain. Is there any way I could be mistaken about Friday night? I had quite a lot to drink, and my memory of the evening is patchy. Could I have been near Charlie's house or even on Cecily Hill for some reason? Perhaps Luke stopped off there when he drove me home. I can't remember much about the drive home apart from a vague memory of the warm smell of leather, Luke's lips on mine, the tang of whisky on his tongue.

But why would Luke have driven to Cecily Hill on the way from Tewkesbury to my house? It makes no sense. It's a dead end and only leads to the park.

I scour my mind, going through the events of that evening again, slowly and methodically.

Everything I told the police was the truth – more or less. I might have left out some tiny details, but the bare bones are correct.

It's true, for example, that it was about six when I dropped Dylan off at his father's. Dylan had whimpered a little and clung to my leg as I tried to leave, and I got a mean and petty satisfaction from the flicker of hurt I saw in Theo's eyes. A small taste of what rejection feels like, I thought. But my satisfaction was short-lived because Harper appeared at the door soon after, looking radiant, young, slender and beautiful.

She had a packet of chocolate biscuits, which she held out to Dylan as if he were a dog she was training.

He stopped crying immediately and took one. He would sell his own grandmother for a chocolate biscuit. He's his mother's son.

'He shouldn't be having a biscuit before his tea,' I said coldly.

'One little treat won't do him any harm,' she replied airily, looking at me as if she saw right through to my hypocrisy. 'Come on, Dylan,' she said, holding out her hand, 'do you want to see what we've got for you in your room? I'll give you a clue. It starts with d . . . and ends in aur.'

'Dinosaur!' yelled Dylan, rushing in.

Ever since Harper moved in with Theo, she's been trying to win Dylan over by buying him a series of ridiculously expensive presents. And I was sure this would be no ordinary dinosaur. This would be the kind that lights up, walks and roars. I wouldn't mind if I thought that she genuinely loved Dylan and wanted to make him happy, but I'm pretty sure she only does it to annoy me.

I sighed and handed her Dylan's overnight bag.

She gave me a small, triumphant smile and closed the door.

I was still fuming as I drove from Theo's to Weight Watchers, so I wasn't really concentrating on my route, but I'm certain that I didn't drive anywhere near Cecily Hill. Why would I have?

Weight Watchers passed uneventfully. Sara monologued a lot as usual, mainly about her troubles at work, and we discussed some new low-calorie recipes. The thing about Weight Watchers is that everyone there is completely obsessed with food and we spend all our time talking about cooking and recipes. It's like going to an AA meeting and talking about the best cocktails to make.

'Anyone fancy a drink?' asked Gaby, as she always does, when we were leaving. Gaby is younger than the rest of us and hasn't got any kids, so she hasn't completely given up on the idea of a social life.

Most people made their excuses – they had babysitters to get back to or their favourite TV series to watch. Normally, I would have made some excuse too. Being woken up at six am by Dylan every morning makes it hard to stay awake after ten o'clock, let alone be good company. But I couldn't bear the idea of going home to an empty house – to the gaping silence of my life without Theo and Dylan. I knew if I went home, all I would do would be obsess over what a bitch Harper is and eat a pile of junk food.

'Sure,' I said. 'Why not?'

'Great.' Gaby beamed at me. 'I know a great little pub. It's a bit of a drive but you'll like it. You might be able to do some research for that book you're writing. It's really old and meant to be one of the most haunted pubs in England. And there's a great band playing there tonight.'

'So, how are things?' Gaby asked, once we were ensconced in a corner of the Black Bear, near the fireplace. 'How's Dylan?'

She rested her chin in her hands and gave me a quizzical look from bright brown eyes. Her hair, as usual, was a dishevelled mass of black curls and it looked as if she hadn't changed after her work at the dog shelter. There were a couple of dog hairs clinging to her black top and what looked like part of a leaf caught up in her curls.

'Dylan's with his dad,' I said picking the leaf out of her hair. 'And things aren't great. I just feel so angry and tense

45

all the time. Harper was there with Theo when I dropped off Dylan this evening.'

I paused for breath. It felt good to offload to Gaby. I knew she was on my side. We'd been friends for a while, bonding over a shared love of food and dogs. Gaby had two German Shepherds of her own, which we sometimes walked together with Delilah. But we hadn't become really close until Theo and I separated. Gaby divorced her husband over a year ago after he cheated on her and she's been supportive, almost enthusiastic, about my separation from Theo.

'That sucks,' Gaby sympathised. 'But you need to try to forget about Theo and Harper. They're not part of your life any more.'

I was about to point out that it's difficult to forget about someone who you share a child with, but Gaby probably wouldn't have understood, not having any kids of her own, though apparently the custody battle over the German Shepherds was long and bitter. Anyway, she was following her own train of thought.

'What you need is a good shag,' she said helpfully, with typical directness. 'When's the last time you had sex?'

I rolled my eyes and smiled. 'That's none of your business,' I replied evasively.

Her big brown eyes widened. 'Oh my God you haven't, have you? Not since Theo.'

'Well, no ... To be honest, offers haven't exactly been flooding in. I can't imagine why.' I patted my still generous belly and thighs and laughed. 'I mean, who could resist this?'

'Don't put yourself down,' Gaby said firmly. Then she inclined her head towards someone sitting nearby, just out of my eyeline. 'What about that guy over there? He's been looking at you since we came in. And he's drop-dead gorgeous.'

I looked over my shoulder. It wasn't hard to guess who she meant. He was sitting by himself, dressed in a suit, as if he'd come straight from work. He was nursing a shot glass, staring broodingly at the liquid inside. As I glanced over, he caught my eye and smiled. His smile was self-assured, bordering on cocky and full of a kind of warm intent that made the heat rise in my cheeks.

'Not my type,' I pronounced firmly.

Gaby laughed. 'What do you mean he's not your type? Look at him. He's everybody's type.'

'Well for starters, he's way too young for me. And I prefer skinny, intellectual-looking men.'

Gaby snorted. 'Like Theo, you mean? Why don't you try a real man for a change?'

I knew that Gaby was just trying to make me feel better by knocking the man who had betrayed me, but I couldn't help feeling vaguely insulted.

47

Angrily, I brushed away thoughts of Theo. I didn't owe him any loyalty now. Why should I feel offended on his behalf? I glanced back over at the man in the suit. He had loosened his tie and was scrolling through his phone. If I was honest, he was undeniably attractive. 'What's he doing here on his own?' I asked. 'It's weird. Anyway, a man like that wouldn't be interested in someone like me.'

'Why not?' Gaby sucked her teeth in irritation. 'Come on, Cat, you're an attractive woman. Don't put yourself down. You're always putting yourself down.'

'I know I'm a beautiful, independent woman with luscious curves,' I laughed, repeating the mantra Sara had taught us.

'Damn right,' Gaby nodded, draining her glass. 'You're a catch for anyone. We both are. Don't sell yourself short.'

'Okay, I won't,' I promised.

'Do you want another vodka and tonic?' Gaby asked, standing up.

'I can't. I'm driving. Maybe an orange juice.'

'So am I. Why don't we get a taxi back together and fetch the cars in the morning? Come on. The night is young. We're young and single and we just likes to mingle.'

'All right,' I laughed. I was feeling reckless and free. I didn't have to get up in the morning, and maybe I was already thinking I wanted to investigate where things might go with the handsome stranger. Against all odds, he did seem to be interested in me. 'You sit down though,' I waved my hand at Gaby. 'It's my round.'

I pushed my way through the crowd to get to the bar to order more drinks. As I was trying to catch the attention of the barman, someone tapped me on the shoulder, making me start, and I turned to find that it was the man Gaby had pointed out. He was laughing at my surprise and holding out a ten-pound note.

'Sorry. I didn't mean to startle you,' he said smoothly, with just a hint of an Irish accent. A Liam Neeson voice. Feral green eyes. He was even better-looking up close. 'But you dropped this.'

I examined the wad of notes in my hand. It was all still there. 'No, I don't think—'

'I haven't seen you in here before,' he said, ignoring me and pressing the note into my hand. I felt a charge of electricity as his hand brushed against mine. His opening line wasn't exactly original. He might as well have said, 'Do you come here often?' But it didn't matter; a man who looked like he did could get away with spouting gibberish and still seem eloquent.

'That's probably because I don't live here. I mean I've never been here. I mean of course, I've been to Tewkesbury, but I've never been . . . er, to this pub, I mean.' I was finding it hard to string a coherent sentence together.

He smiled as if he was used to grown women falling

to pieces in his presence. 'It's the most haunted pub in England did you know?'

'Yes, I heard it was haunted . . .'

'It's built on the intersection of two ley lines – one that comes all the way from Stonehenge. There are at least five ghosts.'

Even mansplaining seemed charming coming from him.

'Five?' I said breathlessly, hanging on his every word.

'Yes, there's a headless soldier who fought at the battle of Tewkesbury who roams the corridors upstairs and . . .' He nodded at a high-backed, dark wood chair near the fireplace. 'No one can sit in that chair because the ghost of old Nick gets angry if someone takes his seat.'

I stared at the empty chair and shivered.

'Do you believe in ghosts?' he asked conversationally.

'I don't know. I don't think so. I thought about my book. I thought about telling him about *Embers*. It would be a natural thing to mention at this point and might impress him, but I chickened out. I could hear my mother's voice. 'Men don't like clever girls, and no one likes a bragger.' A part of me can't help wondering if things started going wrong for me and Theo after *Embers* was published. Was he threatened by my success? It was either that or the extra weight I piled on after Dylan was born. Who am I kidding? It was the weight, of course.

All I could think of to say was, 'How about you? Do you believe in ghosts?'

He shrugged. 'I don't know either. I sort of do. I believe most ghosts manifest through the living. While they're remembered, they're still alive in a way. Do you see what I mean?'

I nod. I know exactly what he means. It's the underlying premise of *Embers*.

'Anyway, I think my date must have got spooked because she hasn't turned up,' he laughed.

'Oh, you're meeting someone,' I said, swallowing my disappointment.

He smiled as if he knew what I was thinking – as if he couldn't blame me for thinking it. 'I don't think she's going to show now. We were going to meet at eight. I stayed anyway for the band, but it turns out the lead guitarist is sick, so they're not going to play. The whole evening has been a washout . . . until now.'

'Was it a blind date?' I asked, pointedly ignoring 'until now'.

'First time I've ever used Tinder,' he said. 'I might not use it again. This is her.' He showed me the photo on his phone – a pretty, dark-haired girl in a red bikini, holding a champagne flute with immaculately manicured nails.

'Too skinny. She looks horrible,' I said, and he laughed.

'Lucky escape, you think?' he said, not taking his eyes from mine.

'Maybe,' I agreed. And I realised that I was flirting and that it felt good. It felt familiar and easy talking to him, and it seemed natural and not at all strange when he joined Gaby and me at our table.

He was soon making us both laugh. He was polite and friendly to Gaby, but made it clear it was me he was interested in, which I couldn't help but find flattering, and when Gaby announced she was tired and ordered a taxi, he suggested that I stay a bit longer. He said that he could give me a lift home.

Alone with Luke, the conversation didn't flag, as I thought it might. It seemed to flow naturally. We talked about everything and anything – books, movies, politics, his travels around Europe when he left university and the scrapes he got into. Though now I come to think of it, he didn't say much at all about his life now. About where he lived or worked.

At the time I didn't notice. I was too busy thinking this man was so attractive, and had a great personality. Too good to be true. And when he dropped me outside my house, I didn't think twice about inviting him in for a coffee.

'You live here alone?' he asked, standing in my kitchen, watching me in a way that made me fumble with the tap as I filled the kettle. He shifted only a little as I brushed past him to the fridge and I caught a whiff of aftershave and something that made me feel weak with lust.

I backed away, startled by the physicality of my feelings. Gaby was right. It had been too long.

'No. I live with my son. But he's not here at the moment. He's with my ex. He's five years old.' I showed him a picture on my phone, glad of the excuse to talk about something safe and about as far from sex as possible.

'No kidding,' he beamed. 'My boy's five too.'

'And his mother?' Warning bells should have been ringing, but they weren't.

'Oh, we split up a few months ago.'

'I'm sorry.' I imagined I saw a hint of sadness in his eyes. Some idiot broke his heart, I thought.

'Don't be,' he said bravely. 'It's a fresh start. A chance to date other women. Play the field. Though I'm quite glad that my date didn't turn up tonight.' He gave me a meaningful look and I was suddenly ambushed by another strong wave of lust.

The kiss, when it came, felt inevitable. His lips were soft and tasted of whisky. The kettle hissed and steam poured from the spout, but we carried on kissing, lost in the moment. And when his hand stole up my thigh, I didn't think about cellulite or about Theo or Dylan. I didn't really think much at all. And I don't remember how we ended up there, but somehow we found our way from the kitchen to my bedroom in a tangle of limbs and clothes.

'Okay?' he murmured, just before he pushed me down on the bed. I didn't answer, just pulled him towards me, unbuckling his trousers and running my hands over the smooth, pale skin of his stomach.

I remember him holding me afterwards, and the feeling of skin against skin after so long was so sweet it was close to pain.

'Thank you,' I said – or something stupid like that because, in the moment, I did feel absurdly grateful.

'No . . . *thank you*,' he said.

Then I must have drifted off to sleep because the next thing I knew he was shaking me awake and the sunlight was streaming in through the window.

'You have to go to work on a Saturday?' I grumbled, still half asleep. What kind of job have you got where they make you work on a Saturday?'

He laughed gently. 'I've got a meeting with some clients about a building I'm designing. I can't be late. It's a really important contract, but I'll call you, okay?'

Of course! Why didn't I remember that earlier? I turn away from the window, from the rain and root in my pocket for the phone number that Littlewood gave me. Then I pick up the phone and call her. She answers after a few rings, sounding hassled.

'Yes?' she says abruptly.

'Hi, yes, it's Catherine. Catherine Bayntun,' I say. 'I just remembered something about Luke – the guy I was with on Friday night.'

'Oh yes?'

'His job. He's an architect. There can't be many architect firms in town. You should be able to find him easily, right?'

Six

Hanging up the phone, I glance at the time in the corner of the screen and realise, with a lurch of dismay, that I'm late for pick-up.

Crap! On Dylan's first day! What kind of mother am I?

I dive into the car and drive through the town centre to school. But the traffic lights are not in my favour, and despite my haste, I'm one of the last parents to arrive. When I rush up to the classroom door, Dylan is sitting with the teaching assistant, Ms Hamlyn, and one other little boy, looking woebegone, clutching a crayon and scrawling half-heartedly on a large piece of paper. I feel a rush of love and guilt so intense it takes my breath away.

'Dylan,' I say. 'I'm sorry, baby.'

He raises his head, his face lighting up when he sees me, and he rushes into my arms.

'Did you have a good day?' I ask, kissing his cheek. And he nods and looks up at me. 'Why is your hair yellow?' he asks with a puzzled frown.

I ignore his question. 'Sorry I'm late,' I say to Ms Hamlyn.

'It's okay, really,' she bounces up, energetically. Young, long-limbed, with overgrown puppy legs, cropped brown hair and wide, caramel eyes. According to the introductory letter we were sent, she started working at the school this term and she seems to have all the enthusiasm and eagerness to please of the newly employed. 'Dylan's been telling us all about dinosaurs, haven't you, Dylan?'

Dylan nods.

'He knows a lot about them,' she adds.

I smile. 'Dylan knows all there is to know about dinosaurs, don't you?' I ruffle his hair proudly.

'He had a little accident, I'm afraid,' Ms Hamlyn whispers in my ear as we're leaving. 'We have some spare underwear, but it would be a good idea if you could put an extra pair of pants in his bag tomorrow and a plastic bag.'

'Oh yes, of course,' I say, feeling like an even worse mother than before. 'I'm sorry. I didn't think. He never normally—'

'It's not a problem,' she interrupts. 'It happens all—' She breaks off because another mother has appeared to pick up her son. It's Georgia, the woman I spoke to this morning.

'Sorry, sorry,' she breezes in, pushing a pram, her brown

hair flying. 'You must think I'm always late. I'm really not. It's just I had a check-up at the clinic for the baby and I had to wait longer than I thought I would.'

'It's okay,' says Ms Hamlyn, cooing over the baby. 'We've been having a great time, haven't we kids? And they've been good as gold.' She folds their pictures and puts them into their book bags.

'Oh, hello, it's you,' says Georgia, noticing me properly for the first time. She does a double take. 'Didn't you have brown hair this morning?'

I nod and pat my hair self-consciously. 'Yes, I just felt like a bit of a change.'

'Well, it looks great.'

'Thank you.'

As we head across the school yard, I fall into step beside Georgia, glancing into the pram at her sleeping baby. It's wearing blue with a pattern of yellow flowers. I'm guessing that it's a girl.

'She's gorgeous,' I hazard.

'Thanks,' she says. 'She's gorgeous when she's asleep. But oh my God, she doesn't sleep at night. She must've woken six times at least last night! And my husband's no good – he just snores though it all.'

Georgia launches into a description of her baby's sleeping patterns and a long complaint about her husband who is a workaholic and apparently is never at home to help with the baby, while her son, Harry, and Dylan run around us, weaving in and out and shooting imaginary guns. I'm only listening with half an ear. I'm wondering if she's seen the photofit yet and if she has, why she's still being so friendly. Clearly, she's still unaware of my status as murder suspect, because the next thing she says is:

'Our boys seem to get on really well, don't they? I was wondering if you and Dylan would like to come round one day? Harry's got a new trampoline.'

I look at Dylan and Harry who are giggling wildly.

'Sure,' I say, trying not to sound too eager. 'Would you like that, Dylan? Would you like to go to Harry's to play one day?'

'Yeah,' he says, barely listening.

'That's settled, then. How about this Saturday? Are you free?' Georgia suggests.

'Um, well, he's with his dad this weekend, but I'm sure we can arrange something—'

'Great,' Georgia carries on talking. 'It seems like a really good school, doesn't it?' she says, and then goes on to tell me that she doesn't know many people in the area yet because they've only just moved here and how her husband has got a new job in town.

We part at the school gate, after exchanging phone numbers and then I drive home with Dylan sitting in the back, singing tunelessly to himself some song he's probably learned at school.

At home, I dump our bags in the hallway and while Dylan scampers off to the living room and turns on the TV, I check my phone. There are a couple of missed calls from my mother. No doubt she's seen the news. I don't phone back. I can't face talking to her just now. She has an uncanny ability to turn a crisis into a full-blown calamity. There's a message from Gaby too, suggesting we meet one day in the week for a coffee. I answer, saying, yes, I'd love to! And then I check Ophelia Black's notifications. There are a couple of new likes and another message from George Wilkinson in Wisconsin.

I should probably just ignore it. He's clearly some kind of nutcase. But curiosity gets the better of me, and I click on the message with a vague, unformed feeling of trepidation. A picture flashes up on my screen. Again, he hasn't written anything, just sent this photo of a park somewhere. There's a lake in the foreground, green fields beyond, with trees and a crenelated church tower in the distance. It looks more like England than America, and in fact, it looks very much like my local park. I enlarge the picture. Yes, I realise, peering at the distinctive yew hedge with arches cut into it; without a doubt, it's the Abbey Grounds – the park in town, just behind the church. That's weird, if not downright creepy. What is George from Wisconsin doing here in the UK – in my hometown of all places? And why has he sent me this photo? Is he stalking me?

I suppose he might not actually be here. He could have found the picture on the Internet and decided I would like a picture of my hometown. But how did he find out where I live in the first place?

I head to the kitchen to find some comfort food, and I'm rummaging at the back of the cupboard trying to find the crisps I've hidden when I hear a door slamming upstairs. The noise makes me start, the chair wobbles and I nearly lose my balance. *Just a draught*, I think, climbing down from the chair. *I must have left a bedroom window open.* But I'm suddenly on my guard and I'm acutely conscious that it's just me, Dylan and Delilah all on our own.

Then, clearly, I hear the whine of the wardrobe door opening upstairs.

Someone is in my bedroom.

Dylan? I look in the living room. Dylan is still in there, watching TV.

A burglar then? My breath snags in my throat. Heart hammering, I fumble in the kitchen drawer and select the sharpest knife. I know they say that carrying a knife isn't smart because someone stronger could easily take it and use it against you. But even so, running my fingers along the sharp blade makes me feel better, braver.

I tiptoe along the hallway, closing the living-room door softly as I pass. Whoever's upstairs I need to keep them away from Dylan. Moving slowly and silently up the stairs, I tug the phone out of my pocket and tap in the emergency services number with a trembling finger.

At the top of the stairs, I freeze. My heart is beating so hard I can feel it in my ears. The bedroom door is ajar. Someone is in there without a doubt. I can hear them rooting around, opening and closing drawers. Clutching the knife tightly in one hand and my phone in the other, I push open the door.

He's bent over a drawer, his bony buttocks in the air. As the door opens, he straightens up and swivels round, clutching his chest and I stare into a pair of startled brown eyes blinking at me from behind black-rimmed glasses.

'Theo. What the . . .' I say, relief flooding through me.

'Jesus, Cat. You scared me!' he exclaims, clutching his heart and laughing 'I didn't hear you come in.'

'I scared *you*? I like that!'

'Emergency. Which service do you require? Fire, police or ambulance?' a woman barks briskly from my phone.

'Sorry, I made a mistake,' I mutter and hurriedly end the call.

'What the hell are you doing here?' I demand, glaring at Theo, my heart rate gradually returning to normal. 'How did you get in?'

He eyes the knife in my hand. 'Do you think you could put that down please? You're making me nervous.'

I place it carefully on the bedside table, the blade glinting in the light from the window. 'What are you doing here?' I repeat firmly. He has no right to be here without my permission.

'I've still got a key, remember? I just came to pick up a few bits and bobs. I hope you don't mind. I thought I'd do it while you were out picking up Dylan. Didn't think you'd be back so soon.'

I make a mental note to change the locks. 'I do mind, actually,' I retort. 'You can't just swan in here whenever you like. This isn't your house any more.'

'Well, technically . . .' he breaks off and stares at me. 'What did you do to your hair?' he asks, as if he's only just noticed.

'Don't you like it?'

He shrugs. 'You look like what's her name – the singer? The one that sings about pavements. Adele.'

'I'll take that as a compliment.'

'It is a compliment. You look nice.' He meets my eyes, and something passes between us. When was the last time he looked at me like that? When we were married, he barely looked at me. We barely looked at each other.

'Anyway,' he says, looking a little flustered. How's my boy? Where's Dylan?'

63

'He's downstairs, watching TV, but I don't think it's a good idea—'

He doesn't wait to hear the end of my sentence but dashes downstairs. I follow, fuming with anger. He has no business coming here during the week. It will only unsettle Dylan. Lead to false expectations. 'Wait. We agreed. No visits during the week,' I say.

But Theo doesn't hear me, or deliberately ignores me. I'm not sure which. And he is already pushing his way into the living room.

'Daddy!' Dylan exclaims delightedly, throwing himself into Theo's arms. The angry tirade I was about to launch into dies on my lips and my heart softens just a little, seeing them there together like that. There's no doubting their love for each other. Whatever else Theo might be, he's a good father.

'Hey, Dyl, I've missed you,' he says, ruffling our boy's hair. 'Have you missed me, mate?'

Dylan nods. 'Uh-huh. Are you staying for tea?' he asks, plaintively.

Theo glances at me. 'Well . . . maybe. It's up to your mother,' he says, glancing sideways at me.

'Please, Mummy, can he?' Dylan fixes his big brown eyes on me.

I bite back anger. Theo has backed me into a corner. Now I'm the bad one if I say no. 'Daddy needs to get back home,' I say. 'Harper will wonder where he is if he's late.'

'Harper's out for the evening, actually,' Theo says. 'I'd love to stay if that's okay with you.'

'I suppose so,' I say tartly. 'If you cook.'

'Great,' he grins. 'What've you got?' He opens the fridge and roots around. 'Mushrooms, pepper, cheese. I'll make pizza.'

'How is Harper, by the way?' I fire a casual shot. I'm sitting with my feet up on a chair, sipping coffee and watching him knead the pizza dough. I hate to admit it, but Theo makes the best pizza. Perfectly light and doughy. Just the thought of it is making my mouth water.

His back stiffens at the mention of Harper. We have a tacit agreement not to talk about her. It only leads to arguments.

'Fine?' he says warily.

'Where is she this evening? Doing her Art Through Music, I suppose?'

Harper is an art teacher at Theo's school. But in her spare time, she paints to the accompaniment of her friend's sitar playing in front of an audience. Apparently, she goes into a sort of trance and paints whatever the music inspires her to paint – judging by the artwork on Theo and Harper's wall, usually a load of squiggly lines that Dylan or any of his peers in reception would have no problem knocking out. It's the kind of thing that Theo used to find pretentious and

65

would have mocked mercilessly when we were together, but now seems to think is inspirational.

Theo frowns. 'Actually, if you must know, she's gone to see a therapist.'

'What? Why?'

'She suffers from depression – always has done. I persuaded her it would be a good idea to talk to someone.'

'What on earth does Harper have to feel depressed about?' I say crossly. As far as I can tell she leads a charmed life. She's beautiful and slim with a great job and a man she's stolen from me.

'It's complicated. Her father left when she was young, and her sister died when she was a baby. She has abandonment issues.'

Theo is a sucker for a damsel in distress. I wonder if Harper's emotional problems were even more of a turn-on for him than her gorgeous blue eyes or her tiny, pert breasts.

'By the way, the police came to talk to me earlier today,' he says, changing the subject. 'They were asking about Friday night.'

Touché, I think. Way to bring the focus back on to me. 'What did you tell them?' I ask carefully.

'The truth of course – that you dropped Dylan off at about six and that's all I know. What's going on, Cat? They don't seriously suspect you, do they?'

'I don't know,' I sigh, thinking of Littlewood's solemn face with a twinge of unease. 'They said it was just routine and that witness testimony was notoriously unreliable, but they still asked me a lot of questions about what I did that night.'

'And what *did* you do?' Theo glances at me curiously.

'I was out with Gaby most of the night. We went to the Black Bear.' No need to mention Luke.

'It's ridiculous,' he pronounces loyally, 'completely ridiculous. What the hell do the police think they're doing? They should be out there finding who really committed this horrific murder, not harassing you. You're the last person who could kill someone. I told the police you couldn't hurt a fly. You're a vegetarian, for Christ's sake.'

I feel an unexpected rush of affection and gratitude. Theo knows me better than anyone. We have so much history together and, after all the suspicious looks today, it's reassuring to hear his faith in me. Despite the unforgiveable things he's done, right this second he feels like an ally and I badly need one of those.

'What did DI Littlewood say to that?'

'She said Hitler was a vegetarian.'

'Hm,' I snort grimly. 'That sounds like her.'

Theo puts the pizza in the oven and comes and sits opposite me at the kitchen table.

'It's just so strange, that's all,' he says thoughtfully.

'I'm trying to think why someone would have given your description to the police. Do you think they could have seen you in the area? The police said the murder victim lived on Cecily Hill. Were you anywhere near there on Friday night?'

I sigh. 'No, definitely not. Maybe the witness saw me somewhere else another time and got muddled.'

'Yeah, it's possible,' Theo chews his finger thoughtfully.

'Or . . .' I give voice to the fears that have been dogging me all day, 'maybe someone is trying to frame me.'

Theo gives a short bark of laughter, then breaks off when he sees my expression. 'Oh, you're serious? That's a bit far-fetched, isn't it? Who would want to frame you? You haven't got any enemies, have you?'

'No.' I shake my head. But it's not completely true, I realise, thinking about a long time ago – things that I haven't thought about in years . . .

'Cat, did you hear me? Are you okay?' Theo is gazing at me, concerned.

I give myself a mental shake. 'Why wouldn't I be okay? I'm only a suspect in a murder investigation. No biggie,' I say, burying my fear under sarcasm.

Theo smiles uncertainly and then shrugs. 'You always did get yourself into scrapes but this one takes the biscuit.' He checks the pizza and starts laying the table.

'Who took the biscuit? I want a biscuit,' Dylan says

coming in, and we both laugh at his unintentionally comic timing.

'Nobody's taken any biscuits. Don't worry,' says Theo, winking at me. I don't smile back. Although Theo has risen in my estimation over the past few minutes and I appreciate his support, I'm not about to accept winking as a form of communication between us.

'You're having your tea in a minute,' I say to Dylan. 'But you can have a Kit Kat afterwards.'

When we sit together around our small kitchen table, it's just like old times. I can almost imagine that we do this every evening – that we're a family again, the three of us. And I must admit it feels good listening to Theo gently teasing Dylan and Dylan chattering away about his day. About the boy who got into trouble with the teacher for not sitting on his carpet space and about the fossil collection Ms Hamlyn showed them.

After the meal is over, Theo insists on staying to put Dylan to bed. While they're upstairs, I turn the volume down on the TV and listen to the low murmur of Theo's voice reading Dylan a bedtime story. It feels like going back in time to a golden era, before Theo left me, before Charlie was murdered – to a time when we were just a normal, happy family. There's a part of me that wants to go back there, to wallow in this warm feeling of security. But Theo betrayed me and destroyed our family, I remind myself. And after that, there can be no going back. 'Once a cheater always a cheater.' That's what Gaby says. And I know she's right.

I turn up the volume on the TV again, so that I can no longer hear Theo, and force myself to remember how I felt when he told me about Harper. How I knew as soon as he returned from the school trip to CERN in Switzerland that there was something different about him, something off-key.

'It just sort of happened,' was his lame explanation. 'Harper and me . . .'

I'm not quite sure how they managed to conduct a steamy affair with a bunch of thirty teenagers in tow, and I certainly didn't want to know details.

'Do you love her?' I asked, feeling strangely detached as my life crashed around me.

And he frowned. 'I don't know. She needs me . . .' he said hopelessly. And I calmly climbed the stairs, neatly packed a selection of his clothes into a suitcase and dumped it by the front door. Within a month of me kicking him out, Theo and Harper had moved into a flat together and the rest, as they say, is history.

'Out like a light,' Theo grins, as he comes down the stairs.

'Yes, his first day at school must have tired him out,' I say. I can barely look at him; the memories have made me so angry. 'Well, you'd better be going, I suppose,' I add coldly as he sits down on my sofa.

'Uh, yes,' he looks at his watch, bouncing up as if he's sat on a bed of spikes. 'I suppose I'd better. He heads to the door. 'Let me know if you need anything. I'm sure Duncan could help you if you need a lawyer.'

Duncan – a man who openly leers at other women in front of his wife and who once sang, 'I like big butts . . .' to me on my birthday – is not my favourite of Theo's friends.

'Thanks,' I say sarcastically. 'I'll bear that in mind. Because Duncan always makes everything so much better.'

'I know you don't like him,' Theo sighs, 'but he's a good lawyer. Think about it, Cat.'

I open the front door, nodding slightly. 'Okay,' I say, just to get him out of the house. I think I'd rather go to prison for life than have Duncan defending me in a court of law.

Seven

It's getting dark and the house suddenly feels empty and quiet after Theo has gone. Something rustles in the bushes outside – a cat, no doubt. But it sets my nerves on edge and I can't shake an odd sensation that there's someone out there, looking in, watching me. Hastily, I draw all the curtains and lock and bolt the doors. Then I go and check on Dylan who is still fast asleep, breathing gently. I gaze at him for a while, marvelling at how a relationship as flawed as Theo's and mine could have created something so perfect and precious. Whatever else has happened, however much he's hurt me, I can't ever regret marrying Theo, because out of our marriage came this miracle – this little person who means more to me than anything else in the world.

'Sleep tight,' I whisper.

And Dylan mumbles and shifts a little in his sleep. I kiss his flushed cheek and then, careful not to wake him, switch off his night light and tiptoe out of the room. Downstairs, in the living room, I turn on my laptop and start typing the next chapter of the *Embers* sequel. Though writing can sometimes feel like work, tonight it feels more like a lifeline – a way to escape from a present that seems increasingly frightening and out of control. I plunge eagerly into the simple world I've created – a world where I pull the strings, where people do what I decide and ultimately, all is forgiven.

'Molly dropped her umbrella,' I type.

> . . . and stared horrified at the doorway. Just when you thought things couldn't get any worse, they did. From one of the rooms downstairs another revenant had appeared and was sliding across the hallway towards her . . .

I type without stopping. The words flow easily, and when I next look at the clock, I've been working for more than an hour. I'm reading through what I've written, deleting a few lines here and there and changing the odd word, when a sudden rumble of thunder jolts me back into reality.

I open the curtains and stare out through the dark window at the rain that has started lashing against the pane and the lightning flaring in the sky. *It's no good*, I think. Writing has only served to delay the inevitable. This whole thing with the photofit and the police is not going to go away by itself. I'm going to have to face up to it at some point.

I try to reassure myself, remembering that I've got an alibi. Luke is my alibi. The police will find him, he'll confirm my story and then they'll leave me alone. But when I think about the way DI Littlewood looked when I was talking about Luke, as if she doubted his existence, I wonder if she'll even bother to try to track him down. Maybe I should do a little detective work of my own. It can't hurt, can it?

Glad to have thought of something positive to do, I Google architects in Cirencester on my phone. There's only one firm in the local area: Anthony Green and Co., and I scroll through their website, looking at the profiles of the people who work there. But there's no Luke. He could be new to the firm, I reflect. Maybe they haven't had time to add him to the website, or perhaps he works somewhere else, like Tewkesbury. That is where we met him, after all. But a brief search of architects in Tewkesbury doesn't yield any results either.

Disappointed and frustrated, I head to the kitchen to make myself a cup of peppermint tea. While I'm waiting for the kettle to boil, I empty Dylan's lunch bag and tip out the empty crisp packet and the half-eaten carrot inside. Then I open his book bag and rummage through. He has a reading book, *Fat Frog*, and a reading record book. Mrs Bailey has written inside: 'Fabulous reading, Dylan. Practise the tricky word "the"' and she has added a silver sticker with a smiley face. Tucked neatly inside the reading book, there's a sealed blue envelope with nothing written on the front and a folded-up picture Dylan has drawn of me, Theo, Delilah and him. We've got circular bodies and randomly placed stick limbs and we're all smiling. One happy family. I feel a twinge of guilt, swiftly followed by anger at Theo. That's what our family should look like, I think. It's his fault it doesn't, not mine. I attach the picture to the fridge with a magnet. Then I tear open the envelope.

Inside is a printout of a photograph on white A4 paper. No words. No explanation. Just a picture of a children's playground – an artistic shot in black and white, oddly angled upwards so that the sky dominates the picture. Rows of rippling grey fish-scale clouds and an ominously looming sycamore above a climbing frame.

There's something familiar about the shape of the climbing frame. And when I examine the picture more closely, I realise that it's similar, if not identical to the climbing frame in the Abbey Grounds park. But what's it doing in Dylan's book bag? Is it a kind of homework or did someone put it there by mistake?

Another picture of the park like the message on my Facebook page. It's strange and unnerving, but I can't quite put my finger on why.

Eight

My sleep is punctured by dark, disturbing dreams. Sharp, horrific images of Charlie blaze through my mind, lit in lurid, searing detail: Charlie crying and whimpering, snot mixing with her tears, her hands stretched in front of her as she makes a futile attempt to ward off her killer; Charlie lying lifeless on the kitchen floor, red blood blooming on her white pyjama top. In my dream, someone bends over to check her pulse and suddenly her eyes fly open like in a horror movie. Then, slowly, she stretches out a quivering hand and makes a gurgling sound in her throat. She's struggling to say something. 'M . . . mm . . .' she chokes out, as the blood trickles over her lips.

'What is it, Charlie?' Someone says. Is it me?

She lifts her head and stares straight into my eyes with such hatred it sucks the air out of my lungs.

'Mm . . . mm . . . Murderer!' she rasps.

I jerk awake, swimming in sweat. There's a piercing pain behind my right eye and my throat is dry. Climbing out of bed, I stumble into the bathroom and take a couple of Nurofen and a sleeping pill. Examining my reflection in the mirror, I realise I must have forgotten to take out my contact lenses last night and they are now stuck to my eyes. When I finally manage to extract them, they pop out with so much suction that for one second, I think my eyeballs are going to come with them. I rub my red eyes and gaze at my blurry image in the mirror. A feeling of guilt and unease gnaws at my belly.

'You just need some sleep,' I tell myself. 'All of this won't seem so bad in the morning.' So I crawl back to bed and lie with a cold flannel to my forehead, trying to keep completely still. Eventually, I drop off into a deep and unbroken sleep until I'm woken by the shrill shriek of my alarm.

After dropping Dylan off at school, I take the long route home through the Abbey Grounds, partly to avoid a group of mothers standing on the corner, but also because I want to see if the photo in Dylan's book bag really was taken there or if it's my imagination.

The park is nearly empty. There are just a few dog walkers doing the circuit of the lake. Everything is damp from the rain last night and there is a low mist hanging over the still, grey water, lending the day an other-worldly feeling. *Just the sort of morning when Molly and her ghostly friends would be out and about*, I think. Through habit, I try to memorise the scene so that I can describe it accurately in my writing as I head over the small footbridge, past the grass-covered remains of the ancient Roman wall, towards the play area.

I stop just inside the fence and, taking out my phone, crouch opposite the climbing frame and take a snap. Then, I sit on the metal bench, and shielding the screen so I can see clearly, I compare the two photos – the one I've just taken, and the one I found in Dylan's book bag.

I suck in my breath in surprise. I didn't really expect to be proved right, but the resemblance is uncanny – undeniable. That sycamore tree is in the same spot exactly. Even its lopsided shape is identical. And the wooden fence that runs around the play area has a panel missing in precisely the same place as in the photograph. Only the sky, today a uniform blanket of grey, is different. There is no doubt. Not only was the photo in the book bag almost certainly taken here, but I believe it must have been taken quite recently.

But who took it? And why?

I check the photo George Wilkinson sent on my phone. The picture of this same park, only from a different perspective. Can it just be a coincidence?

I look around the park feeling suddenly scared, as if someone might be here, waiting for me, watching me. *Are you there, George?* I think with a shiver and I peer into the thick bushes and trees that separate the park from the main road behind. But there's no one around, apart from a couple of teenagers in school uniforms hanging out by the swings, swilling cans of Coke. *They should be in school by now,* I think. As I look at them, they eye me sulkily, as if I'm going to snitch on them, and they slope off towards the gates, dragging their school bags. I watch them go, absent-mindedly. They look thin, slightly feral. They remind me of me and Charlie at that age.

Charlie and I came here many times over the years. We came here as dreamy adolescents, sitting by the lake and poring over books about star signs, working out who was compatible with who. Charlie was a Pisces and I was a Gemini. Not generally seen as well-matched signs. But we got on so well that we agreed there must be something in our ascendant signs. When we were older, we came here with bottles of cider from the off-licence to smoke spliffs and get off with boys.

The last time we came here was just after we finished our A levels. The night of 28 August 2002. The night of Nessa's party.

As I remember that night, I feel a sharp pain in my heart – like a shard of glass has lodged there. I haven't thought about what happened for a long time. It's been buried at the bottom of my mind, locked away safely. But now the memories are resurfacing, things I would rather forget, bubbling up like sewage from a drain.

I walk over to the swings and sit gingerly on the middle seat. And suddenly I'm a teenager again, feeling the breeze against my face as the sun dips behind the trees.

Charlie was sitting on the swing next to me, puffing away on a spliff, her hair glowing amber in the sinking sunlight. She looked beautiful and brave, like a Celtic warrior queen. Jenson and May Ling were here too, sitting on that bench over there, snogging. We'd just finished our A levels and there was a feeling of freedom in the air – a fizzing in my veins and the sense of our lives stretching out before us, full of possibility.

I was holding a roll-up awkwardly in my hand, wondering what to do with the butt once I'd finished. I didn't want to drop it on the floor and grind it under my heel like I'd seen Jenson do, but then again would I look uncool if I threw it in the bin? More than anything, I didn't want to seem uncool. May Ling and Jenson were so cool, effortlessly cool. I knew they only tolerated me because I was Charlie's friend, and I didn't want to stuff it up. I didn't want to let Charlie down.

Charlie had arrived late in our school in Year Eight, when we were thirteen. She'd moved from a posh private girls' school in Cheltenham after her father died. We were drawn together partly because we were both outsiders. Charlie because of her plummy accent and me, well, because I was overweight and nerdy, and my parents insisted on dressing me in second-hand clothes.

We were inseparable for a couple of years. But in Year Ten, Charlie changed. She cultivated a west-country drawl and made friends with a bunch of cool kids. She didn't exactly drop me, but we drifted apart, and I was left alone, feeling hurt and betrayed. It was only in the last year of school, in the sixth form, that she deigned to become part of my life again and persuaded her new friends to allow me into their group.

'She's quite a laugh when you get to know her. She's just shy,' I overheard her saying in the toilet once.

That evening in the park, Jenson and May Ling wandered over and started talking about a band they'd seen the summer before. I kept quiet. I'd never heard of the band, never even been to a concert, except for classical ones with my parents, and I didn't want them to know. People always tell you to be yourself, don't they? 'Just be yourself,' they say, 'and everything will be fine.' Well, in my experience, being yourself was not always enough, or maybe it's more accurate to say it was too much. Sometimes I knew I said things that were too thoughtful, too honest or just too plain weird. By the age of seventeen, I'd learned that you had to filter yourself, keep things hidden, bury the part of you that didn't fit with the group.

Of course, I understand now that I was luckier than them in many ways. I had a mother and a father who loved me, even if they sometimes had a strange way of showing it. Jenson's father was in and out of prison, May Ling's parents were divorced, and Charlie's father had died when she was thirteen, leaving her mother unable to pay the fees for Charlie's expensive school. I didn't fully realise it at the time, but Charlie must have still been mourning her father and all her bravado and reckless behaviour were probably, at least in part, a symptom of her grief. At the time, I'd just thought she was very cool, and I wanted to be like her. I let her down, I think. I bought into the myth that she portrayed to the world – that she was invincible. I didn't see the little girl inside who was crying out for help.

'I'm sorry, Charlie,' I say aloud under my breath. 'I didn't understand. I should have helped you.' And tears roll down my cheeks as I realise that I'll never be able to say it to her now. Because Charlie is dead.

I brush the tears away angrily. I was young. I had my own problems. I can't be blamed. But even as I make these excuses to myself another voice, a cool and ruthless voice inside my head, is insisting otherwise. *You were eighteen. Old enough to know better. You destroyed her life and you never took responsibility.*

'I'm bored,' said Charlie. She was standing on the swing.

And as she spoke, she stretched her arms out, letting go of the chains, making me worry she was going to fall.

'What shall we do now?' she asked when she finally grabbed hold of the chains again and sat down. 'There's a party at Nessa's. Shall we go?'

'Sure, why not?' said May Ling, lazily.

'I don't know,' I hesitated. I had promised to help my mother at a charity auction the next morning and would need to get up early.

'Please come.' Charlie gave a mischievous grin. 'James will be there.'

I shot her an angry look. I'd been infatuated with James since I was eleven and had never told anyone. But recently, in a moment of weakness, eager to please and to maintain our new-found closeness, I'd told Charlie. I had made her promise to keep it a secret, but here she was making it obvious in front of May Ling and Jenson that I had a crush on him.

'Do you fancy James?' May Ling asked curiously.

'No, he's just a friend, that's all.'

'Yes, you so do. You're going red,' said Jenson, laughing.

'Shut up, Jenson,' said Charlie. 'He's just her friend, that's all. Please come with us. It won't be the same without you. Besides, we need someone to drive.' She clasped her hands together as if she were praying. 'Please, Cat.'

I hesitated just for a second. Then I smiled and nodded.

'All right,' I said.

What made me say yes? It wasn't that James would be there. I had given up on James ever being interested in me in that way. I think it was the fact that Charlie said she wanted me there. I could never say no to Charlie.

What if I had said no? What if I had never gone to Nessa's party? If only I could go back in time and just change that one decision; what happened next would never have happened. Charlie and I could have stayed friends and so many lives wouldn't have been destroyed.

I stand up and walk briskly towards the park gates. There is no point in brooding and wishing things could have been different. Nothing can be changed. Time travel only happens in science fiction.

As I walk past the yew hedge, I look again at the picture of the park on my phone. *It's just a coincidence*, I think, dismissing my misgivings as paranoia, the product of a guilty conscience. The picture couldn't be a reference to that night. Even if someone else knew what had happened back then, how would they know we'd come here earlier in the evening? And besides, no one could possibly know about that night.

There are only two people who ever knew what happened. One of them is me and the other is dead, stabbed four times in the chest.

Nine

'Ah, finally, Catherine.' Mum embraces me on the doorstep and looks me up and down critically. 'You haven't been answering your phone. Your father and I have been worried about you.'

'I'm fine,' I lie. 'I've just been busy, that's all.' I've dropped in to see my parents on my way home, because I know if I don't, my mum won't stop ringing. I know I will have to explain the photofit eventually, and I'd rather do that in person than over the phone.

'Well, you look nice, darling,' she says dubiously. 'You've changed your hair. You look as if you've lost some weight too, have you?'

'A little.'

Thin as a rake, my mother has never been able to understand how she could have a fat daughter. When I was a child, she used to weigh me before every meal and proclaim in mystification at my inevitable weight gain. She didn't know that I was spending the money she gave me for after-school gym class on sweets and crisps.

I follow her into their long, dark kitchen – the result of a badly thought-out extension in the seventies – and sit at the large pine table.

My mother doesn't sit down. She rarely sits. She's one of those people who keeps busy all the time. Just now she's bustling about making me a coffee and wiping invisible crumbs off the kitchen counter.

'How are Dylan and Theo?' she asks.

I roll my eyes. It annoys me the way she insists on talking about them as if we're still a family unit. 'Dylan's fine. I don't know how Theo is,' I say pointedly.

'Well now, there's no need to be like that,' she says huffily.

'Like what, Mum?'

'Theo is still my son-in-law. I care about him, you know. I can't just switch off my feelings, unlike some people.'

God knows I'm aware of her feelings about Theo. Mum adores him and refuses to believe anything bad about him. She knows that he was the one that cheated on me, but somehow has rationalised this in her mind as my fault. She assumes that I didn't treat him right – and I probably didn't by her standards, if the way she treats my father is anything to go by. My mother subscribes to an old-fashioned view of marriage, where the women look after the men and the men are helpless babies, unable to do simple housework and slaves to their sexual urges.

'As far as I know he's fine,' I say in a conciliatory tone. 'Harper's moved in with him.'

My mother makes a strange noise of frustration in her throat. 'That woman,' she says.

Mum has never actually met Harper but in her opinion, she is the incarnation of evil and if anyone is more to blame for the break-up of my marriage than me, it's Harper. In her mind, Harper is a siren who lured in poor, unsuspecting Theo with her promiscuous ways. 'You need to stop her,' she adds crossly.

'How am I supposed to do that?'

'I don't know. If you made more effort . . .' She breaks off. I suppose by making more effort she means losing more weight. 'I dread to think what all this is doing to poor Dylan,' she continues, shaking her head. 'I can't bear to think of my grandson living with that woman.'

'Dylan's okay. Harper is actually quite nice to him to be fair,' I say. It's a testament to my mother's ability to bring out the contrarian in me that I find myself defending Harper of all people.

'Hmm,' Mum says doubtfully. 'And how's my little grandson settling into his new school?'

'So far, so good. He likes his teachers, and he seems to be making friends.'

'Good.' Mum's face softens and she slops my coffee down in front of me, then starts taking out cooking ingredients and placing them on the table. 'You don't mind, do you darling? I promised Gillian I'd make some lemon tarts for the WI bake sale. It's in aid of – oh, I forget what it's in aid of, but it's a good cause anyway. I've got so much to do this morning I don't know how I'm going to fit it all in.'

'That's okay,' I say, relieved that we seem to have abandoned the topic of my divorce. 'Do you want any help?'

'No, thank you. But please don't put your feet up on the chair, she gives my leg a friendly pat and smiles. 'And I do wish you'd sit up straight.' I automatically straighten my shoulders. (It's another disappointment to her that she has a daughter who always slouches.)

There is a lengthy silence, broken only by the slap of the rolling pin against the dough. Both of us are reluctant to mention the subject that's really on our minds.

'There's a photo I found the other day,' she says at last. 'It's on that shelf there. It's of you and Charlotte Kent. You must have been about thirteen when it was taken.'

I pick it up and stare at it. It's of me and Charlie sitting on the bench in Charlie's garden with our arms round each other. Charlie has a flower in her teeth as if we're about to do a tango.

'That girl always was trouble,' she says, and gives a sigh. 'You know the police came here the other day.'

'They came here?' I repeat with a lurch of dismay.

Mum nods firmly. 'Yes, and they asked me a lot of impertinent questions. I didn't like that woman one bit. Now what was she called? Smallforest or Littletrees, something like that.'

'You mean DI Littlewood?'

'Yes, I think that was her name.'

'What did she ask?'

'Oh, about your friendship with Charlotte Kent – or Holbrooke now, I should say.'

'And?' I hold my breath. 'Did you tell her that I barely know her any more, that I haven't seen her for over seventeen years?'

'Um, no, actually I forgot that. It seems like only yesterday you were both sitting in this kitchen here, stuffing your faces with my fairy cakes. I told them that she was always a troublemaker – that she treated you badly.'

I make a small, exasperated sound in my throat. 'You shouldn't have told them that,' I say.

'What? Why?' My mother looks affronted.

'Well, don't you think they might construe that as a motive?'

'For murder?' She gives a small, tinkling laugh. 'You are joking, aren't you, Catherine? They can't seriously suspect you.'

'Well, I think they do.'

She puts her spoon down and stares at me.

'Nonsense, darling,' she says. She starts cutting the dough into small circles, frowning. She's placing it in the category of things she doesn't believe because she doesn't like them. My mother is good at that. For example, she doesn't believe in automatic checkouts in shops and she doesn't really believe that Theo and I are going to get a divorce.

'I never liked that girl,' she continues. 'I told you she would get you into trouble one day. Do you remember when she drove my car and dented it? We never did get the money for the repairs. And then there was the time you both nearly got arrested for trespassing.'

I remember.

'Yes, but that wasn't Charlie's fault,' I point out. 'The house looked derelict. How were we supposed to know there was a crazy old man living there? Besides, I don't think we can really blame her for getting herself killed.'

'Hmph. Can't we?' Mum purses her lips. 'She probably had it coming to her. I've no doubt she was mixed up with the wrong people. Drug dealers, I shouldn't wonder.'

'Mum, she smoked marijuana when she was a teenager. Big deal. By all accounts, she was a perfectly respectable young woman. She'd just married and had a thriving business – you know the shop in town, Charlie's Choice. You must have been there.'

Mum gives a disapproving sniff. 'Never been there. Lots of overpriced trinkets and all that New-Age stuff: crystals and joss sticks and whatnot. Load of stuff and nonsense, if you ask me. There used to be a lovely wool shop there. Now you can't get wool anywhere.' She sighs. The modern world has never agreed with my mother.

'Anyway –' she frowns – 'I don't understand why the police think you were involved. Do you know anything about why she was murdered?'

'I really don't. As you know, I haven't seen her since we left school.'

'I told the police, I wouldn't be surprised if it was her husband,' she sighs. 'I don't understand why they aren't investigating him, instead of wasting time bothering you. It's almost always the husband or partner in murder cases.'

'You've been watching too much true crime,' I say.

My mother looks annoyed. 'I certainly haven't. Nasty exploitative programmes. But I'm serious, Catherine. Charlotte inherited that house from her mother. It must be worth quite a lot of money now. And there was her business; that was doing well, as far as I know. They should look at her will. Who benefits?'

'The police should hire you,' I say sarcastically.

'I'm just trying to help.' My mum sniffs.

And though I hate to admit it, my mother has a point. The police seem to be getting nowhere with this investigation.

Why haven't they been looking at money as a motive for her killing? Why isn't the husband a serious suspect? Charlie was stabbed four times, according to the news reports, which suggests a crime of passion, which, in turn, suggests that she was killed by someone close to her. Why not the husband?

When I get home, I ignore a message from my editor politely asking when I will be finished with the *Embers* sequel, and if I need to extend the deadline. Instead of replying, I type the name Adam Holbrooke and Gloucestershire into my search engine. He's the first person to come up on LinkedIn. In his profile photo, he looks handsome and clean cut with floppy blond hair, dimples, white teeth and a pleasant, friendly smile. I peer closely at his face, trying to decide if he looks like a wife killer. It's a pointless exercise. Psychopaths and serial killers look just like anyone else. You might as well try to tell if an egg is rotten just by looking at the shell.

Perhaps I could find out more by meeting him in person. But how, without arousing his suspicion? I still have my press card from when I used to work at the *Gazette*. I could pretend I want to write a piece on Charlie. But I imagine he's sick of reporters by now and there's no guarantee he would agree to meet me. I decide it's probably better to approach him in a professional capacity. According to his profile, he's a clinical dietician and nutritionist and he has a wealth of experience in treating all kinds of disorders. On the website there's a quote from a satisfied customer who suffered for a long time from depression and abdominal bloating. 'Adam has literally transformed my life,' she says.

I note down his contact number and call straight away before I have the chance to chicken out.

'Hello, Holbrooke Nutrition, how can I help you?' Adam has a slight Northern accent. I can't place it. Maybe he's from Manchester.

'Hello, yes,' I say nervously. 'I'd like to make an appointment for a consultation. Um, I've been suffering from bloating and . . .' I might as well stick to the truth. 'I'm trying to lose weight.'

'Sure, I can help you with that. Can you give me your name?'

'Er, yes. It's Catherine Bayntun.'

'I give consultations in my home. I hope that's not a problem.'

'No, that's okay.' *Even better*, I think. It's an opportunity to see where Charlie died. Perhaps seeing their home will help me get a feel for their relationship and enable me to assess the viability of Adam as a suspect.

'So how about Friday at eleven o'clock?'

'That's perfect,' I say. 'See you then.'

'Wait. Don't you want the address?'

Damn. I need to be more careful. I give a light, silly-me laugh. 'Yes, of course.'

'Where are you coming from?'

'Uh, Swindon,' I lie.

He gives me some long- winded instructions on how to get to his house from Swindon, which I pretend to write down.

As soon as the call ends, the phone leaps to life in my hand. It's DI Littlewood.

I answer, my heart in my throat. What does she want now? Have they found Luke?

'Hi Catherine,' she says sounding polite and briskly efficient. 'Sorry to bother you. I hope this is a convenient time?'

'I was about go and pick up my son, but I've got a few minutes.'

'I've got some good news and some bad news. Which do you want first?'

'The good news, please.'

'Well, the good news is we managed to track down the man you met on Friday night.'

'Great.' I say, hope surging. 'That's fantastic. How did you find him?'

'We examined the security footage of the Black Bear and when we showed his picture to the bartender, he was able to identify him.'

I exhale with relief. 'Does that mean I am no longer a suspect? He told you he was with me that night?'

95

DI Littlewood doesn't answer straight away.

'Not exactly,' she sighs. 'He confirmed that you met and chatted at the Black Bear and that he gave you a lift home. But the bad news is that your accounts of the evening from that point on differ. He claims that he dropped you off at your house and then drove straight home.'

'What? But that's bullshit!' I exclaim, outraged. 'I'm sorry about my language, but he's obviously lying.' I'm trying to breathe, trying to stay calm, but my mind is spinning. Why would he lie?

'I'm just repeating what he told us,' says Littlewood calmly.

'But if you look at the security footage,' I say, 'you'll see that his car was parked outside my house all night.'

'I'm afraid we don't have any CCTV coverage of your street.'

'What about his drive home? Did you see his car? Because I'm willing to bet that you didn't.'

'We don't have cameras on the route he took either.'

He must live close by, I think. Otherwise, surely it would be a route with at least some surveillance.

'What's his full name?' I demand. 'I need to speak to him.' *I need to give him a piece of my mind*, I think. I'm furiously angry. *How dare he?*

'I'm afraid that information is confidential.'

I sigh with frustration. 'Where does he live, then? Can you tell me that?'

'Unfortunately not. I'm sorry, Catherine,' Littlewood clears her throat. 'We'd like you to come in for an interview at the police station to give your side of the story. An official statement. Can you come tomorrow at ten o'clock?'

I turn the phone call with DI Littlewood over in my mind as I walk to Dylan's school. Why did Luke, assuming, of course, that Luke is his real name, lie to the police? I can think of only two possible reasons: one, that he's married or in a relationship and doesn't want his partner to find out that he was cheating; two, that he's setting me up for some reason. The thought shudders through me. *Could Luke be the person who gave the police the photofit?*

Ten

The reading corner has been transformed overnight into a magical forest with paper leaves trailing from realistic-looking branches. There's a grass carpet and cushions that look like logs.

'Isn't it fantastic?' Mrs Bailey agrees when I compliment it. 'Ms Hamlyn was here until late last night creating it. 'She's so artistic, isn't she?'

Ms Hamlyn looks up and smiles. She and Dylan are huddled together over a book on one of the log cushions, Dylan leaning against her and her long, overgrown puppy legs stretched out in front of her.

'It's your mum, Dylan!' Ms Hamlyn announces, snapping the book shut. Dylan lets out a yelp of happiness, jumps up and launches himself at me, his little head butting my stomach, trying to wrap his arms around me.

'He's been a very good boy,' Ms Hamlyn beams as Dylan fetches his bag. 'And he drew a great picture of a dinosaur, didn't you, Dylan?'

Dylan smiles up at her adoringly and I feel an irrational twinge of jealousy. I should be happy that Dylan is bonding with his teachers – that he's happy at school. And I am. But I suppose Dylan and I have spent so much time alone together since Theo left that I feel a little possessive.

'He's got a new book in there for you to read with him,' Mrs Bailey says, running a frazzled finger through frizzy grey hair, and I'm reminded of the photo of the park. I rummage in my handbag and show it to her.

'I found this in Dylan's book bag yesterday,' I say. 'Is it homework? I'm not sure what we're supposed to do with it. There weren't any instructions.'

Mrs Bailey frowns and peers at the picture through her reading glasses.

'We didn't give them any homework, apart from the reader,' she says. She calls to Ms Hamlyn, who has wandered off and is tidying up toys on the windowsill. 'Any idea what this is?' she asks.

Ms Hamlyn shakes her head. 'That's odd,' she says.

'It was probably in the scrap paper box. We try to get them to reuse as much as possible.'

'Maybe. Or perhaps someone else put it in there by accident. One of the parents?' I hazard.

Mrs Bailey shrugs. 'I suppose it's possible. We hang them up on their pegs outside the classroom so anyone could easily pop something inside when they come to pick up their kids. But why would they?'

'I don't know. Maybe it was intended as a gift for someone else and they got the wrong bag.'

'Mm, could be. I'll ask around, see if anyone knows.'

'Thank you.' I take Dylan's hand. 'Say goodbye, Dylan.'

As I'm leaving, closing the gate that separates off the little ones from the rest of the school, Ms Hamlyn comes running up after me.

'Mrs Bayntun, I'm sorry to bother you – I almost forgot, I need to talk to you,' she says breathlessly. She clears her throat and blushes slightly. 'This is a bit awkward, but I felt you ought to know that some of the parents have complained . . .' she tails off.

I bristle. 'About what?'

She looks at Dylan and lowers her voice. 'About the murder investigation – the woman killed on Cecily Hill. There are rumours—'

'That I'm a suspect?' I say, losing patience with the way she's pussyfooting around the subject.

Ms Hamlyn looks startled. 'Well, yes. Apparently, there was a photofit on the news and some of the parents have got it into their heads that it looked like you. Ridiculous of course but . . .' She gives me an anxious look.

I feel a pressure in my chest. It feels like all the suspicion is closing in on me like a clenching fist and it's suddenly hard to breathe.

'It's true,' I say sharply. 'The police came to talk to me, but it was just a formality and they haven't arrested me.' I can feel my voice rising, anger overcoming caution. 'And do you know why they haven't arrested me?'

Ms Hamlyn shakes her head and takes a step back. She looks alarmed and I realise that she's a little afraid of me. With an effort, I try to control my temper and lower my voice.

'Because they've got absolutely no evidence – that's why.'

'I'm sure, I'm sure,' she murmurs soothingly. 'It's just that some of the parents aren't happy about you being around their children. It's nonsense, of course.' She takes a breath. 'But just to keep the peace, I was wondering if maybe Dylan's father could come and pick Dylan up from school instead? Just until this all dies down.'

I shake my head. Theo doesn't finish work until an hour later and he often has meetings and after-school clubs. 'He can't pick him up. He has to work,' I say. Besides, I fought hard to retain the right to have more access to Dylan. If I start giving Theo more time with him, it'll be the thin edge of the wedge.

'Is there anybody else?' she asks.

My mother, I think. I feel incredibly weary, but I really

don't want to ask her. She would do it, of course, but I'd never hear the end of it. 'Maybe I could come earlier to pick him up before everyone else arrives,' I suggest.

Ms Hamlyn smiles, 'That's a good idea. I'm so sorry about all this. I'm sure it'll all blow over soon.'

'Yes,' I agree, hoping that she's right. I'm suddenly aware that Dylan is staring up at us open-mouthed, listening to our conversation. I wonder how much he's heard. How much he's understood.

'Come on Dylan, let's go,' I say brightly, and I clasp his hand in mine. Inside, I'm fuming with anger and humiliation. *Some people are so narrow-minded*, I think. *So quick to judge and condemn. They don't even know me. How dare they? Whatever happened to innocent until proven guilty?*

I hesitate when I see Georgia standing at the school gate, talking to another woman with short blonde hair. I want to slide out of here unnoticed but they're blocking my path and there's no other way. I decide to brazen it out and I stride up to them with a confident smile plastered on my face. They're talking quite intently but break off abruptly when they see me.

'Hi,' I say breezily. 'How are you?'

'Hi,' says Georgia looking embarrassed and unsure. 'Cat, this is Marsha. Marsha this is Catherine. Marsha's daughter, Willow, is in Butterflies class with Harry and Dylan.'

'Nice to meet you, I'm Cat,' I say holding out my hand.

The other woman gives me a sharp look and pointedly ignores my hand. I let it fall awkwardly by my side and feel myself shrinking inwardly. But I plough on regardless, smiling so brightly that my cheeks hurt.

'Do either of you know what this could be? I got it in Dylan's book bag yesterday.' I take out the photo and hand it to Georgia.

She gives it a cursory glance. 'No, I've no idea, do you, Marsha?' Georgia says and Marsha shakes her head slightly, her eyes as cold as stones.

'Why?' Georgia asks.

'Never mind,' I say. 'It doesn't matter.' And I slink past them feeling about two inches tall.

When I get home, all I want to do is go to bed and curl up under the duvet. I want to forget about Marsha and Georgia, about Luke's lie and the fact that I'm going to have to talk to the police tomorrow. But I can't, because Dylan is here, tugging my hand, demanding that I play with him.

'Don't you want to watch TV?' I say, but he shakes his head firmly. Typical. Normally I can't drag him away from his cartoons, but today, just when I could do with some space, he seems particularly clingy and he's got it into his head that he wants us to do a jigsaw puzzle together. He drags one out from the cupboard and tips out the pieces on to the floor.

'I need you to help me,' he says, rummaging through them.

'Don't forget to start with the corner pieces,' I advise him absent-mindedly. I'm scrolling through the messages and posts on my phone. There's nothing much. An invitation from my cousin to the christening of her son and some posts from Gaby about dogs that need rehoming. Theo has been tagged in a post from Harper – a picture of them posing at an exhibition of Harper's paintings. God, that's just what I don't need right now – a reminder of their perfect life. I haven't bothered to unfriend Theo because he never posts anything, but now I think that was an oversight and I'm just clicking on his profile, working out how to delete him when my phone pings, and a message pops up. There's a bubble on my screen, a picture of a man in a baseball cap with a moustache. George Wilkinson again. I click on it angrily. What does he want this time? Why can't he just leave me alone?

'Mummy, help me,' Dylan says plaintively. 'Where does this one go?'

'Hold on a minute, sweetheart.' The message fills the screen and I grip the phone tightly, trying to remain calm and convince myself, yet again, that it's a coincidence.

'Remember this?' he's written, and underneath there's a photo of a pub sign, the Royal Oak. It's a pub in the town centre near the church. I haven't been there for years, but we used to go there all the time in the sixth form. And we went there that night, after the park – before Nessa's party.

I saw her the other day from the car window. We were driving home from the hospital, and we had stopped at the traffic lights near the marketplace. She was standing on the kerb waiting to cross the road. And she was so close I could've almost reached out and touched her.

I couldn't quite believe she was there. I thought I must have conjured her up from some dark recess of my mind. But it wasn't my imagination, it was her. I watched, in helpless rage, as she smiled and waved at someone on the other side of the road. She actually smiled, and my heart clenched like a fist.

Why haven't they locked her away? What right has she got to liberty after all that she's done? It made my blood boil, seeing her there, sauntering along the street, free as a bird, without a care in the world. I wanted to get out of the car and run after her – to confront her. I wanted to smash her face until that peachy-smooth skin was bruised and battered to a pulp. But of course, I didn't. I let her cross the road, stop and pause to look in a shop window. One day I'll make her pay for the things she's done but not yet. For now, I need to be patient. Good things come to those who wait.

Eleven

I haven't slept well in days. I drop off in Dylan's bed reading him a bedtime story and wake up two hours later with a crick in my neck and drool running down my chin. Forcing myself up, I stumble across the landing and crawl into my own bed. Then I spend another night tossing and turning before I finally fall asleep again, just as it's getting light.

The sound of a leaf blower outside my window drills into my head and I wake, bright sunlight streaming in through my window. A quick glance at my phone confirms that it's already nine o'clock. Shit! I leap out of bed, pull on the pair of shorts and t-shirt lying on the floor next to my bed and find Dylan downstairs watching cartoons in his pyjamas.

'Why didn't you wake me up?' I groan in frustration.

'What?' He looks confused.

'We're late for school. Oh, never mind. Put these on.' I throw him his school uniform.

'No!' he yells, as I turn off the telly and drag him upstairs to brush his teeth. 'It's not finished!'

'That's too bad,' I say grimly, buttoning his shirt. Then I shove his shoes on his feet and bundle him, whining and wailing into the car. Outside, Eileen's husband, Bob, is collecting up the leaves in a refuse bag. He stops and stares with sharp, critical eyes. *Anyone would think I was abusing my son,* I think, bitterly. 'Stop crying,' I hiss at Dylan. 'You're embarrassing me.'

'We're late for school,' I explain cheerily to Bob over the sound of Dylan's screams and Bob nods slightly but doesn't smile.

When I get to the school, it's already first break, and all the children are outside in the playground, running and shrieking. Ms Hamlyn is on duty, standing by the wooden pergola in the centre of the playground, a whistle around her neck. She's deep in conversation with another teacher, a woman with dark, curly hair, but breaks off when she sees us.

'Oh, hi Dylan,' she coos sweetly, crouching down to his level. 'We missed you in phonics. Where have you been?'

'Sorry,' I say breathlessly. 'We overslept.'

She straightens up, the sweet smile vanishing. She doesn't tell me it's okay this time. I've been late already twice for pick-up in just the first week and now this. It looks like even Ms Hamlyn's good nature is not inexhaustible. Three strikes and you're out with her, I suppose.

'Did you inform Nicky in the office?' she says coolly. 'She'll need to add Dylan to the register.'

'Not yet, but I will.'

'Where's his lunch? I'll put it in the fridge,' she adds, as Dylan runs off to play with Harry and a couple of other children who are kicking a ball around on the small football pitch.

Crap! I forgot. 'It was just on the side,' I lie, feeling mortified. 'I'll go home and fetch it.' I haven't even given him a water bottle.

'No need. Don't bother. He can have a school dinner. There are always a few extra and I can give him one just this once. Are you okay?' she says with sudden sympathy as I turn to leave. 'You look a bit peaky.'

'I'm fine,' I say, scurrying away before I start bawling in front of Ms Hamlyn and the other teacher. 'Thank you.'

At home, I just have time to feed Delilah and shower and change before I have to head to the police station to give a statement. As I'm leaving the house, I glance in the mirror and examine myself critically. My hair is still sleekly blonde, but it's starting to get greasy and clump a little. I haven't washed it since the haircut yet. I'll never be able to blow dry it the same way. But I've dressed smartly in a new summer dress with purple butterflies. *I look respectable and honest*, I think, tucking my hair behind my ear. I give myself a friendly, trustworthy smile. They have to believe me over Luke, surely.

The police station is near the centre of town, just behind Boots on the high street. I've only ever been inside once before, years ago when I found a stray dog with Charlie. Knowing that our parents wouldn't be willing to keep it, we took it to the police station. I can't remember much about what happened, except that we left the dog with a friendly policeman and that he gave us badges.

There's no badge this time, and the policeman who greets me is not so friendly. A stocky, young officer, he fills in a form with grave formality and then shows me through without ceremony to a bare, grey office where DI Littlewood and Sergeant Fisher are waiting.

'Thank you for coming,' Littlewood smiles coolly – as if I had any choice in the matter. She takes a sip of water from a plastic cup. 'We'll try to take up as little of your time as possible. Please take a seat.'

'Would you like a drink, Catherine?' asks Fisher, all friendly bumbling as if I'm a guest in his house.

I smile at him gratefully and shake my head. If I accept a drink, I won't be able to hide the fact that my hands are trembling, and it will be obvious how nervous I am.

'If you don't mind, we'd like to run through your account of Friday night again, just to make sure we've got everything straight,' says Littlewood smoothly as I perch on the edge of the chair.

'Sure, no problem,' I say with false bravado.

Littlewood switches on a tape recorder, announces the date and lists the names of the people present in the room.

'So, Catherine Bayntun,' she says, 'for the recording, please tell us in your own words what happened on the night of Friday the thirtieth of August.'

Cautiously, I run through the events of that night again. But I've been through it so many times now in my head it sounds false – like a rehearsed speech – and I try to ignore the sceptical expressions on their faces as I recount what happened: dropping Dylan off, Weight Watchers, the pub and then the drive home.

'I invited Luke into my house, and he accepted,' I finish firmly. 'He stayed the whole night.' I repeat that several times, so that there can be no doubt.

'Do you have any evidence that he was at your house?' asks Fisher.

'Like what?'

He shrugs, 'Something he left behind maybe, or some proof that you and he were intimate.'

'He has a birthmark on his thigh,' I say, with a sudden flash of inspiration. 'How would I know that if I hadn't slept with him?'

'A birthmark?' Littlewood looks interested. 'Can you describe it?'

I picture his smooth, muscular leg. The bedroom was dimly lit, so I only had a vague impression. I tell them, 'It was brown, I think,' suddenly doubting myself. 'Sort of long, like a cigar.'

Littlewood nods and smiles, as if I'm a child who needs encouragement.

'Anything else you can remember?'

'Not really.' I shake my head.

'Well, that's it for now,' Littlewood switches off the recorder and says 'Thank you very much, Catherine. That was helpful.'

'Oh, one more thing,' she adds casually, as I stand up to leave.

'Yes?'

'We'd like to take a DNA sample. You don't mind, do you? It's a simple process. It'll only take a minute. Purely routine.'

I hesitate. I don't like the idea of having my DNA on a police database, but it would look suspicious if I refused, and it could only be to my advantage, right? They won't find any of my DNA at Charlie's flat. I'm certain of that.

'Sure, no problem,' I say smiling. I am nothing if not co-operative. Co-operative and trustworthy.

Littlewood wasn't lying. The DNA sample didn't take much more than a few minutes – a simple swab of my mouth – and before I know it, I'm back outside the police station inhaling fresh air, blinking in the sunlight, feeling like a prisoner who's been released after years in jail.

Did the police believe me? I wonder as I walk home. It's impossible to tell. Fisher maybe did, but Littlewood gives nothing away and she's the one who counts. Will they even bother to check up on the birthmark? My mind is working overtime, analysing the interview, wondering what impression I made and trying to figure out what my next step should be. But I can feel a migraine coming on – that familiar nagging pain just above my right eye – and when I get home all I can do is take a couple of painkillers and crawl into bed.

I'm woken after what seems like only a few minutes by my phone ringing persistently on the bedside table.

'Cat, where are you?'

It's Gaby and she sounds annoyed. I can hear the clatter of crockery in the background, the murmur of voices and the hiss of an espresso machine.

'We were supposed to meet today for a coffee,' she says testily. 'I'm waiting for you here in the bookshop café. Have you forgotten?'

I rub my eyes, sitting up. At least my headache has gone.

'Shit, sorry, I fell asleep. I'll come now,' I say. The way things are going I need all the friends I can get and the last thing I want to do is piss Gaby off. 'I'll be about ten, fifteen minutes.'

My mouth feels stale, so I brush my teeth, run a comb through my hair and then dash out into town.

I enter the bookstore through the back entrance in the car park and find Gaby sitting in a corner of the café, sipping a latte and scrolling through her phone, a pensive expression on her face.

'I'm so sorry,' I blurt, kissing her cheek. 'I completely forgot. It's no excuse, but I've had the worst few days.'

She runs a hand through her hair, which looks even wilder than usual, and frowns. 'Yes, I heard about the news story and the photofit. The police called me to talk about Friday night. It sounds like you're having a bit of a nightmare. Are you okay?'

'I've been better,' I try to laugh.

Gaby's big, brown eyes meet mine and they are steady and sympathetic. There's no judgement or suspicion in them. Just empathy and curiosity.

'Poor you,' she says, and I feel the tension in my shoulders relaxing slightly. She pats me on the knee and grins. 'I know what'll cheer you up,' she says, and she bustles off to the counter and returns a few minutes later with two coffees and two cinnamon buns. 'I won't tell Sara if you won't.'

I bite into the sweet, sticky bun, letting the delicious blend of cinnamon and sugar swirl around my mouth. Gaby's right. It does make me feel better. It's not called comfort food for no reason.

'I had to go into the police station this morning,' I tell her. 'They wanted me to go through what happened on Friday night. They seriously think I might have murdered that woman.'

Gaby looks at me directly. 'But you didn't,' she says. It's a statement of fact not a question.

'No, of course not.'

'Well then. Sooner or later the police will find out who did, and you'll be in the clear.'

'Yes, but I'm worried that even afterwards, after this is all sorted, this will stick to me like a bad smell. I'll always be the woman who was suspected of murder.' Murder. It's such a frightening and dramatic word. A word that's used on true crime programmes and in thrillers. It shouldn't have anything to do with me. It doesn't belong in my life.

She shakes her head, takes a bite of her bun, chews slowly and swallows. 'People will forget, Cat, you'll see. They've got short memories. Anyway, whatever happens your friends will stick by you.'

I feel tears of gratitude welling up in my eyes. Gaby is a

true friend – one of the few people I believe is really on my side. She was so good to me after Theo left. She brought me flowers and cajoled and badgered me to get out and get on with my life. I'm not sure what I would have done without her. I'm not sure I deserve a friend like her.

After coffee with Gaby, I pick up Dylan from school, a little early, as agreed, before all the other parents have arrived.

'Do you want to go to the park, Dylan?' I ask as we scurry out of the gate.

'Yeah!' he exclaims, swiping an imaginary sword through the air. And so we head to the Abbey Grounds. I sit on the bench for a while and watch Dylan play. He looks lonely there, his little face a mask of dogged, solitary determination as he scales the climbing frame, and I find myself wishing Theo and I had got around to having another child. But I found Dylan so exhausting as a two- and three-year-old, I couldn't even contemplate another, and by the time he was nearly five and becoming much easier, Theo had already met Harper.

On our way home, we stop at the kiosk near the gate and I buy Dylan some sweets and a packet of fudge for me. I've already broken my diet today, so I might as well pig out, make the most of it and start again tomorrow. We munch in happy silence on the way home, fingers sticky and lips grainy with sugar. Life is too short to worry about calories all the time, I think. We need a treat after the past few days. The sun is shining, and I feel refreshed and buoyed by my conversation with Gaby. In the sunshine it's easy to feel more optimistic. Gaby's right, this whole thing will all blow over; people will soon forget and move on to the next scandal. I hold Dylan's warm, sticky hand in mine, and he smiles up at me. *We'll be all right together*, I think. I need to get my priorities straight. So long as I've got Dylan and he's got me and he is well and happy, I don't need anything else.

'What's that?' Dylan asks as we turn into our street. He points towards our house at something written on the front wall in large red letters.

'I don't know,' I say. I can't read it from here. *Bloody kids*, I think with annoyance. *How dare they?* Because our house is on the end and is near to the pub it occasionally gets vandalised by drunks. Sometimes the fence gets kicked in or the flowerpots tipped over at night. But no one has ever written graffiti on it before. Besides, it's the middle of the day. That surely wasn't there when I left the house.

As we get closer and the letters come into clearer focus, my heart plummets. The paint has dripped in places, making it look as if the words have been daubed on in blood, but the message is still abundantly clear. Shockingly, heart-stoppingly clear.

'What does that say?' Dylan pesters me as I hurry him up the path to the front door. 'Wait –' he tugs at my hand

and tries to sound out the letters the way he's been taught at school – 'm . . . u—'

'Never mind. Come on inside,' I say, trying to cover his eyes and bundling him through the door as quickly as I can, my heart racing. 'Someone naughty has written a bad word, that's all.'

This is bad. Very bad.

'Ow, Mummy, you're hurting me,' he complains as I drag him through to the living room. I want to read the word. I can read really well now.'

'I'm sure you can,' I say through gritted teeth. But I need you to just sit tight in here for a bit while Mummy takes care of something.'

I switch on cartoons and plonk him on the sofa. 'Don't move,' I say firmly. Then I head outside to the shed and find a large paintbrush and a half-full tin of paint. It's Magnolia – not the same colour as the wall, but it will have to do. I lug the tin around to the front of the house and splash paint on the wall in broad brushstrokes. I haven't bothered changing. I paint in what I'm wearing – my new summer dress. I don't care if I ruin it. I just want to obliterate that hateful writing. As quickly as I can, I cover the letters, layering on several coats of paint until you can no longer read the word underneath, painted in red:

MURDERER.

In the toilet, I wash the paint off my shaking hands with turpentine, scraping off the bits that have already dried with my nails. Then I head downstairs to check that Dylan is okay.

'Will the naughty man be in trouble?' he asks, round-eyed, looking up from his cartoons.

'Big, big trouble,' I say, kissing him on the head. 'Just a sec. Wait here. I'm going to pop round next door to see if Eileen or Bob saw anything.'

I leave the front door open so that I can hear Dylan if he needs me and hop over the low wall to the neighbours. Outside their front door, I take a deep breath and try to steady my shaking hands. I don't want Eileen to see how agitated I am.

Eileen answers, but only opens the door halfway.

'Yes?' she says warily.

What does she think? I'm going to barge in and hack her to death? Not such a bad idea, come to think of it. 'Um, I was wondering if you saw anything earlier today. Someone wrote some graffiti on my house and I thought maybe you might have seen who did it?'

She purses her lips and shakes her head. 'No, I didn't see anyone,' she says.

Like hell, you didn't, I think. *Like you're not always nosing into the coming and goings in the neighbourhood.*

'Are you sure? What about Bob? Maybe he—' I say.

'Bob didn't see anything either. I'm absolutely sure,' she says and slams the door in my face.

I should have known Eileen wouldn't be any help. *For all I know, she wrote the message herself,* I think angrily, as I clamber back over the wall and shut myself in my house. I feel a wave of frustration, rage and despair. Just when I thought things were going to be okay, this happens.

I manage to hold it together long enough to feed Dylan and put him to bed. Fortunately, he hasn't learned to tell the time yet, so I'm able to convince him it's an hour later than it is. But once Dylan is safely in bed, all the fear and anger I've been bottling up for the past few days surge out of me and I curl up on my bed, finally giving in to tears. I cry like I haven't cried in years – big sobs that shake my body and leave me breathless. I cry until I'm all cried out and then I sit up and wipe my eyes, fetch some toilet paper from the bathroom and blow my nose. I feel as if I'm under siege. It's so unfair. What did I do to deserve this?

This isn't going to stop until the police find the real killer. But when will that be? I could be waiting for ever. They've made no progress as far as I can tell and they are wasting their time interviewing people like Gaby, Luke and me.

Staring in the mirror at my red, swollen eyes, I experience a sudden clarity. I can't afford to wallow in self-pity and wait for Littlewood to ride in on her white charger and rescue me. If I want this to go away, I'm going to have to do something about it myself. I need to find out who gave the police the photofit and who murdered Charlie for myself.

I ignore the discouraging voice inside my head that says, *Who are you kidding? What makes you think you would find anything the police have missed?* But I have something the police don't have, and that's motivation. Clearing my name; it doesn't get much more motivating that that. Where should I start though? I brush my teeth, get undressed and climb into bed, thinking all the time. Of course, the answer is obvious. There's really only one place.

Twelve

It's Friday – a week since Charlie was murdered and I am standing on the pavement in front of her house. From the outside Cecily House hasn't changed much since I was last here. It's is a large, elegant Georgian building perched at the top of the hill on the edge of the Bathurst estate – or the big park, as we used to call it. You would never guess from the old stone façade that it's been divided up into flats inside. The only changes are subtle and in keeping with the historic character of the house: a small extension has been added, blending discreetly with the stonework and there's a ramp curving around the stairs up to the front door, but otherwise it seems much as I remember it from when Charlie and I were kids.

I do a one-eighty, taking in my surroundings. There's a large, black wrought-iron gate to the park and a wide footpath leading up to the monument. Opposite Cecily House is a row of smaller houses. They have a clear view of the entrance. Anyone in those houses could have provided the police with that photofit or it could have been someone walking up the hill into the park, or someone in Cecily House itself . . .

Bathed in September sunshine, the house looks pretty, not menacing at all, but even so, I suppress a shiver as I approach the entrance and the nightmare I had the other night comes back to me in vivid detail. Images of Charlie dead and dying crowd into my mind. Charlie's eyes bulging as she begs for mercy. The blood on her shirt spreading like an ink blot.

Quashing the voice inside my head telling me this is a bad idea, I press the buzzer for number one, Adam and Charlie's flat. After a couple of seconds, the intercom crackles.

'Who is it?' asks Adam.

I clear my throat nervously. 'It's Catherine Bayntun. We spoke on the phone the other day? I have an appointment for a consultation.'

He hesitates for just a second. 'Sure, yes, come on in,' he says and buzzes me in. I push my way through the heavy door, and it swings firmly shut behind me. Finding myself suddenly enclosed in a dark, windowless corridor, I fight a wave of panic. What if Adam recognises me from the photofit? Or what if my mother is right and he killed Charlie? What kind of danger am I getting myself into?

'Hi, Catherine, come on in,' Adam says, opening the door to his flat and making me jump. He looks a little older and scruffier than the photograph on his LinkedIn profile. Less put together and handsome, and paradoxically less like a serial killer. And he looks taller than in the pictures on TV. Of course, Charlie had that effect – of shrinking a person; most people seemed diminished in her presence. She was always so bright and so vibrant.

His eyes are slightly bloodshot, I notice, as he ushers me into the living room, and he smells strongly of after-shave.

'You look familiar,' he says, doing a double take as I step into the light from the living-room window. 'Have we met before?'

'I don't think so,' I say cautiously, putting a self-conscious hand up to my face. I should have done more to disguise myself. What if he works out where he's seen me before? I hold my breath. Then sigh with relief as he shrugs.

'Maybe not.'

'I've got that kind of face,' I say lightly. 'I'm always being mistaken for other people.'

'Take a seat,' he says politely. 'Would you like a drink? I have a selection of herbal teas or coffee.'

'Do you have peppermint?'

While he's making drinks in the kitchen, I perch nervously on the edge of the sofa and look around the room. It's exactly the kind of place I would have expected Charlie to live in. There are brightly coloured rugs on the floor, battered old books on a bookshelf, a tree painted on one wall, a guitar flung on the armchair and a keyboard dominating one corner of the room. They must be Adam's, unless Charlie learned an instrument after she left school. That explains the attraction, I think. Charlie was always a sucker for a musician. I remember when we were thirteen, she was obsessed with the drummer in the school band. Despite the artful, cosy chaos, the place is scrupulously clean and there's a faint odour of bleach. *Of course*, I think with a flicker of fear. *They would have had to clean up all the blood.*

On the wall, there's a photo of Charlie and Adam; the same one that the press released. She's smiling down at me with an expression I remember – that flirtatious smile she gave everyone, half mocking, half challenging. I stare at it feeling uneasy. When she smiled at me like that, I always felt as if she knew exactly what I was thinking.

'So,' Adam says as he comes back into the living room carrying two steaming mugs, plonking them on the coffee table and making me jump.

'Sorry, I didn't mean to startle you,' he says pleasantly. He sits down opposite me and glances at the notes in front of him and then at me. 'You want to lose weight, right?'

He looks at me appraisingly. 'I wouldn't say you need to lose too much.'

'I've already lost quite a bit, but I can't seem to shift the last couple of stone,' I say. Not surprising, I suppose, considering all the packets of fudge and chocolate biscuits I've eaten lately, but he doesn't need to know about that.

He clears his throat. 'The first thing I should say is that diets don't always work – not long term. People who diet might lose it at first but tend to gain weight over time. The best thing you can do is aim to lead a healthy lifestyle, increasing the amount of protein and vegetables you eat, cutting down on refined sugar and carbohydrates.'

'That sucks,' I pout. 'Sugar and carbohydrates are two of my favourite things.'

He smiles wanly. 'Why don't you start off by telling me what you eat on a typical day?'

Hmm, I think. *Yesterday, a slice of toast for breakfast, a salad for lunch, then a cinnamon bun, a whole bag of fudge, a whole pizza and a packet of ginger biscuits and half a large tub of strawberry ice cream.*

'I don't really have a typical day,' I say.

'Well, that could be part of the problem.'

He goes on to discuss the different types of proteins, carbohydrates and fats for a while. He talks in such a natural, easy way and seems so normal that I forget to be afraid of him. Instead, I start feeling sorry for him. I notice his nails, which have been bitten to the quick and the dark shadows under his eyes. This is a man clearly struggling to come to terms with the death of his wife and bravely trying to carry on with his life. But I mustn't forget the purpose of my visit. I didn't come here just to chat about nutrition. I came here to find out more about Charlie's death, and during a pause in the conversation I decide to broach the subject directly.

'I'm so sorry about Charlie,' I say. 'I can't imagine what you must be going through.'

He frowns and blinks at me with dark, startled eyes. 'You knew Charlie?'

'We were friends at school.' I wonder if he will find it weird that I've decided to consult the husband of my recently murdered school friend, but on balance I decide it's worth the risk of telling him I know her, so that I can get him to talk about her death. I rummage in my bag and pull out the photograph Mum gave me. 'I found this the other day. I thought you might be interested,' I say. 'That's me and Charlie when we were about thirteen.'

He takes the photo but doesn't really look at it. He seems distracted. His hand is trembling a little and I wonder why. It could just be natural emotion on seeing the image of his murdered wife or it could be something more sinister.

'I don't know if she ever mentioned me?' I ask tentatively.

'Catherine? Catherine Bayntun? I don't think so.' He shakes his head slowly.

'Bayntun is my married name. I was called Hawkins at school. Cat Hawkins.'

'Cat Hawkins,' he murmurs. 'Yes, now I come to think of it. She did mention you.' His eyes narrow and I feel a twinge of unease. How much exactly did she tell him?

'What did she say about me?' I ask.

'Um . . .' He frowns. 'Just that you were a good friend at school. Some of the scrapes you got into – like the time you were arrested for trespassing.'

'So, she told you all our deep, dark secrets?' I say lightly, as if it's a joke.

He doesn't answer. There's a long pause. He shifts uncomfortably and clears his throat. 'Listen Catherine, this is all a bit strange, don't you think? I didn't know you were a friend of Charlie's. I don't mean to be rude but why exactly are you here? You didn't come here to talk about nutrition, did you?'

He stands up and I'm worried that he's going to show me to the door.

'I know it must seem odd,' I say rapidly, 'but I honestly didn't know you were Charlie's husband until you gave me your address, and when I realised who you were, I did consider cancelling the appointment, but then I changed my mind. I thought you might welcome the chance to talk about Charlie to someone else who knew her well and who loved her too.'

My voice breaks a little on that last part and it seems to have the desired effect because he hesitates and then sits down again with a heavy sigh.

'How did you two meet?' I ask, trying to turn the conversation down a less dangerous path.

He rubs his forehead and eyes. 'At uni. We met at a gig. I used to play in a band.' He smiles – a sad, lopsided smile – and looks suddenly sweet. 'She was very drunk, and she got up on stage and tried to grab my guitar to sing happy birthday to one of her mates.'

'Yep, that sounds like Charlie.'

'I wasn't impressed at first, but later I got to know her sober and – well, you know what she was like.'

I know what he means. He fell under her spell. Everyone who ever met Charlie fell under her spell.

'Whenever you were with her life was an adventure,' I say.

'Yes, that's it exactly,' he exclaims, surprised. His eyes light up and he looks at me – really looks at me for the first time. Then a cloud passes over, and for a second, I think he's going to cry.

'Well, it's good to meet a friend of Charlie's.' He stands up again. It's a cue for me to go, I realise. But I'm not ready yet. I need him to keep talking.

'I still can't believe she's dead,' I say, not shifting from the sofa. 'I mean, why would anyone want to kill Charlie? She was such a lovely person.' This is not entirely true. Charlie always tended to provoke strong emotions in people, both good and bad. There was that boy at school who was so obsessed with her he attempted suicide when she broke up with him; and she once had a full-on fist fight with Amelia Blake by the school gates.

Adam's face blackens. 'I don't know,' he says, looking at his feet.

I can tell he doesn't really want to talk about this, but I press on regardless. 'Was it a break-in? Was anything stolen?'

'No. The police think it was someone she knew. There was no sign of forced entry. She must have let them in.'

'It was somebody she knew?' I say, my breath catching in my throat.

'I suppose so.' He sits back down looking winded. 'I keep thinking who would she have let in at that time of night? Who did she trust that she shouldn't have? Do I know them? Do you know what that feels like – to look at everyone you know and think, could you have done this horrible thing? Could you have killed my wife?' He squeezes his eyes shut, as if there's a piece of grit in them – a bid to ward off intense pain or an attempt at fake emotion? It's hard to tell.

'It must be horrible. I can't imagine.' I murmur. 'What

about the rest of the people who live in the building? There are three other flats, right?'

'Yes.'

'Do you know them well? Do you trust them?'

'Do I think they murdered Charlie, you mean?' He frowns and looks as if he's considering the possibility. Then he shakes his head slowly. 'In flat two there's Meg Darley. She's a lovely person and she's disabled – severely disabled. Aside from having absolutely no reason to kill Charlie, she wouldn't have been physically capable.' He pauses and frowns. 'Then there's Ben Wiltshire in flat four. Charlie found him begging on the street and offered him a place to live free of charge.'

'Completely free?' I suppose I shouldn't be surprised. Charlie was always generous with the little money she had. I remember her in the pub buying rounds for everyone when we finished our A levels.

Adam nods and presses his lips together. 'I warned her against taking in people like that. He's an addict. It wouldn't surprise me if he killed her for drug money.'

'Was any money stolen?'

'Maybe. I don't know how much she had lying around, but the medicine box was out on the table and all the contents had been tipped out. Charlie had strong painkillers in there. I think he could have been looking for medication, anything to get a fix.'

'Or I suppose Charlie could've been looking for a bandage, something to stop the bleeding?' I suggest tentatively.

'Yes, only there was no blood on the box. There was blood everywhere else but none on that box.'

I shudder, trying to block an image of Charlie dying and bleeding, desperately trying to survive. *Charlie would have fought to her very last breath*, I think.

'What about the other flat?' I say, trying not to cry. If Adam can hold it together, then I can too.

Adam shrugs. 'Flat three is empty. They moved out a couple of weeks before Charlie died. They went to Newcastle. I don't think they could have had anything to do with Charlie's death.'

Then casually, carefully, 'Where were you on Friday night?'

Immediately I regret asking him because he gives me a sharp, angry look. Clearly, I've gone too far. I sound almost like I'm interrogating him – as if I suspect him of murdering Charlie. Which of course I do.

'I'm not sure that's any of your business,' he says coldly. 'But if you must know, I was on a stag weekend in Paris. Turns out it was the worst decision of my life.'

'You couldn't have known what would happen.'

Adam continues, shaking his head, almost as if he's talking to himself. 'I didn't even like the guy. He's just some idiot I used to know at uni. One of those people you never seem to shake off.'

'So, who found her . . . I thought—'

'Oh, I found her.' He winces at the memory. 'When I got back from the trip. She'd been dead for nearly a whole day.' His voice comes out bitter and harsh and the eyes he fixes on me are dark with anger. 'But it took her several hours to die.'

'She didn't die straight away?' I feel deeply shocked. Poor Charlie. She must have been so frightened and in so much pain – I wonder how it's even possible that she was still alive after being stabbed four times in the chest.

'No, she was attacked in the kitchen,' he says. 'But she somehow manged to drag herself through to the living room. The police think she was trying to get to her phone.'

So, she died in this room, I think with a shudder. *Where exactly was the body?* I think about the dream. Charlie in those white pyjamas, blood on her chest. 'What was she wearing?'

He gives me an odd look. 'I don't remember. Her night-shirt, I think,' he says. 'Why?'

'Oh, no reason.'

I return to what Adam told me about the police thinking Charlie was killed by someone she knew. 'Did she have any plans to meet anyone that night?' I ask.

'Not to my knowledge. I called her at about eight o'clock

the night she died,' he says. 'That was the last time I spoke to her. The last time anybody spoke to her – apart from her killer, of course. She said she was going to have a quiet night and watch a film on Netflix.'

'And do you know if the police have any leads?' My mouth is dry, waiting for his answer.

'Not really,' he wipes his nose and glares at the coffee table. 'They don't tell me much. They treat me as if I'm a suspect.'

You and me both.

There's a pause. Adam frowns and stands up abruptly. 'Right,' he looks at his watch again. 'Well, it's been nice to meet you, Catherine. Thank you for this photo. Let me know how you get on.'

Thirteen

Outside Adam's flat I wipe away the tears of anger and fear that are welling up in my eyes. I can't imagine what kind of pain and terror Charlie must have experienced in those last few hours of her life. Did she know she was going to die, or did she keep hoping and clinging on until the last minute? It doesn't bear thinking about. One thing is clear – whoever killed her is dangerous and it's more important than ever that I find out who it was.

Adam obviously believes, or at least is pretending to believe, that the man that lives in the flat upstairs could have murdered her. And I wonder if the police have been looking into him as a suspect. Surely, they must have at least interviewed everyone in the building. But have they missed something? I ball up the tissue in my hand, shove it in my pocket, take a deep breath and climb the carpeted stairs to the first floor and flat four. There's no answer when I ring the bell, so I thump loudly on the door until it flies open. Loud rock music blares out and a thin, young man eyeballs me suspiciously.

'Ben Wiltshire?' I shout over the music.

'That's me,' he says. 'How can I help you?'

'Er . . . I'm Catherine Bayntun. I flash my press card. Hopefully, he won't notice that it's out of date. 'I'm from the *Wilts and Gloucester Standard*. I just want to ask you a few questions about the death of Charlotte Holbrooke.'

'No journalists,' he says, shaking his head firmly as he starts to close the door.

'I can pay you for your time,' I say desperately.

He opens the door again just a fraction. 'How much?' he asks.

I rummage in my purse. I have sixty pounds cash in there. I hold it out to him, and he grasps it eagerly.

'Can I come in?'

'Sure,' he steps back to let me in.

His flat is the same layout as the downstairs one, but the walls are plain white and the furniture is bland – Ikea standard. From what Adam told me, I'd expect it to be a dingy, sordid drug den, but in fact, it's quite clean and tidy, if rather bare, and the large windows let in a lot of light. In the living room the music is deafening, and I put my hands over my ears.

'Sorry,' he says, and he presses a button on a remote and the music stops.

'Thanks, that's better.'

Now I can hear myself think I examine him more closely. He has a stubbly brown beard and a solid covering of tattoos on his neck and arms. At a guess, I would say that he can't be much more than twenty-five, but he's stringy and haggard-looking and there's a dull, disillusioned look in his eyes that you'd expect from a much older man.

Aside from his skinniness and his eagerness to accept my cash, there are no obvious signs of drug addiction. He seems with it, and his hand is steady as he moves a PlayStation controller from the one chair in the room. 'Take a seat,' he says, and I hover uncertainly.

'Where will you sit?' I ask.

'I'm sorry – I don't get many visitors,' he says. 'Don't worry about me.'

He fetches a chair from the kitchen and sits on it back to front, legs straddled, hugging the back rest and gives me a direct, challenging look.

'Well. What do you want to know?'

Did you kill Charlotte Holbrooke? I think. *Did you murder my friend just so that you could get high?*

'Did you know Charlotte Holbrooke well?' I ask out loud.

He jiggles his leg. 'You could say that, yeah.'

'What was she like?'

He gives a deep, sad sigh. 'What can I say about Charlie?' he says. 'She was one of a kind. I've never met anyone quite like her.' He winces in what looks like genuine pain and to my surprise his eyes fill with tears.

'How do you mean?' I ask gently.

He taps his fingers on his knee. He doesn't seem to be able to keep still. 'She was an angel, that's all. If it weren't for her, I'd still be on the streets. In fact, I'd probably be dead by now.'

'Really?'

'Oh yeah. I was fucked up when Charlie found me. There's no doubt about that.'

He stares down at the carpet.

'How did you meet her?' I ask.

He turns to look at me. 'It was about two years ago. I'd just been kicked out of my flat and I had nowhere to live. I was mainly couch-surfing and staying in hostels. Anyway, I was sleeping rough in Cheltenham and I got talking to Charlie. She said she had a place empty and that I could use it if I wanted—' He breaks off. 'Why aren't you writing any of this down?'

'I'm recording it on my phone,' I say.

He looks dubious. 'Well, I don't want you misquoting me.'

'I won't, I promise.' I'm wondering what brought about this change in Charlie. True, she was always generous, but the Charlie I knew was more interested in having a good time than in charities and causes. Plus, it seemed reckless, even for Charlie, to invite someone she didn't know into her home.

'I thought there'd be a catch,' he continues. 'There usually is. But with Charlie there wasn't. Not only that, but she persuaded me to go to rehab. She paid for me to go to this expensive clinic and well . . . here I am now. Three months clean. All thanks to her.'

Clean. This isn't the picture Adam painted.

'What about her husband, Adam? Do you know him?' I ask.

He frowns. 'Not so well. And I don't really like what I do know, to be honest.'

This is interesting. Adam didn't like Ben and clearly the feeling is mutual. 'Why not?' I ask, leaning forward.

'He wasn't good enough for her. He didn't appreciate her like he should have.'

Ben looks furiously angry for a moment and it occurs to me that he was jealous of Adam. His feelings for Charlie seem to be stronger than the usual tenant–landlord relationship. I even wonder if he was a little in love with her.

'What do you mean by that?' I ask.

'Oh, nothing,' he sighs. 'Probably nobody deserved her. She was . . . Well, I can't explain to someone who didn't know her.'

But I did know her. Sighing, I stand up and walk over to the window. From his living room I can see the park, the wide, straight path flanked by chestnut trees, a family trailing dogs and children striding up to the top of the hill. There is also a clear view of the road outside the front entrance.

'What about the night Charlie was killed – did you see or hear anything?' I ask, turning back towards Ben.

He gives me a sudden sly look and I supress a shiver of fear. What if it was him who provided the police with the description of me? But that's nonsense. He doesn't even know me. What reason could he have to want to frame me?

'Yeah, I did, as a matter of fact. I didn't hear anything, but I heard a car drive up and park outside at about one o'clock in the morning. I assumed it was Adam back from his trip.'

'What made you think that?'

'I don't know. Who else would visit so late at night? And anyway,' he bites his lip. 'Whoever it was didn't ring the buzzer. They let themselves in with a key.'

I inhale sharply. 'Really? Are you sure? How would you know?'

He looks annoyed. 'Yes, I'm sure. I heard the sound of the key in the lock.'

'You could hear it from up here?' I say doubtfully.

'Yes, it was hot that night and the windows were open. I couldn't sleep so I came in here to have a smoke.

I sit down again, feeling winded. If he's telling the truth, this is dynamite. It suggests that someone in the Cecily House flats killed Charlie. But it couldn't have been Adam. He had an alibi. The police must have checked that, surely.

'Who else had a key to the front door?' I ask as casually as I can.

'I don't know,' he shrugs. 'As far as I know, just me, Meg and Sophia in number two and Charlie and Adam, of course.'

'Sophia?'

'Meg's care worker, companion or whatever you call it.'

I grip the armrest tightly. My hands are shaking with excitement. 'Did you tell this to the police?'

'I did. But I don't think they believed me. Police don't tend to take people like me seriously.'

I'm not surprised. He comes across as shifty and untrustworthy, though I believe that his feelings for Charlie were genuine.

'Did you hear anything else after that?'

'I went to bed and finally got to sleep. But later I was woken up by a scream.' He shudders. 'I didn't realise what it was at the time, but now I think it must have been Charlie.'

I didn't sleep well last night. I kept seeing her face in my mind, smiling and waving by the side of the road. When I did finally get to sleep, I had nightmares. I dreamed I was walking along the street, a child's small hand clasped in mine. I'm not sure where I was going but I knew I had to get there quickly and that there was something very important I had to do. Something terrible had happened and I had to put it right.

'Are we nearly there?' the child asked plaintively, and I looked down and saw that it was Daisy looking up at me with her innocent blue eyes – those eyes that grab on to me like claws and won't let go.

'Daisy!' I exclaimed, my heart bursting with joy and relief. 'But I don't understand . . . you're alive. How are you alive?'

She didn't answer. She just grinned at me revealing the pink gums where her baby teeth had fallen out.

'It's your fault,' she said airily. Then she let go of my hand and before I could stop her, she ran out into the road.

'Daisy, no!' I screamed, as a huge truck loomed out of nowhere and ploughed into her, shattering her small body. I watched in horror as the pieces turned into jigsaw-puzzle pieces and scattered in the wind.

I woke up silently screaming, my pillow drenched in tears. Daisy is dead and nothing will ever bring her back. Somehow, I have to live with that.

Fourteen

Ben Wiltshire is probably full of shit, I think, as I climb down the stairs.

Even so, I stop thoughtfully outside flat two and I notice that the patio doors are flung wide open. The radio is blaring and there's a woman sitting in a motorised wheelchair on the patio under the shade of a maple tree. Her grey hair is neatly bobbed, her mouth is hanging open slightly, her head tipped to the side and her hands resting limply on the edge of the chair.

I recoil slightly at the sight of her and am immediately ashamed of myself for my reaction, so I overcompensate by smiling broadly and saying an unnecessarily loud 'Hello.'

She doesn't respond immediately, just makes a strange gurgling noise in her throat and I think she can't speak or that maybe she's mentally disabled. But her eyes seem to be flicking up and down, looking at the monitor on the portable stand next to her computer and then the computer next to her speaks in a cheerful American woman's voice.

'Hi there.'

'I'm Catherine,' I say, taking a cautious step towards her, holding out my hand for her to shake, then I drop it, flushing with embarrassment as I realise that of course she can't lift her arm. 'I'm an old friend of Charlotte's – the woman who lived in flat one. Did you know her?'

Again, there is an unsettling silence as her eyes move purposefully across the monitor.

'Nice to meet you, Catherine. I'm Meg. Yes, Charlie was a good friend,' she says at last. 'She was a special person,' the machine voice continues.

'Yeah, Charlie was one of a kind,' I agree. 'I still can't believe anyone would want to hurt her. I mean who could do something so despicable . . . so . . .' I search for the right word. 'So *evil?*'

'Why don't you take a seat for a minute? I'd offer you a drink, but I can't move. I'm paralysed from the neck down in case you hadn't noticed.'

I'm not sure if this is meant to be a joke and I smile awkwardly.

'It's okay, I'm not thirsty,' I say, perching on the edge of the garden chair. As I turn and face the road, it occurs to me that this is a good vantage point to see anyone coming and going. Meg has an even better view of the entrance than Ben.

'I wish I knew what happened to her,' I sigh.

'Yes, me too.'

'You didn't see or hear anything the night she was killed? Or in the days before she was killed, anything out of the ordinary?'

There's a silence. I watch a sparrow flutter down to the bird feeder hanging from the maple tree and a car crawl past along the road.

'I went to bed early that night. I had a headache,' Meg says at last. 'The only unusual thing about that weekend was that Adam was away.'

'Did Charlie have any visitors?'

'Just the man who came that afternoon.'

'The man?' I lean forward. My heart is thumping with excitement. 'Who was he? What did he look like?'

'He had dark hair, dark complexion. Good-looking. He brought flowers – a bunch of irises.'

'And do you know who he was?'

'No, but I've seen him here before.'

So, someone Charlie knew, a friend, then. Or maybe even . . . Is it possible Charlie was having an affair? It seems unlikely. She and Adam hadn't been married long.

'How long did he stay? Did you see him leave?' I'm aware that I'm firing questions at her, but she doesn't seem to take offence or become defensive; though it's difficult to tell – her eyes are the only clue to what she's thinking and at the moment they seem bland and friendly.

'I didn't,' she says simply.

So, it's entirely possible that this man, whoever he is, didn't leave at all. It's possible he was still here in the early hours of the morning when Charlie was killed. He could have killed her. I feel a twinge of excitement. This is the first real lead I've had.

'Did you mention him to the police?' I ask.

'I did.'

So why hasn't his picture been broadcast on all the news stations? I think bitterly. *Why only mine?*

'Did you hear anything later in the night?' I ask. 'Ben Wiltshire said he heard a car drive up about one o'clock in the morning.'

'No, I was sound asleep. I take pills to help me sleep. I didn't hear anything. But I did notice Charlie's car was still parked outside the next morning and I was surprised because she usually goes in to work at the shop on a Saturday. But I just assumed she'd decided to take the day off. She was the boss so she could do what she liked.'

I want to ask more about the man Meg saw visiting Charlie that weekend, but at that moment we're interrupted by another woman who emerges from inside. She's in her forties, stocky with dyed black hair and a tough,

145

belligerent face like a bulldog. She has rubber gloves on, and her sleeves are rolled up, as if she's been cleaning.

'Are you okay, Meg?' she asks, staring at me suspiciously. 'What are you doing here?'

'I'm fine, Sophia. It's okay,' says Meg. 'This is Catherine. She was a friend of Charlie's.'

'I see.' She nods curtly at me, but her eyes still glitter sharp and watchful. It's easy to see that she feels very protective of her charge.

'This is Sophia,' Meg says. 'She's my nurse, cleaner, friend and my own personal Sergeant Major.'

Sophia laughs gruffly. 'She thinks I'm a bully just because I make her do her exercises every day.'

I wonder what exercises Meg can possibly have to do. She can barely move.

'Nice to meet you, Sophia,' I say, holding out my hand to shake hers.

She takes it, frowning stiffly. Then she seems to soften slightly. 'Sorry. I probably seem rude to you, but we're all a bit on edge lately with what happened just next door – and the killer still out there. The police are useless. They've done next to nothing. I asked them for a guard, protection for Meg, but nothing. Nada. And I can't be here all the time. I've got my own family to look after.'

How much more terrifying it must be if you're stuck in a wheelchair, unable to move, literally unable to defend yourself? I wonder how Meg seems so calm. She seems so stoical, humorous even. If I were in her situation, I probably would have given up long ago. But perhaps we all have reserves of strength and endurance inside us that we are unaware of until we're tested.

'I don't think you're in any danger though,' I say. 'The police seem to think that it was a personal attack – that they targeted Charlie.'

Sophia sits down at the table next to Meg.

'Who on earth would want to hurt that sweet, young woman?' she says shaking her head.

'That's what we were just saying,' I agree. 'It makes no sense.'

'Were you here that night?' I ask as casually as I can.

She shakes her head. 'No, I don't usually sleep here. Meg can contact me or her daughter any time if there's an emergency. I only live a couple of minutes away, but like I said, I've got my own family to look after.'

'But did you notice anything unusual,' I ask, 'in the days leading up to the murder?'

Sophia's eyes narrow. 'Not really. Adam went away on the Thursday evening. Charlie kept up her usual routine – work, therapy sessions. I told her she should slow down, take it easy, given her diagnosis, but she insisted on going into work. She was worried the shop would fall apart without her there. And judging by what's happened since, she was probably right.'

'Her diagnosis?' I say and as soon as the words are out of my mouth, I realise I've made a mistake.

Sophia stares at me, suspiciously. 'You didn't know? I thought you were her friend.'

I shake my head and hurriedly explain. 'We were old school friends. We'd been out of touch for quite a few years. What was wrong with her?'

Sophia presses her lips together and folds her arms across her chest.

'Charlie was very ill,' she says. 'She had stage four bowel cancer.'

Fifteen

'Charlie had cancer?' I repeat. My head is spinning.

Sophia nods gravely. 'Yes, she was dying. But she was determined not to give up without a fight, bless her.'

Neither the police nor Adam had mentioned anything about cancer.

'Did Adam know?' I ask.

'Of course. How could he not know?'

Weird that he didn't mention it, I think. *But perhaps he thought it wasn't relevant or, more likely that it was none of my business.*

'How long did she have to live?'

'The doctors had given her about four months. That's right, isn't it, Meg?'

'Yes,' Meg agrees.

'Just four months?'

Sophia nods. 'It's ironic but her killer probably saved her from a lot of suffering.'

I digest this new piece of information, still reeling from the shock. It opens up all kinds of possibilities I hadn't previously considered. Charlie was facing months of pain and anguish with no prospect of recovery. She must have been shattered. 'Do you think her murder could have been a mercy killing?' I suggest tentatively.

Sophia gives me a sharp look. 'I don't think so. I don't think anyone would choose to die that way, do you – stabbed four times in the chest?'

'No,' I shake my head and laugh inappropriately. 'You're right. Stupid question.'

There is a silence. Meg drools a little at the corner of her mouth and Sophia wipes it away with a tissue. 'I think that Meg is getting tired now,' she says pointedly.

'I'm all right, I like the company,' Meg protests but Sophia's eyes are boring into me and I like to think I know when I'm not wanted.

'Thank you for your time,' I say, standing up. I'm staggered by what I've just discovered. Poor Charlie. She found out she was dying just when her life was falling into place. She'd set up her own business, just married Adam. Who knows? Maybe they were thinking of having kids. It must have been a devastating blow. Is it possible she took her own life? But that's ridiculous. I almost laugh out loud at the idea. She couldn't have stabbed herself in the chest. Besides, that didn't fit with the Charlie I knew.

When I get home, I notice with a twinge of guilt that the lawn is covered in small piles of dog poop. I haven't taken Delilah out for a walk in a while. Feeling contrite, I clean up the lawn and give Delilah a dog biscuit, promising I'll take her out this evening. She gazes at me with big, reproachful brown eyes, then curls up in her basket with a heavy sigh of resignation.

The house looks like a bomb's hit it. I clear up some toys, load the dishwasher, hoover the carpet and clean the bathroom. I scrub the bath vigorously, trying to remove the ring of grey grime near the top of the tub, and I mop the kitchen floor. It feels therapeutic, as if cleaning the house can also clear out my mind and give me some clarity. But everything I've learned at Cecily House has just raised more questions. Who was the man Meg saw visiting Charlie on Friday afternoon? And did Ben Wiltshire really hear a key in the door and a scream in the early hours of the morning? How much can I trust what either of them says? And what about Adam? He seems suspicious to me. Have the police really checked his alibi carefully?

My head is spinning, so I make myself a cup of tea, take a piece of paper from the printer, fold it over and write a list:

1. Who visited Charlie on Friday afternoon? (I underline that twice as it seems key to me.)
2. Who did Ben hear arriving at one o'clock in the morning?
3. Why was the medicine box out?
4. Who gave the police a description of me and how can they claim they saw my face so clearly when it must have been dark at one o'clock in the morning?

I add three more question marks to the end of the last question. I can't believe the police haven't picked up on that. I need to talk to DI Littlewood. I pick up my phone to ring her. But it's as if she's read my mind. And her name flashes up on my screen along with a little green phone symbol before I get the chance to call.

'Hello?'

'Yes, hi. This is DI Littlewood. I hope I haven't caught you at a bad time,' she says politely.

'No, it's fine. Actually, I was just going to call *you*. I wanted to talk about the photofit,' I say.

'Oh yes?'

'Charlie was killed in the early hours of the morning. It would have been dark. How could the witness have seen my face clearly enough to give such a detailed description?'

There's a short silence. 'What makes you think Charlotte was killed in the early hours of the morning?'

Shit. I don't want her to know I've been talking to the residents of Cecily House. 'Well, wasn't she?' I say lamely.

'I can't disclose that information, Catherine,' she says tartly. She gives a loud, angry sigh. 'And you really just need to let us get on with our work.'

'Well, the fact that you're so interested in the time Luke was with me from eleven o'clock onwards suggests that Charlie was killed after that,' I retort testily. 'And by the way, have you talked to him again yet? You know that he's lying, don't you?'

'Er, no, actually. I know nothing of the sort.' Littlewood sounds annoyed, her usual icy calm cracking a little. 'This has nothing to do with Luke. There's something else – something we'd like you to take a look at. Something that has come to light.'

'Oh?' My gut clenches uneasily.

'We've received a new piece of evidence and we'd like to discuss it with you. Could you come to the station today?'

'What time?'

'As soon as you can get here. Let's say in about half an hour?'

What am I supposed to say? I can't exactly refuse, can I? It's a Friday and Theo is picking up Dylan from school so I can't even use him as an excuse.

'Okay.' I agree wearily and then add, with a short, explosive burst of anger, 'But I'm getting sick and tired of this whole thing. You need to do your job properly. Find the real killer. None of this has anything to do with me.'

DI Littlewood doesn't respond. 'Right then,' she says in a tight, deliberately calm voice. 'See you soon.'

Why the hell did I snap at Littlewood? I berate myself as I walk into town. I need to keep her on my side – if she ever was on my side, which is doubtful. And what is the new evidence she was talking about? It's got to be good for me, right? I didn't kill Charlie and I wasn't anywhere near Cecily House on the night she died, so any new evidence should point to someone else. But then why do the police want to discuss it with me? My thoughts spiral and my stomach churns with anxiety until I reach the police station and push open the blue painted doors.

I'm shown to the same interview room as before. And DI Littlewood and another male officer, not Sergeant Fisher, are sitting chatting. They stop abruptly when they see me and DI Littlewood addresses me gravely.

'Take a seat please, Catherine.'

'I'm sorry about earlier,' I say. 'I'm sure you're doing your best. I'm just under a lot of stress right now, that's all.'

'Don't worry about it,' says Littlewood coolly. 'Sit down.'

I hesitate in the doorway, fighting the urge to turn tail and run. Everything is so formal and serious. I hadn't expected this, and I can't help feeling ambushed.

'What's going on?' I blurt. 'Am I under arrest? Do I need a lawyer?'

DI Littlewood smiles soothingly. 'You're not under arrest and we're not charging you with anything, but of course you have the right to speak to a lawyer if you want.'

I step into the room and perch on the only empty chair gingerly. It's slightly wobbly and it crosses my mind that they've given me an unstable chair deliberately to unsettle me. 'No, it's okay,' I say airily. If I'm not guilty why would I need a lawyer? It will just make me look suspicious if I started demanding representation now.

'Good. Then we're okay to proceed?'

I nod and DI Littlewood presses record on the tape recorder on the table.

'I'd like to show you something, Catherine and for you to tell us if it means anything to you.' She speaks loudly and clearly into the recorder. 'For the record, I'm showing Catherine Bayntun photograph 16A.'

She pushes a clear plastic envelope with a photograph inside across the table to me and I peer at it without touching it, my hands clasped in my lap. It shows a picture of an old stone country house next to a river. Next to it is what was once a stable, converted into a garage with large, dirty white doors and a gravel driveway. It seems faintly familiar, but that's probably because it looks like hundreds of other houses in this part of the world.

'Um, I don't think so,' I say cautiously. Under the table my leg is jiggling out of control. I feel as though I'm falling into a trap, but I don't know what the trap is. 'Why, what is it?' I ask.

'Look again. Carefully. Are you sure you don't recognise it?' Littlewood laces her fingers together under her chin and regards me in that unnervingly icy-cool way she has.

'Um . . .' I'm thinking rapidly, glancing at the picture again, and I flush because now I realise that I *do* know it, and it's going to look as if I was lying if I admit that.

'Now I come to think of it, I've been there before,' I say cautiously. 'It's in South Baunton, right? It's the house of a girl I was at school with. I don't know if her family still lives there – Vanessa Price, she was called.'

'A family called Carter lives there now. Do you know them?'

I shake my head.

Littlewood leans forward. 'You said you attended the same school as Charlotte Holbrooke. Did she know this Vanessa Price too?'

'Yes, she knew Nessa, she was our classmate.'

I didn't know Nessa very well, but she was always near the top of the class, always ambitious. I expect she's in some high-flying job in London by now. I can't imagine her sticking around here in this backwater for long.

'So, when did you go to this house?' asks the other police officer, introducing himself as DI Clarke. He leans forward and his impassive brown eyes bore into me as if he can see through to my lying core. I wonder where Sergeant Fisher is. I don't like this new guy. He's not at all friendly and he has a smooth, observant manner like a cat watching its prey.

'I went there once or twice when we were at school, but that was more than seventeen years ago.'

In truth, I only ever went to that house once, on the evening of Nessa's party. Chill creeps into my bones. Can it be a coincidence? After the pub, Nessa's house was our next stop. The possibility that this is all unrelated – the picture of the park in Dylan's book bag, Nessa's house, the photofit, Charlie's murder – is receding rapidly.

'So, just to be clear for the purpose of the tape, you're stating that you haven't been to this house recently?' Clarke taps the desk, drumming his fingers in a slow, deliberate rhythm.

'Right.' I nod firmly. 'I haven't even been to South Baunton – not for years. Why are you asking me, anyway?' I ask, meeting his eyes defiantly, not sure if I really want to hear the answer.

'We received this yesterday, along with a note.' DI Littlewood hands me another piece of paper. Just a scrap really, torn at the edges. The message is written in capitals in blue biro. ASK CATHERINE BAYNTUN.

'Who sent it?' As I place the note back on the table, I can't help noticing that my hand is trembling, and I don't want them to see that. Clarke spots it anyway. I catch him taking it in, as if it's a plump, tasty mouse. I can almost imagine his tail twitching under the desk.

'We don't have any idea,' he says, folding his arms and leaning back in his chair. 'We thought maybe you might know.'

'Don't you have ways of tracing the paper or the handwriting?' I say, fear making me angry. 'Did it occur to you that the person who sent that note could be Charlie's killer, trying to pin the murder on me?'

'What makes you think this has anything to do with Charlotte's death?' says DI Clarke, pouncing. His eyes glitter with the thrill of the chase.

'Nothing really,' I say, mentally kicking myself. 'I just assumed. Well, doesn't it?'

'We really don't know,' says Littlewood. 'We were hoping you could tell us. Think carefully, Catherine. You don't have any idea who wrote this and why?'

I shake my head and shift uncomfortably in my chair. 'No, I haven't a clue,' I say firmly.

Sixteen

2002

We piled into my mum's old Ford Fiesta and wound along the country lanes towards Nessa's. 'Get the Party Started' by P!nk was blaring out of the CD player, the windows were wide open, the wind rushing in our hair and the sinking sun was casting a golden glow over everything. It was one of those evenings when everything felt right with the world. I felt as if anything was possible. I felt invincible.

The party was already in full swing when we arrived at Nessa's, loud music swelling out into the quiet of the village. There was no sign of Nessa, but her brother was sprawled across the porch, drunk or high, muttering something incomprehensible about spiders. We clambered over him into the hallway where a couple were snogging on the stairs.

'Get a room,' May Ling shouted, cackling with laughter as we flounced past.

The living room was smoky and crowded, lit only by fairy lights draped over the doorway and windows. It was difficult to make out who was who, but as soon as we entered, Charlie nudged me sharply in the ribs.

'Look who's here,' she hissed in my ear and nodded towards the corner where a small huddle of boys were passing around a bong made out of a plastic bottle. My heart leaped to my throat because among them, with his back to us, was James. He'd recently had his hair cut and just the sight of the shorn hair and the small mole at the base of his neck made me feel weak at the knees with what I thought was love.

Charlie nudged me. 'This is your chance. Why don't you go over and say hi?'

'I can't,' I muttered and dashed into the kitchen before James could turn round and see us.

'Do you want me to talk to him for you?' Charlie asked, following me into the kitchen.

'Oh my God, no!' I wailed. 'What would that look like? Like we're little kids. "My friend fancies you." Don't you dare!'

'What's the problem?' asked Nessa, who was in the kitchen pouring crushed ice into a big plastic container of beers.

'There's a boy she likes here, and she won't talk to him because she's chicken,' Charlie said, removing the lid from a bottle of beer and taking a swig. 'Tell her she's being an idiot.'

I threw her a dirty look and she raised her eyebrows. 'What? I haven't said his name.'

'Why don't you have a drink to give you confidence?' suggested Nessa.

'I want to, but I can't,' I said sadly. 'I'm driving.'

'Just one won't hurt,' Nessa said.

'I need more than one to get the courage to speak to him. I need about a million drinks.'

'You can both stay here the night, if you like,' said Nessa expansively. 'Then you can drink as much as you like.'

'Are you sure?' asked Charlie.

'Course I'm sure. Lots of people are sleeping over. My parents are away for the weekend and I've got spare bedding. You'll have to sleep on the floor though. Just enjoy yourself, Cat. We deserve it after all the work we've been doing.'

I willingly accepted the drink she poured me, took a swig and then spluttered it out while Charlie and Nessa cracked up laughing. It had a strange strong taste, something like liquorice.

'Oh my God, what's that?' I said, choking, the alcohol burning the back of my throat.

'Pernod,' said Nessa. 'Don't you like it?'

I took another experimental sip. 'No, I do like it. I just wasn't expecting it, that's all.'

I downed a couple of glasses of Pernod in quick succession. And then moved on to margaritas, which Nessa was lining up on the kitchen counter.

After that, the rest of the evening was a bit of a blur. I lost track of Charlie, May Ling and Jenson and ended up talking to a bunch of friends of Nessa's brother on the stairs. One of them, a boy called Josh, made a clumsy pass at me and we kissed on the stairs, teeth bumping awkwardly. Feeling buoyed by his attention and drunk enough not to really care what happened, I decided to go and find James.

'Have you seen James White?' I asked, wandering into the living room.

No one seemed to have seen him for a while, but eventually someone pointed me in the direction of the garden. 'He's out there, I think.'

Outside, the air was deliciously cool, and it was breathlessly quiet. There was no traffic noise, just the chirrup of crickets and frogs from the garden pond. The moon was like a fat gold globe above the trees and the stars were clearly visible in the velvet-black sky. Solar lamps were surrounded by a haze of moths and other insects hung from the trees. It felt magical, like stepping into another world. A night for falling in love, I thought, drunkenly as I stumbled down the garden path. Maybe I'd ask James for a kiss. We'd kissed once before but that had been in a game of spin the bottle and was just a peck on the lips, so it didn't really count. About halfway down the path, I heard laughter and someone murmuring in a low voice. The end of the garden was divided off by a high hedge and surrounded by trees. It was darker than the rest of the garden and difficult to see. But as I pushed my way through the gap in the hedge, I heard a strange, guttural noise.

I blinked, my eyes adjusting to the darkness and made out a bench, a white statue of an owl and two naked bodies entwined. It took me a while to make sense of what I was seeing. James was facing me but blind to everything, his face contorted in what looked like pain. The girl he was with was sitting, legs straddled across his thighs. Her head was thrown back, long red-brown hair tumbling down her white, curved back.

I gave a small involuntary gasp and the girl froze, then turned and stared at me, her eyes wide with shock.

'Cat . . .' she said. But she didn't need to speak, and I didn't need to see her face to know that it was Charlie.

Seventeen

I must admit that I wasn't completely honest with the police. It's true that I have no idea *who* sent them the picture – God knows I wish I did. But I may have an inkling about *why*.

In the car on the way home, I try to examine my theory in a calm and rational way, but my stomach is churning with anxiety and my hands are gripping the wheel as if I'm holding on to a lifebelt. Everything seems to be spiralling out of my control. The messages from George Wilkinson, the photo of the park in Dylan's book bag and the photo of Nessa's house. Were they all sent by the same person? And if so, why? The only possible connection between the two places that I can think of is the night of Nessa's party, the summer of 2002. The park, the pub and then Nessa's house. It's almost like someone's creating a photographic record of my movements that night. They're sending me a message and the message is clear: they know what happened.

But why? For what purpose? Revenge? Blackmail?

By the time I'm almost home I've convinced myself that I must be mistaken. How could anyone possibly know? Only Charlie and I know what happened that night and Charlie's dead. I cling on to this fact and the idea that it's all in my head. It's so much better than the alternative.

Feeling calmer, I park opposite my house. There's a van blocking my parking space, but I'm so preoccupied that I don't immediately clock that it's a news van.

Stepping out of my car, I'm bombarded by a barrage of reporters. There's at least six of them, including photographers holding cameras with large lenses. And they chase me across the road, thrusting microphones into my face.

'Mrs Bayntun. Catherine Bayntun. Can we have a quick word?'

'No, I'm sorry.' I duck my head and keep my eyes firmly on the ground, shielding my face with my handbag.

As I scramble to my gate, I notice the van has the logo of a national TV news station on it.

Shit.

'Mrs Bayntun,' a man shouts after me, as I dash up the path and fumble with my key in the lock. 'Do you know anything about the murder of Charlotte Holbrooke? You were school friends, is that right?'

'Can you explain why you were seen outside her flat on the night of her murder?'

'Did you kill Charlotte Holbrooke, Catherine?'

I don't answer. I lunge through the door, slamming it behind me, my heart pumping hard. For a few seconds I lean against the door, trying to breathe, trying to work out what to do. Should I phone someone? Theo maybe? Or the police? Are these reporters even allowed to be here? Isn't this tantamount to harassment? After a few moments, paralysed by indecision, I go to the front room and peer out of the window. Bastards. They are hanging around outside, chatting and laughing, waiting for God knows what. I can't believe I was ever part of this profession. They're parasites, feeding off the misery of others. I remember with an uncomfortable churning in my belly a time when I was working at the *Gazette*. A two-year-old boy had been killed by a falling pylon. I wrote a short article describing simply what had happened, but my boss said it was too dry and wanted me to get a quote from one of the relatives. Even though it was only a local paper, the atmosphere at the *Gazette* was fiercely competitive and cutthroat, so against my better judgement, I rang the distraught parents and was told in no uncertain terms to fuck off. Then I rang the grandparents and the uncles and aunts and neighbours until eventually, I got the quote I needed. I remember that now with shame.

I don't scream at the reporters. Instead, I draw the curtains and sit in the darkened room, my head buried in my hands, trying not to cry.

After what seems like an age, I hear them packing up and driving away and I feel safe to open the curtains again and let in what's left of the daylight. The man that lives across the street is gawping at me. I repress the urge to give him the finger and turn away abruptly. God only knows what Eileen and Bob will have made of this.

I don't want to think about it all any more. I retreat to the back room and try to forget the only way I know how. I switch on my laptop, open the *Embers* file, and write until the real world recedes, until I'm absorbed into Molly's world and the simple battle between good and evil. The words flow easily, and my fingers fly over the keys, my word count steadily climbing. I'm not sure how long I sit there writing but when I finally stop, my bum is sore from sitting still for so long and it's already getting dark.

I look at the time in the corner of the screen. It's seven-thirty and Dylan will be heading to bed soon. I miss him a lot when he's not here. The house feels so lonely and empty without him. But I'm relieved he wasn't around to witness those reporters. The poor boy must be confused enough as it is.

When I ring Theo's to say goodnight to Dylan, I can hear the burble of the TV and Harper talking in the background and I imagine the three of them cuddled up cosily on the sofa. I picture Dylan leaning against Harper as she ruffles his hair and Theo pouring her a glass of wine. In my imagination, Harper's wearing a simple white slip dress, her hair is down and she looks beautiful and slim. Beautiful, slim and innocent. Everything I'm not.

'Sleep tight, don't let the bed bugs bite,' I say to Dylan, biting back tears.

'What bugs?' Dylan sounds alarmed.

'It's just an expression. There aren't any bugs, really. I just mean I hope you sleep well, and I'll see you tomorrow. Night night, sweetheart.'

'Night night, Mummy.'

'Can you just get your daddy for a minute? I want to speak to him.'

'Hello?' Theo takes the phone. He sounds impatient, no doubt annoyed to have his perfect evening with Harper interrupted.

I want to tell him about the press and about the interview with the police today. I need to talk to someone about all the craziness in my head. But he doesn't sound like he wants to talk. He sounds like he can't wait to be rid of me.

'I just wanted to remind you that I'm taking Dylan to play with his friend tomorrow,' I say in the end.

He sighs. 'Okay. I haven't forgotten. I'll see you tomorrow, then.'

'Yes, see you tomorrow.' I hang up.

Without really being aware of what I'm doing I head to the kitchen, make myself a cup of tea and open a large bag of salted peanuts. Then I switch on the TV and sit down, shovelling peanuts into my mouth, tears of self-pity rolling down my cheeks. I catch the end of an old comedy show, which washes over me and then the evening news comes on. I brace myself for what's coming. I'm terrified that I'll be on, but I need to know. Maybe it'll be a busy news night. If there's a lot happening around the world, maybe they'll skip the story about Charlie. You never know, I could be lucky.

The lead news item is about the upcoming elections, and then they bang on about Brexit and the economy again for a while. The half hour is nearly up, and I'm beginning to think I might have got away with it, but my hopes are quickly dashed when Charlie's picture flashes up on the screen, her big hair, big smile – lots of teeth. Of course, they were never going to drop a story like this. An attractive young woman dies under mysterious circumstances in a posh country house. It's like an Agatha Christie. This is catnip for the press.

'An "angel" who was loved by everyone,' runs the caption underneath. They show an interview with Adam during which he tears up and says that he can't imagine life without her, then a short clip of Ben Wiltshire basically saying what he told me – that she was 'an angel' and he owes his life to her.

'Charlotte Holbrooke was much loved by friends and family, described by those who knew her as selfless and caring,' concludes the male news anchor. 'Police aren't ruling anything out and couldn't be drawn to comment on a woman that was seen close to the Bathurst estate on Friday night.'

The photofit of me appears on the screen and there's a split screen of me dashing to my house chased by reporters. *Oh, God – I look guilty as hell*, I think. *Why else would I be so unwilling to talk to the press?*

The news reporter moves on to a light story about a dog that was rescued from a well somewhere in Africa. I'm just turning off the TV and heading up to bed when my phone beeps, making me jump.

It's a text from Georgia.

Just checking you're still on for tomorrow. ☺

She obviously hasn't seen the news.

The last thing I want to do at the moment is socialise and

make small talk with someone I barely know, but Dylan has been looking forward to this playdate and I don't want to disappoint him

I hesitate, then tap in:

Sure. See you tomorrow. ☺☺ 🍷

Eighteen

Dylan's hand is slippery in mine as we walk up the path to Georgia's house.

'Mummy, your hand is wet,' he complains.

'Is it? I'm sorry.' I let go and wipe my palms on my jeans.

I'm sweating because I'm nervous, I realise. That news report from last night is playing on my mind. Why hasn't Georgia cancelled Dylan's playdate? I wouldn't have blamed her if she had. Any normal person would have second thoughts about making friends with a suspect in a murder case.

Outside the plain white front door, I take a deep breath and ring the bell. Then I wait with bated breath for Georgia to appear. I'm half expecting her to slam the door in my face when she sees me. *Please not in front of Dylan*, I beg silently.

She doesn't shut the door in my face. Instead, she greets me with her usual warm, friendly smile and I'm ridiculously grateful.

'Cat! Dylan! Come in, come in,' she bubbles. 'Sorry about my appearance. I was up late last night and didn't have time to put on any make-up.' She's wearing a grey sleeveless t-shirt and jogging pants and her face is, as she says, bare of make-up but even so, she looks beautiful. Her eyelashes are thick and black, and her black hair is falling in sleek sheets over smooth, tanned shoulders.

'Wow. You look fantastic,' I say. 'You should see me without make-up. It's like a car crash.'

She laughs lightly. 'I'm sure it isn't.'

'Well, I don't look like you, that's for sure.'

I wonder if I'm laying it on too thick. But I'm really so grateful to her for treating me like a normal human being.

She leads us through her open, airy home, talking nineteen to the dozen, firing questions that don't require answers, leaving no space for social awkwardness.

'How are you, Cat? It's a gorgeous day, isn't it? I was thinking we could sit outside, and the kids could play in the garden. Harry's out there already on his new trampoline. Would you like to see it, Dylan?'

Dylan nods shyly and we follow her out through the French doors into a smallish garden, totally dominated by the large trampoline. Harry is bouncing around on it in a

173

bored, desultory way. When he sees Dylan his face lights up and he jumps off, running up to him holding out a pine cone he has found.

Georgia pulls up an expensive-looking garden chair for me. Then disappears inside and emerges a few moments later with a clinking tray. We sit under the shade of a parasol, watching the boys tumble and shriek on the trampoline, sipping cold lemonade and nibbling ginger biscuits. Georgia's baby is asleep in a rocker next to us.

Georgia talks so easily and comfortably that I gradually relax.

'Sorry about the mess, by the way,' she's saying. 'We moved here just a few months ago. I haven't got around to sorting all the boxes yet. I've been so busy what with trying to get Harry into a school and with the baby. I think we were lucky to get places at Green Park Primary, don't you? It's meant to be one of the best. It has a very good Ofsted rating and the teachers are brilliant, don't you think? Especially Lizzie Hamlyn. Harry loves her. Did you know she's got a master's degree? She could have got any job she wanted, but she wanted to get into teaching because she wanted to make a difference. I mean that just shows how caring she is, don't you think?'

'Where did you live before you came here?' I ask, when I can get a word in edgeways.

'We lived in Oxford. I loved it there, but my husband

had a new job opportunity, so we decided to move. I miss Oxford and all my friends. It's nice round here but, you know, it's difficult starting again somewhere new. Though I must say everyone has been very friendly . . .' She breaks off and a faint pink colours her cheeks. 'I'm so sorry about Marsha the other day at the school gate. She was so rude to you. I didn't know what to do with myself I was so embarrassed. I don't believe a word she says, by the way,' she adds hastily.

'What *does* she say?' I ask tightly, the churning in my stomach starting up again.

Georgia frowns. 'It's so ridiculous. She's got this crazy idea in her head,' she laughs lightly, but doesn't quite meet my eyes. 'She thinks you look like a suspect in that murder near the park. You must have heard about it? It's been all over social media.'

I nod. 'Yes, I heard something about it,' I say vaguely. 'A woman was stabbed, right?'

She shivers. 'That's right. I don't watch the news as a rule. It's always so negative, but this story's been difficult to avoid.'

So, Georgia didn't see the news report last night, I think. *That explains a lot.*

'Everyone's been talking about it,' she continues. 'The woman who was murdered, she was in her own home too. Apparently, she let him in.' Georgia shudders. 'It doesn't bear thinking about, does it? Anyway, Marsha is convinced they had this photofit on the news that looked like you.'

'Really?' I try to laugh. I look around the garden searching for another topic of conversation. 'Where's Harry's dad, by the way? Is he working?'

'Don't ask,' she says, rolling her eyes and smiling. 'It's a sore subject at the moment. He's a dentist and he's always at work, that man. I feel like he puts his work before me and the kids. How about your ex? What does he do? Have you been divorced long?'

'Dylan's father is a teacher – a maths teacher. We're separated, not divorced yet. We broke up a few months ago.'

Georgia looks sympathetic. 'Oh, I'm sorry. What happened? Tell me if I'm being too nosy.'

'No, it's okay. He cheated on me with another teacher at the school where he works. They went on a school trip together to Switzerland and, well, one thing led to another, I suppose.'

'Oh my God – that's terrible. Poor you. I don't know what I'd do if Luke did something like that. I think I'd chop off his balls.'

I laugh uneasily. Did I hear correctly? Did she call her husband Luke? It must be a coincidence.

From the front of the house, we hear a muffled thud of the door slamming.

'That'll be him now,' says Georgia. 'Speak of the devil.'

I stand up, my heart hammering. 'Well, I probably . . .' I begin nervously. But the words die on my lips as a tall, handsome man breezes out through the French doors.

'Hey,' he says, then breaks off, standing stock-still in the doorway. The flabbergasted look in his beautiful green eyes mirrors the shock and panic that I'm feeling. It can't be . . .

But it is.

Nineteen

I'm staring at him, unable to move or speak, opening and closing my mouth as if all the oxygen's been sucked out of the atmosphere.

Fortunately, at that moment, the baby spits out her dummy and starts crying, and Georgia doesn't appear to notice anything because she's busy trying to pacify her.

'Luke, this is Cat, Dylan's mum,' she says, glancing up at her husband with an amused smile. 'There's no need to look so surprised. I told you Harry was having a friend round.' She lifts the baby out of the rocker, sucks on the dummy and then pops it back in the baby's mouth. 'I apologise for my husband, Cat. He doesn't have any manners sometimes.'

He recovers before I do. 'Nice to meet you, Cat,' he says, holding out his hand and smiling blandly.

I stand up and take it automatically, 'Nice to meet you too,' I mutter, trying to censor an image of that hand on my naked thigh and simultaneously trying to avoid his eyes, which seem to be burning into me.

'Well, how was work?' Georgia asks him, seemingly oblivious to the tension in the air.

And he's chatting smoothly about patients, fillings and root canals, but I can't really hear what he's saying. There's a drumming in my ears and I feel dizzy and nauseous, as if I'm about to pass out.

'Are you okay, Cat?' Georgia is asking.

'Um, actually I feel a bit sick,' I blurt. 'I couldn't use your toilet, could I?'

'Sure. It's upstairs. Second door on the right. The downstairs is broken, sorry.'

I dive into the house and dash upstairs. It wasn't a lie. I do feel sick. The man I slept with the other night is downstairs. I should have realised he was married. But to Georgia? I could never have guessed that.

I lock the toilet door, remove the child's seat and stand over the toilet bowl heaving. But nothing comes out, just phlegm. I wipe my lips. Then I pull the chain, close the lid and sit down, thinking hard.

Of course, I feel terrible about Georgia and incredibly embarrassed, but if I can get over the initial shock and humiliation and look at this in the cold light of logic, then

179

this is actually a piece of luck. I now know who Luke is. There's no hiding for him any more. I can make him explain why he lied to the police and I can force him to provide me with an alibi. I stand up and wash my hands, splashing cold water on my face and staring at my reflection, trying to work out how to get him on his own so that I can confront him and get him to tell the truth.

As it turns out, I don't need a plan because, as I leave the bathroom, he's barrelling towards me across the landing. His face is like thunder. The polite veneer completely gone. He looks furious and quite frightening.

'What are you doing here?' he hisses savagely, grabbing my arm, digging his fingers into soft flesh.

'I didn't know Georgia was your wife, I swear,' I whisper, trying to extricate my arm.

He loosens his grip a little and looks at me as if he's trying to decide whether to believe me or not.

'I had no idea,' I say. I'm not sure why I'm being so defensive. It's me who should be angry. Not him. And I *am* angry, I realise. Furiously angry. How dare he blame this on me?

'Anyway, why did you lie to the police?' I blurt.

He glances over his shoulder. Georgia has moved inside. I can hear the baby grizzling downstairs and Georgia talking to her in a sing-song voice. Luke looks panicked. 'We can't talk about that now,' he says. 'Meet me tomorrow.'

'All right. Where? When?'

'At my surgery. I work at Cotswold Dentists on Blackjack Street. Come at lunchtime, twelve o'clock, and I'll be there. In the meantime, don't you fucking dare say anything to Georgia.'

'I won't, I—' I start. But he's not listening. He opens the door to his bedroom and slams the door firmly behind him before I have to time to finish my thought.

'You poor thing,' says Georgia, as I walk unsteadily down the stairs. 'Can I get you anything?'

'No, I'll be all right,' I murmur weakly. 'But I think I need to get home.'

'What, really?' She looks dismayed. 'But you only just got here. Do you want Dylan to stay? Luke could drop him off at his dad's later.'

'No thank you. That's really kind, but he doesn't like staying places without me or Theo,' I lie. 'Another time, okay?'

I can't wait to get out of there. The thought of making polite conversation with Georgia and pretending everything's okay, with Luke just upstairs, makes me feel nauseous. To my relief, Dylan doesn't make a fuss when I tell him we're leaving, and Luke stays upstairs in his room.

'I'll call you,' Georgia says, as I bundle Dylan into the car. 'Hope you feel better soon.'

Twenty

'That was quick,' says Theo when he opens the door to his flat. He ruffles Dylan's hair and gives me a questioning smile.

I don't smile back. 'Yeah, we left early. I wasn't feeling too good.'

'I have to say, you don't look so great.'

'Thanks a lot.'

'You know what I mean,' he sighs. 'Why don't you come in for a cup of coffee? Do you need any painkillers?'

'No, I'll be all right. I should probably go home, have a lie down.' Seeing Harper is the last thing I need right now.

'Harper's not here,' he says, as if he's read my mind. 'Come in . . . please,' he puts his hand on my shoulder and I stare at it until he drops it awkwardly. 'It's been a long time since we had a good chat.'

'Well—'

'Please Mummy,' Dylan chimes in, tugging my hand. 'I want to show you my new dinosaur.'

I weaken, 'Oh, all right. Just for a minute.'

Dylan drags me by the hand to his room. He has everything in there: a bed like a space rocket and matching space-themed bedding and curtains, a night light that spins around and casts moving images of the planets on the ceiling. There's a large flat-screen TV with a PlayStation attached and even the latest iPad. *Why does a five-year-old need all this?* I think, wearily. *And how in hell am I supposed to compete?* But I don't have the energy to get annoyed. I'm still in shock about Luke and just generally worn down by the constant stress I've been under.

I sink on to Dylan's bed feeling dizzy. My head is throbbing.

'Look. This is Dino,' says Dylan, fetching the dinosaur from an overflowing toy chest.

'Cool,' I say weakly. He shows me the dinosaur's features which, as I suspected, include walking and roaring.

'Ms Hamlyn gave me this,' he says flitting around from object to object, unable to focus. He hands me a smooth, rounded stone; one side has broken off, exposing a dark spiralling pattern. 'Do you know what this is, Mummy?'

I nod, glancing at it absent-mindedly. 'It's a fossil. An animal that lived a long time ago.'

Dylan picks up his PlayStation controller. 'Can I play Minecraft now?'

'I expect so.'

I wander into the kitchen where Theo is spooning fresh-smelling coffee into a cafetière and I sit down at the table. He plonks a glass of water and a packet of Nurofen on the table in front of me and I swallow a couple.

'So . . .' Theo says, turning his dark eyes on me, searching my face.

'So . . .'

'How is everything?'

'Okay,' I say defensively. 'How about you? How's Harper?'

'I saw the news report.' He ignores my question. 'What's going on, Cat?'

'Nothing.'

'It doesn't seem like nothing to me. My God, Cat. Those journalists. I couldn't bear to watch those bastards hounding you.' He runs his fingers through his hair. 'My offer still stands, by the way. I can get Duncan to help you, if you want. I'll pay any legal fees.'

I look at the tired bags under his eyes, the stubble on his chin and find myself longing for a time when we were everything to each other, when I could tell him anything and he would always have my back.

'There's no need for that. It will all be sorted very soon,' I say. 'I've got a watertight alibi.'

He raises his eyebrows, 'That's great. Why didn't you mention this before?'

I explain about Luke, meeting him at the Black Bear with Gaby. Theo winces when I reach the part about him staying the night. 'Spare me the details,' he mutters under his breath.

I don't spare him the details. Why should I? And I enjoy watching him squirm. But then I get on to how Luke lied to the police and he listens wide-eyed when I tell him I just found out that Luke is Dylan's friend's father.

'He's terrified that his wife will find out,' I continue. 'So I think I can persuade him it's in his best interests to tell the police the truth.'

Theo looks worried. 'Threaten him, you mean?'

'Well, yes, if you want to put it like that.'

'Do you want me to come with you to talk to him? You don't know how he'll react. He could become violent.'

It's tempting to accept his offer. I think about how angry Luke seemed on the landing and I have to admit I am a little scared of him. But I can't keep running to Theo every time I have a problem.

'I can manage,' I say stiffly.

Theo shakes his head. 'What were you thinking of, inviting a stranger into your house, Cat? He could have been dangerous. Look at what happened to Charlotte Holbrooke.'

I bite back my anger. What gives him the right to advise

me on who I can and can't have in my own house? 'The police think she was murdered by someone she knew, not a stranger,' I say coldly. 'Anyway, I can look after myself. I've had to for quite a while now,' I add pointedly.

'I'm sure you can. I just thought—'

'How's Harper? Where is she, anyway?' I interrupt.

He frowns and looks down at his shoes. 'She's gone back to her place. We had an argument just last night.'

I stare at him in surprise and wonder how I feel about this piece of information. It's something I've been hoping for, praying for, for months but now it's happened I feel strangely flat.

'So – what? You've split up?'

'I don't know.' He lifts his eyes reluctantly to mine. 'We're having a break for a little while to think things through.'

I wonder who initiated the break. My money's on Harper. I doubt she was ever seriously interested in Theo. Objectively, he's punching above his weight with her. Besides which, she must be at least ten years younger than him. My theory is that she picked him up like a new toy and played with him for a while, but now she's bored and wants to move on to the next new, shiny thing. Well, it serves him right. He'll get no sympathy from me.

'That's a shame,' I say sarcastically.

'Yes, I'm sure you're gutted,' Theo smiles wryly. Then he gives himself a little shake. 'I was going to take Dylan to the park to hunt for the Gruffalo before you organised that playdate,' he says. 'We could still go. You could come too, if you want.'

'I don't think that's such a good idea, do you?'

'Why not? Just think how happy it would make Dylan for us to spend the day together as a family.'

We're not a family any more, I think. *Because you destroyed it. You destroyed it the moment you jumped into bed with Harper.* But he's played the Dylan card and I know he's right. It would make Dylan happy – and if Dylan's happy, I'm happy.

So that's how I find myself in the car, driving Theo and Dylan to the park. On our way, we stop at the house to pick up Delilah and spend the next few hours tramping around the park, sploshing through muddy puddles, making dens and throwing sticks for Delilah. Delilah, delighted to finally be out of the house, dances around crazily, like a puppy, and Dylan careers after her, chuckling like a loon. There's something soothing and healing about being outdoors and close to nature, and slowly, I feel myself shedding some of the stress and anxiety of the week. For whole minutes at a time, I forget about Charlie and the police investigation and it almost feels like we're a normal, happy family on a day out.

It's getting late by the time we get back and Theo persuades me to stay to dinner and put Dylan to bed.

'Stay. Have a drink,' Theo says, after Dylan has nodded

off to *The Gruffalo's Child*. He's sitting on the armchair, his arm splayed expansively over the back and he's opened a bottle of Californian red and has already started drinking.

'No thanks. I can't. I've got to drive,' I say primly.

'You can stay the night here. Why not? You can sleep on the sofa bed.'

'Well, I—'

He senses me weakening. 'Go on, Cat. I'd have thought you need a drink or two after the week you've had. Besides, I worry about you all alone in that house. For all we know, there's some psychotic killer on the loose. I'd feel much better if you were safe here with me.'

I know that I should keep my dignity intact and refuse, but I'm tired and scared and the thought of a drink to blunt the edges is very enticing. I don't want to be alone any more. I want a respite from the constant fear that's been dogging me lately.

'Why not?' I sink wearily into the sofa and accept the glass of wine he pours for me.

'Do you remember we drank this on the first date we ever had?' he says, draining his glass and pouring himself another.

'How could I forget when you knocked the bottle over on my white skirt?'

He chuckles. 'Yeah, I was so nervous. I was trying so hard to impress you.'

'Really? You didn't seem nervous.' Theo never seems nervous to me. It is one of the things that attracted me to him – his lazy, unflappable humour, the way nothing seems to faze him. (The first time I met him I interviewed him for the local paper because a huge pet python had escaped from someone's house and had turned up in his garden. I remember he recounted the whole episode as if it was no big deal, as if these kinds of things happened to him all the time.)

There's a short silence. I suppose you could call it companionable. I certainly feel no pressure to talk. I just slump back in the chair, sipping wine, waiting for the numbness to kick in.

'So, this Luke—' Theo says, at last, topping up my glass.

'What about him?'

'Is there anything between you?'

I snort at the stupidity of the question. 'Obviously not. He's married and he's got me into trouble by lying to the police. Not exactly boyfriend material, I think you'll agree.'

He gazes at me with serious brown eyes. 'I can't help feeling jealous when I think of you with him,' he says.

I swallow a tight ball of anger. 'Well, you have absolutely no right to be.'

'I know I don't. But I can't help the way I feel. Sorry.'

I don't answer. I just go to the kitchen and open another bottle of wine.

Theo sighs as I return to the living room. 'I suppose, at least it means you've got an alibi. Do you think the police will leave you alone after he talks to them?'

'I don't know. I hope so. They took my DNA too.'

I slump back in my chair, fighting back tears. Suddenly, I am overwhelmed by it all. By the constant fear and paranoia that have been stalking me for days.

'Everything's just completely fucked up.' I give a shuddering sigh. And to my mortification I start crying.

Theo shuffles around beside me and puts his arm around my shoulders. He has that helpless, confused look he always gets when people are upset. Emotions are not Theo's thing. Give him a mathematical puzzle or a practical problem to solve and he's your man. Upset ex-wives? Not so much. It's strangely endearing.

He rubs his thumb on my shoulder and then gently wipes away the tears from my cheeks. 'It's going to be okay, you know,' he says.

'I hope so,' I say, looking up into his eyes. Then, next thing I know we're kissing. Theo's lips are soft and familiar. It feels sweet and safe being in his arms, and I feel the hard shard of ice inside me crack just a little.

'I've missed that,' he says softly, breaking off and cupping my cheek with his hand.

There's a part of me that still loves him, I realise, as I look into his warm brown eyes. If I'm honest, I have never stopped loving him. Why should I fight it? It feels right. But then I'm brought up short when I glance over his shoulder and notice the photo on the mantelpiece – Theo, Harper and Dylan at the zoo, sitting on the wall by the penguin enclosure – and I swipe his hand away, angrily. *What the hell am I doing?*

'Stop! This is not happening,' I blurt, shoving him roughly backwards.

He tumbles off the sofa on to the floor and sits there rubbing his head, looking bemused and drunk.

'You're right. God, I'm sorry. Shit,' he says, scrambling to his feet. 'We must have drunk too much.' He avoids my eyes. 'We'd better go to sleep. I'll make up the bed for you.'

I wake next morning to the sound of a phone ringing. It's raining, a steady tapping on the window, and I'm lying on the couch in Theo's t-shirt. I can't even remember him giving it to me last night. I feel exhausted, hung over and there's a crick in my neck.

Theo answers the phone and I can clearly hear his sleepy voice. I can tell straight away from his tone, which is soft and intimate, that he's talking to Harper.

'Yes, right. You're right,' he says. 'Yes, me too, okay.' Then, more softly, 'I'm sorry.'

They're making up, I realise, with a sinking feeling in my gut. Their argument was just a lover's tiff, after all. I roll

191

over and clamber out of bed, feeling like I've been scraped off someone's shoe. What was I thinking last night? Why did I let Theo kiss me? Have I got no self-respect? Thank God I didn't end up sleeping with him. At least I can hold on to that and leave with some dignity. Wanting to get out before Theo comes in, I scramble into my clothes and collect my stuff together, but I'm really thirsty and my mouth feels like it's been scraped out with sandpaper, so before I go, I head to the kitchen to get some water.

While I'm filling my glass from the tap, I'm distracted by Dylan's school bags on the kitchen chair. They look as if they were just dumped there on Friday and haven't been touched since. Sure enough, when I open his lunch bag, I see that Theo hasn't even bothered to empty it. Inside, there's Dylan's half-eaten sandwich and some apple slices going brown. I toss them into the bin and rinse out the bag, turning it inside out to dry. Then, as an afterthought, I check his book bag. *I bet Theo hasn't bothered to read with him*, I think crossly, flicking through his reading record. I'm incensed to see not only that Theo hasn't read with him, but that Harper has. That's even worse than nobody reading with him at all. *Super reading today!* she's written in her swirly, girly writing, and she's drawn a large smiley face. I snap it shut and empty out the rest of the bag on to the counter.

Along with the book, some scrunched-up paper and,

strangely, an acorn, a blue envelope falls out. My breath catches in my throat. I turn it over in my hands afraid to open it, afraid of what might be inside. This time someone has written the words 'For Catherine' on the front in printed blue biro, just like the note that was sent to DI Littlewood.

I scrabble in the cutlery drawer, trying to stay calm and taking out a sharp knife, then, with a single swift movement, I slit the envelope open and slide out the contents. Another printout. I unfold it and flatten it on the kitchen counter. Blinking as the picture comes into focus, I try to make sense of what I'm seeing. *Is that . . .?* I bend over double, trying to breathe and force myself to look at it again.

It's an empty stretch of road in the middle of nowhere: a grass verge and a gate, an oak tree with a twisted trunk. There's nothing remarkable about it and yet . . .

This is the spot, I think. *This is where it happened.*

I grip the edge of the kitchen counter. It's as if a huge explosion has gone off in my head, creating a massive shock wave. I feel as if I've been electrocuted. For a moment, I think I might be having a stroke.

'That was Harper on the phone.' Theo sidles sheepishly into the kitchen wearing boxer shorts and a t-shirt, hair all mussed up. He rubs his eyes and blinks at me sleepily. 'She's on her way. She's going to be here in a few minutes.'

I can't speak. I'm still staring at the picture. I can't drag my eyes away.

Theo misinterprets my silence. 'I'm really sorry, Cat. I know this is an awkward situation. You can stay if you want, I just thought you'd want to know.'

'What?' I manage. My voice seems far away. 'No, sure, I'll go. I don't want to see Harper. You don't have any idea where this envelope came from, do you?'

Theo glances at it and shrugs. 'No. Cat, are you all right?'

'Never better,' I say vaguely, as I scoop up my jacket and shove the envelope in my handbag.

'See you later, Theo,' I say, as I head to the door.

'Cat? Is there—?'

Outside, I gulp in fresh air and retch into a plant pot. Then I get into my car and drive blindly, as if I can escape the demons chasing me. But I can't escape. I will never escape. There's no doubt now. They've caught up with me. The photos, Charlie's death, the photofit. They're all linked. Someone knows what happened and they want me to pay.

Twenty-one

2002

Charlie and James.

The shock of it was like something sharp stuck in my throat.

Charlie and James sitting in a tree, K-I-S-S-I-N-G. The rhyme drummed in my head, taunting me. Charlie and James sitting in a tree. Except they weren't just kissing.

At that moment, a flash of lightning lit up the sky and the whole scene was illuminated in stark, unforgiving detail. The look on Charlie's face was pure deer-in-headlights. Caught in the act. It would have been almost comical in other circumstances.

'Cat . . .' she said. And James, finally realising something was wrong, opened his eyes and blinked in confusion.

'Oh my God!' he exclaimed, as Charlie pulled away from him and I stood there, rooted to the spot, unable to look away.

'Cat . . .' Charlie said again, scrambling to get dressed.

'What the fuck, Charlie?' I blurted, having at last found my voice – and the use of my legs, as I turned and blundered away.

'Wait, Cat!' Charlie shouted, as I stumbled down the garden path. But I didn't stop. I ran sobbing out of the garden gate, across the small footbridge towards the village. I ran and ran, not really thinking about where I was going. I just knew I had to get away from there – away from my best friend who'd betrayed me and the boy I'd liked ever since I was eleven. At that moment, it felt like the worst thing that had ever happened to me.

I would never speak to Charlie again, I told myself. She was a bitch who didn't deserve my friendship. She knew how much I liked James and she'd deliberately stolen him from me. For what? Just because she could? To prove she was better than me?

After a while, I ran out of breath and tears and I stopped running. I found I was heading along the lonely country road out of the village back towards Cirencester. The street lamps had petered out and now the only light came from periodic flashes of lightning and a faint glimmer of grey morning on the horizon. I carried on walking briskly, slowly becoming aware of how far I had to walk and of how chilly the morning air was in my sleeveless summer dress. Not only was it cold, but thunder was rumbling ominously, and it looked increasingly likely that it was going to rain. My anger was subsiding and slowly bleeding into fear as it dawned on me that I was in the middle of nowhere, all alone in the early hours. It didn't matter, I told myself defiantly. I could get raped and murdered for all I cared. Then they'd be sorry. But as I walked further, and the alcohol began to wear off, the silence seemed to stalk me and small noises in the hedgerow set my imagination reeling. When I heard a car on the road behind me, my body went into fight-or-flight mode.

The car was driving unnaturally slowly. Every now and then it would stop and then start up again with a loud roar of the engine. It was weird and creepy. But I resisted the urge to escape by diving into the woods and instead carried on walking, my back rigid, heart pounding. Probably just a drunk driver, I told myself. It will just drive on past. But it didn't. It swerved around me and stopped dead just ahead, lurching into the bushes, as if the driver had suddenly lost control. Then the car door flew open and I froze in terror. I wished I'd drunk more to dull the horror of whatever was going to happen next. This is it, I thought. This is how I die.

Twenty-two

Eileen Robinson is in her front garden watering the flowers in her hanging baskets when I arrive home.

'Don't know why I'm bothering. It looks like it's going to rain,' she comments, glancing up at the darkening sky.

'Mm-hm,' I mumble neutrally.

She leans on the wall as I'm opening my door, looking me up and down, taking in my messed-up hair and crumpled clothes.

'There were a lot of reporters outside yesterday,' she says with a spiteful gleam in her eyes.

'Were there?' I feign surprise, fumbling with the lock. Go to hell, you old bitch is what I want to say.

'I thought they were here to see you,' she begins. 'Wasn't it something about that murder in—'

'Sorry, can't talk now. I'm not feeling all that well,' I

interrupt and dive into the house, slamming the door behind me.

Inside I take some painkillers and down a couple of glasses of water in quick succession. My throat is so dry after all that red wine last night. My head is pounding and I want to just lie down in a darkened room. But that photograph is preying on my mind. I have to know. I have to be certain.

I make myself a coffee, sit at the kitchen table and switch on my laptop.

After a quick search, I find the *Wilts and Gloucester Standard* archives on my phone and quickly, before I have the chance to chicken out, I type in 'hit and run 2002' in the 'search key words' bar.

And there it is. The page appears straight away. I inhale sharply as I read the headline, 5 July 2002: *Five-year-old girl killed in hit and run.*

Underneath the headline there's a photo of an empty stretch of road. And when I hold up the printout from my handbag with a trembling hand, I confirm what I knew already: they are practically identical. There's the same oak tree with the twisted trunk, the same grass verge and wooden gate. But what really takes my breath away is the picture next to it. A head shot of a little blonde girl giving a shy, gap-toothed smile to the camera. Underneath it says *Daisy Foster, five years old.*

Bile rises in my gullet and my stomach roils, but I swallow the bitterness and force myself to read.

In the early hours of last Sunday morning, Daisy Foster was hit and killed by a car on the road between South Baunton and Cirencester. Five-year-old Daisy had wandered away from her home. It is believed she was looking for her dog.

I close the page. I can't read any more. I can't look at that picture – those innocent eyes boring into me, piercing my soul. She was five years old – the same age as Dylan. I close the window, my stomach heaving, a wave of dizziness and nausea washing over me, and I rush to the toilet and throw up.

I stand up shakily. A bit of vomit has got caught in a strand of my hair.

Daisy Foster. I never knew her name before. I never wanted to know. Knowing her name would have made her real and I didn't want her to be real. I wanted to pretend that she had never existed. For all these years, I've been quite successful at kidding myself. When friends talked about small prangs, I found it easy to say that I'd never had an accident or so much as a speeding ticket. And I almost believed my own lies. I've buried this secret, like nuclear waste sealed in concrete deep underground. But now all the poison is leaking out. Someone else knows what I did, and they haven't forgotten or forgiven. I can't really blame them. Daisy Foster was only five. She hadn't even started her life. I think about how I would feel if someone killed Dylan. I wouldn't forgive them. I would want to kill them.

Twenty-three

2002

The car ground to a halt and the door flew open. I was rooted to the spot, bracing myself for what was to come. Pure fear surged through me, sharp, cold air caught in my lungs, making me suddenly terrifyingly sober. I'm too young to die, I thought. Please. Please don't let me die.

I don't know why I didn't recognise the car. It was dark, I was drunk and panic was scrambling my brain. So, when a young woman climbed out and tottered unsteadily towards me, it took me a few terrified seconds to realise that it was Charlie and not some mad, axe-wielding lunatic.

'Not bad after two driving lessons,' she said hiccupping. Her words were slurred. She was obviously even more drunk than I was. 'I think you'll agree.'

I gaped at her in amazement, at her wildly dishevelled hair and the t-shirt, which in her rush to dress, she'd put on back to front and inside out. My heart rate was slowly returning to normal, my breathing becoming more regular. On the one hand, I was incredibly relieved to see her; on the other, now that I was no longer in mortal danger, I remembered why I was out here in the first place – how she'd betrayed me. She was my best friend and she'd betrayed me.

'The keys were in here,' she held out my handbag. 'You left it in the kitchen.'

Realising I was being ridiculous, I snatched the handbag without a word and carried on walking past her, head held high, nose in the air.

She came lumbering after me, half laughing and half crying. 'Jesus, Cat what are you doing? You can't walk all the way home. It must be about ten miles.'

'Fuck off, Charlie. I don't want to speak to you.'

'I'm sorry, Cat. I'm such a fuck-up. Please forgive me.'

I stopped and turned on her.

'Why did you do it? You know how much I like him.'

'I know. I'm sorry. I don't know. It just happened.' She staggered a little and steadied herself by grabbing my shoulder. I got a whiff of her perfume, musky and sexy. The scent enraged me, and I shook her hand away angrily.

'You don't even care. You broke the code.'

'It's not as if he was your boyfriend.'

I think I was more hurt by how easy it had been for Charlie to betray our friendship than by the fact it had been with James. James was just a fantasy. Charlie was real. 'I've loved him ever since I was eleven,' I said bitterly. 'You were never interested in him until I told you I liked him. Oh, I can't even be bothered to talk to you. I'm never ever going to talk to you again.'

Charlie grabbed my arm. 'Don't be so dramatic, Cat. Look, I'm sorry. I'm so, so sorry. Please forgive me. I love you, Cat. I can't lose your friendship. I'll make it up to you, I promise.' She was crying now, drunken tears rolling down her cheeks. 'Let's just get in the car and go home. It won't seem so bad in the morning.'

I hesitated. It was a long way home. I was tired and I already had a blister on my heel. Not to mention the fact that it was scary as hell walking along this lonely country road by myself.

'All right, but I'm driving. I'm not sure how you even made it this far,' I said. 'And this doesn't mean I forgive you, by the way.'

She threw me the keys. 'It's all yours.'

I was still drunk. I knew that driving home was a bad idea, and for a second, I thought about phoning for a taxi and leaving the car where it was. But the thought of explaining to a taxi driver where we were, and the thought of explaining to my mother why we'd abandoned her car in the middle of nowhere didn't bear thinking about. It wasn't far to Cirencester and the roads were empty at this time in the morning.

'Give me a hug,' said Charlie as I got into the car.

I didn't answer.

'We should never let boys come between us again,' she said as we drove off.

I pressed my foot on the accelerator – I was still seething with rage. She wasn't even taking the whole thing seriously. I couldn't bear being in the car with her. The sooner I dropped her at her house the better.

'I think I'm going to be sick,' Charlie announced as we were driving. And she wound down the window and stuck her head out, letting the wind rush in.

'Get in, Charlie. You're going to kill yourself!' I shouted.

But she just laughed and leant further out. 'Live a little, Cat. You know what they say . . .' she yelled.

I never did find out what they say because at that moment something so terrible happened, it blew Charlie and James into insignificance.

Out of nowhere, an animal flashed in front of the car. Then, a split second later, a small child appeared, running up behind it.

I didn't have time to react. No time to think. Just before impact, the girl turned, and her eyes met mine. Her expression didn't register any shock or alarm. It all happened too quickly for that. It must have been merely a matter of seconds, but her image was frozen in time, her face white, illuminated in the headlights. It was the sharpest, most permanent thing I'd ever seen. Still, even now, I remember every detail. From the grubby-looking white dress she was wearing, to the two missing front teeth and the wispy blonde hair, lit up like a halo around her head. She held out her hand as if to ward us off, as if she could stop fifteen hundred kilos of metal with one tiny little hand. And I stamped desperately on the brake. But it was too late. There was a sickening thud and then she was flying, vaulting through the air, her legs skyward. My car screeched to a halt and I watched, horrified, as she slammed into the hard, tarmac road.

There was a silence – a silence that stretched out like a scream.

Charlie was the first to recover. 'What the hell just happened?' she said. Her eyes were rolling in their sockets like a startled horse.

I couldn't speak. My hands were glued to the steering wheel. The breath had left my body. It felt as if all my organs had fallen out and I was nothing but a hollow shell.

'We have to see if she's okay,' I muttered finally. I was trying to get my limbs to move without much success. When they eventually got the message from my brain it felt like an out-of-body experience, as if I was watching someone else clamber out of the car and walk over to where the girl was lying in a small, limp heap.

Strangely, one shoe had come off her foot and had rolled a few feet away and the animal that had sped across the road – a black schnauzer, as it turned out – had come back and was sniffing around her, licking her face.

She was so young, I thought. Her arms were flung carelessly out by her sides, her little hands still padded with baby fat. Her face was strangely peaceful, her eyes shut, as if she were sleeping. But beside her head a large pool of dark blood was soaking into the tarmac and there was no movement in her chest. No sign at all that she was still breathing.

Please God, let this not be happening, I prayed, sinking to the ground beside her and touching her neck lightly with trembling fingers. Her skin was warm, but I couldn't feel any pulse.

'I think she's dead,' I said. And my voice seemed to come from a long way away, drowned out by the rain that suddenly began falling, like some cosmic judgement. Rain pattered down on us, soaking the girl's blonde hair, rolling off her soft, unblemished cheeks like tears.

'Shit, shit. Is she dead?' Charlie appeared beside me. She looked like the Joker, mascara-blackened tears rolling down her cheeks. She tugged at her hair, as if she wanted to pull it out at the roots.

'Yes. I think so.' I tried to gather my wits. 'I suppose we need to call an ambulance,' I said. 'Have you got a phone?'

Charlie stared at me, her features frozen in horror. 'I left it at Nessa's.'

'It's okay. Mine's in my handbag.' I stood up and walked to the car in a dream and fumbled for my phone.

'Shit,' I called out to Charlie.

'Did you get hold of them?' she asked as I got closer. She was shivering, whether from shock or cold, I couldn't tell.

'No,' I said through the rain. 'I couldn't. My phone's run out of battery.'

'Oh my God, what do we do? This is bad.' Charlie fell to her knees beside the little girl and pressed her head to her chest. 'She's dead, Cat,' she wailed. 'We've killed her.'

My head felt like it was about to explode. 'Shut up, shut up. Let me think. What are we going to do?'

I looked around. There was a house across the field. All the lights were glowing yellow in the windows and very faintly I could hear music playing. It sounded as though they were having a party.

'Maybe we should go to that house?' I said. 'Knock on a door. Ask if we can use their phone.'

'Wait,' said Charlie. She had stood up and was dusting herself off, brushing away her tears. 'Slow down. Let's think about this a minute.' Her face was pale and grimly resolved.

'She's dead already. There's nothing we can do. There's nothing anyone can do for her.'

'Right,' I nodded, my mind working frantically.

'Think about it, Cat. You've been drinking. Drink driving. Manslaughter. If people know about this, you'll go to prison for a long time. It will ruin your life.'

I sank down on the damp grass verge, blinking away the rain. I could see it all with a terrible crushing certainty. My future ruined. The anger and disappointment of my parents. The disgust and condemnation of my friends and acquaintances. Charlie was right. We couldn't help the little girl. She was dead. Nothing would change that. And my life was as good as destroyed if people knew about this.

'Come on,' Charlie said, suddenly urgent. 'We should go before another car comes and sees us here.'

I nodded blindly, stood up and climbed back in the car. I didn't look at the girl lying in the road again. With a heavy heart, I turned on the ignition and drove away. I felt so tired. All I wanted was to get home and forget this had ever happened.

In the end, it was surprisingly easy to do – to just drive away and pretend the whole thing was just a bad dream. There was a slight dent in the car that I explained away to my mother by saying Charlie had attempted to drive and had hit a post. She didn't question my explanation. No police came to my house. A few weeks later, we both went our separate ways: Charlie to Cambridge and me to Manchester University. There was no fuss. We never spoke of it again. The road to hell isn't always paved with good intentions. Sometimes the road to hell is the easiest route – the path of least resistance.

Twenty-four

Outside there's a crack of thunder and it starts raining hard. Wind and rain batter the bathroom window.

I want to drink myself into a stupor, take sleeping pills – do anything to erase the image of that little girl. Daisy Foster – the little girl who never got to grow up or have a life. She's never going to have a job, get married or have children of her own. All because of me. I want to forget her, but it's impossible. Her face is tattooed on to my mind and nothing I can do will ever change that. I rummage in the bathroom cabinet and find the packet of Xanax which I persuaded the doctor to prescribe me after Theo left. I swallow a couple, washed down with water from the tap. Then I splash cold water on my face and rinse out the vomit from my hair, staring at my reflection in the mirror. It's strange how the turmoil inside me doesn't show on my face. I'm a little pale and there are dark shadows under my eyes. But that's all. I look normal, which is good because I've arranged to meet Luke at midday.

I check the time on my phone. It's nearly eleven already. Shit. Meeting Luke is the last thing I feel like doing right now, but I can't afford to miss this opportunity. Who knows if or when he'd agree to talk to me again? So I shower quickly and change into clean jeans and a shapeless green t-shirt. Then I scrape some eyeliner around my eyes, smear some cover-up over the dark shadows and pull my hair back into a ponytail. When I've finished, I smile at myself in the mirror with grim satisfaction. I look battle ready, resolute. There's no way I'm going to let Luke get away with his lies. But I'm not taking any chances. After all, Luke is at least seven inches taller than me and I know that if things get physical, I don't stand a chance.

Downstairs, I google homemade pepper spray on my phone and follow the instructions, making a simple mix of crushed-up chilli, black pepper and water, heating it in the microwave and then pouring it into an empty perfume bottle. I screw on the lid, put it in my pocket and practise drawing it out quickly and squirting it like a gunslinger in the Wild West. A real gun would be more useful, I think, but how on earth do you get a gun in this country? If I lived in America I could probably just go to the local Walmart and buy one off the shelf. But here, in the UK, I don't know. Farmers and hunters must have guns. There must be a way. I'm halfway through typing *how to get a gun* into Google, when I'm brought up short. How can I be so stupid? Everything you do on the Internet can be tracked and it won't exactly help me prove my innocence if the police find out that I've been looking into buying a firearm. Taking a deep breath, I delete the search. I can't believe it's come to this. Only a few weeks ago, everything was normal. I was getting used to the idea of life without Theo. Okay, I wasn't exactly happy, but I was managing – everything was under control. Now my world seems to have imploded. I'm a suspect in a murder case and I've become so paranoid that here I am making pepper spray and considering buying a gun.

I don't need a weapon, I tell myself as I'm leaving the house. Luke isn't dangerous. He's just an arsehole who cheats on his wife and thinks he can get away with it. Even so, I pop the bottle of pepper spray in my handbag just in case.

There's no one at reception or in the waiting room at Cotswolds Dental surgery. I stand in reception and look around the room at the pictures on the walls of people's open mouths and rows of teeth in various stages of decay. It's Sunday, of course, so it's natural that there's no one here. But still feeling slightly unnerved, I ring the bell on the desk, and after a few seconds, Luke appears from a back room. His sleeves are rolled up and he's shaking off his hands as if he's just washed them.

'Cat, hi,' he says, leading me into a small back kitchen with a table and a fridge.

'Please take a seat,' he says neutrally, as if I'm a patient. He perches on a stool opposite me and meets my eyes directly. There is no shame in them, but there's something else I can't quite read. I force myself to look at him dispassionately – the perfect dimpled chin, the beautiful, murky green eyes. I try to block the memory of the weight of him on top of me and the thrust of his hips. I feel a thrill of fear. We're all alone, I think. I know how strong he is. This man could easily overpower me. I should have agreed to let Theo come with me. I finger the phone in my pocket, wondering whether to call him now. But then I think about last night, about Harper. I can't call Theo. It's too humiliating.

He watches me carefully and I fidget uncomfortably under his scrutiny.

'Why an architect?' I ask, staring out of the window at the rain sluicing against the pane. It's hard to look at him directly. The atmosphere is tense. The air is crackling with it. Anger? Fear? From me or from him? Maybe both.

'What?'

'When you were . . . at my house, you told me you were an architect.'

He shrugs. 'If I'd told you I was a dentist, you might have been able to find where I worked. Architect was the first thing that came into my head.'

And of course, he's arrogant enough to believe I would have sought him out and what? Created a scene when I found out he was married. Perhaps it's happened before with other women.

'Is it something you do a lot, pick up women? Cheat on your wife?' I'm trying to sound tough, aggressive, but my voice comes out whiny, hurt even.

'No, you were the only one.'

'I find that hard to believe,' I say angrily. 'Why should I believe anything you say? You've done nothing but lie.'

'Fair point,' he shrugs.

I blush to think how easy it was for him to seduce me. He barely needed to say anything. If I'm honest, if I'd stopped to think about it, I could have guessed that he was married. But did I ask? No. I was too busy feeling flattered that someone so handsome and charming could be interested in me. Basically, I've done to Georgia what Harper did to me. Of all people, *I* should know what it's like to have a faithless husband and I feel an uncomfortable twinge of guilt at the thought.

'Why did you do it?' I blurt. I mean Georgia's beautiful and such a nice person. You're so lucky. Don't you love her?'

He winces. 'Yes, of course I love her. What can I say?

It was a mistake. Probably one of the worst mistakes I've ever made.'

'You couldn't help yourself, you mean,' I say sarcastically. He doesn't answer.

'You caught me at a weak moment,' he says, at last.

'Oh, give me a break.' I feel a welcome surge of anger. 'You realise that I'm in deep trouble because of your lies. The police think that I'm involved in a murder.'

'Yes, I know,' he chews the end of his thumbnail and observes me thoughtfully. 'Why do they think that?'

It seems he's the only person in this town who hasn't seen the photofit.

'There was a news report,' I say carefully. 'A witness saw a woman who looked a lot like me at the scene of the crime on the night that Charlie was murdered. But it wasn't me, obviously,' I add hastily.

He's leaning forward, listening intently.

'Anyway,' I continue firmly, 'it doesn't matter because I have an alibi and that's you. You were with me that night. *You're* my alibi.'

He frowns and tips his chair back, staring at me through narrowed lids. 'If there's no other evidence against you, then you don't need an alibi. They can't use a witness statement in a court of law.'

'You're missing the point,' I say angrily. 'They may not be able to arrest me, but I have to live with their suspicion

216

and everyone else's. Do you know my son's teacher asked me not to pick him up from school because the other parents don't like me being around the school? And I've had reporters hassling me day and night.' Not quite true, but it feels true in this moment. My voice cracks a little and I feel tears welling up. *Not here. Not now*, I think. *Don't start crying now. Not in front of him.*

'I'm sorry about that,' he says more gently. 'But you have to understand my point of view. I can't risk Georgia finding out about the other night. I'd lose everything. You know Harry is not actually my son. I have no rights over him. She'd take him away from me.'

'There's no reason the police would need to tell Georgia.'

He shakes his head. 'How can I know that for sure?'

I ball my hands up in my lap, digging my nails in. The next thing I say I say quietly but firmly.

'You don't. But if you don't tell the police you were with me that night you can be sure that she will find out . . . because I'll tell her myself.'

It takes a moment for my words to sink in. Then he looks suddenly ugly – his handsome features twisted with anger.

'You wouldn't do that,' he says.

'Try me. I don't want to hurt Georgia, but I'm prepared to do whatever it takes.'

He stands up and takes a step towards me around the desk. He stands over me, glaring down at me, breathing quickly through his nose. *He's trying to intimidate me*, I think. *Well, it won't work.*

'You have to tell the police the truth,' I say, reaching for the pepper spray inside my bag.

His hands are clenched by his sides. For a moment, I think he's going to hit me. I can see it crossing his mind and I brace myself for the impact, clutching the perfume bottle, ready to retaliate. Then he gives a deep sigh and walks back round the table and slumps in his chair.

'All right,' he says, at last. 'But you have to promise me that you will never ever mention any of this to my wife. If you do, I won't be held responsible for my actions.'

'I promise,' I say, breathing deeply and loosening my grip on the pepper spray. I will agree to almost anything if only he will tell the police the truth.

'On your son's life,' he says.

There's no way I'm going to swear anything on Dylan's life. 'Don't worry,' I say. 'I'm good at keeping secrets.'

Twenty-five

It's true that I'm good at keeping secrets. If keeping secrets was a sport, I'd be an Olympic champion – a gold medallist. But clearly Charlie wasn't. She must have told someone about the accident. I don't see how else they could have found out. But who did she tell? I mull this over as I dash through the rain to my car. I suppose the most likely person is her husband, Adam. I'm guessing that he was the person she was closest to. If she confided in anyone, it probably would have been him.

I sit in the car, listening to the rain drum on the metal roof and thinking about Adam, his smooth, boyish face and his seemingly genuine grief. I need to talk to him again and find out what he knows. But that will have to wait. There's something else I need to do first – something I should have done a long time ago. I start the engine and head through town towards the ring road. I drive slowly, blinded by the driving rain, past the petrol station and the garden centre until I reach South Baunton. Then I stop on the small stone bridge and look at Nessa's house through my windscreen, the wipers swishing backwards and forwards. The house hasn't changed much. There's a slide and a playhouse in the front garden that weren't there when Nessa lived here, but that's about it. I shrink down in my seat as the garage doors swing open. A car rolls out and a woman drives past over the bridge. Then everything is quiet again and I picture myself as a teenager running round the side of the house down that gravel driveway, tears streaming down my face. I wish I could go back to that moment and warn my younger self. I would tell her to turn around and go back into the house. I would explain that what happened between Charlie and James wasn't important – that it would mean nothing to me years later and that I was running towards a cataclysm that would scar my life and the lives of so many others for ever.

It's too late. The past can't be changed. There's nothing to be done. Taking a deep breath, I turn the car around and drive back over the bridge. This time I follow the route I took seventeen years ago when I ran away from the party. As I drive, the rain eases and I bump over ruts and divots in the road, the low-hanging branches of trees brushing against my windscreen. I grip the wheel tightly as I get closer, fighting off a wave of panic.

I turn a bend in the road and suddenly, I'm back there – and it's all exactly as it was: the tree with the twisted trunk, the wooden gate and the grass verge. I swerve into a lay-by and kill the engine. Sitting in the car for a few moments, I try to control my breathing. Then I get out and walk through the drizzle a short way up the road. When I reach the tree, I stand still, my heart hammering. I can't turn my head. There's the strong, superstitious sensation that someone is behind me. I'm afraid that if I turn, I'll see *her*.

Ghosts don't exist, I think. There's no such thing as ghosts, I repeat to myself firmly, and clenching my fists, I swivel round swiftly. As though if I turn quickly enough, I might catch her – like that game 'What's the time, Mr Wolf?' Or those moving statues in *Doctor Who*.

I breathe out slowly. There's no one there, of course. Just the empty road and the tree shifting a little in a breeze. Out of nowhere, a car whizzes past, splashing through a puddle, kicking up spray. I step back, but too late to avoid being splattered with dirty water. I brush down my jeans, then I take the photo out of my bag – the printout from Dylan's book bag. Raindrops land on the paper, creating dark grey spots that spread and wrinkle the page. But it matches exactly, as I knew it would: the tree, the gate, the long grass. The faded white lines.

*

In the distance, at the far end of a yellow corn field there's a church spire and a small white house – the same house I saw with Charlie that night. It has never occurred to me before, but Daisy Foster must have lived there. Where else? There are no other buildings near by. Five-year-old girls don't just appear out of nowhere in the middle of the night. I close my eyes, trying to block out the image of her small, startled face lit up in my headlights – her limp body lying on the hard, cold tarmac and the tiny, yellow shoe left on one foot.

'What were you doing, Daisy? Why did you rush out in front of my car like that?' I murmur aloud.

Then I remember the article I read online and think about the dog that dashed across the road immediately before the crash. *She was chasing him*, I think. Though what she was doing out and about at five in the morning in the first place is a mystery. *Where were her parents? Who lets a five-year-old wander about alone like that? They have to take some of the blame. I'm not the only one responsible.* The thought should be comforting, I suppose, but somehow it isn't.

I glance back at the small white house. Who lives there now? Could Daisy's parents still be there? Seized by a sudden idea, I get back in the car, turn on data roaming and Google house prices. Then I lock the car and head across the fields, retracing what I think must have been Daisy's steps that morning. The corn has recently been cut and is wet from the rain. It's full of crows pecking at the grain. Disturbed by my arrival, they rise into the air, a black cloud of thrashing wings, cawing loudly. It feels like an ominous sign. And as I get closer to the house, my courage wavers. What if I'm wrong? Or worse, what if I'm right and her parents still live in here? Are they the ones trying to frame me? What if I'm walking into a trap?

In the front yard there is a rusty old caravan with one wheel missing, balanced on a pile of bricks and a skip on the lawn full of random junk. A vicious-looking Alsatian runs up barking and snarling as I open the gate and I walk quickly up the overgrown pathway and press the bell. There's no answer.

The windows are dark, smeared with grime and I can't see in, but I sense movement inside. Maybe the doorbell isn't working. I rap on the door instead and listen to the sound of someone stirring within. A few seconds later, a flabby-looking middle-aged man with a shock of wild grey hair and a prominent, round belly emerges from the gloom, blinking at me as if he hasn't seen daylight in years.

I plaster a smile on my face. 'Hello,' I say brightly. 'Are you Mr Foster?'

'That's right, Doug Foster,' he nods slowly and my heart leaps to my mouth. My knees start trembling and I steady myself by leaning against the doorjamb. I was right. Daisy

Foster lived in this house. This must be her father. He is the right age – in his late fifties, at a rough guess.

'Who wants to know?'

'I'm Amanda Potter, from Cooper estate agents.' I hold out my hand. It's only shaking a little. I'm getting used to lying.

'Oh yeah?' he picks at his teeth and stares at me. There's something not entirely friendly in that look, but there's no sign of recognition, nothing but a faint, generalised hostility. I take a deep, shaky breath. *It's okay*, I think. *He has no idea who you are.*

'We're doing free valuations of properties in the area and I was just wondering if you would like to take advantage of the opportunity,' I continue. I'm breezy and professional. My voice sounds alien to me.

'Not really, thank you very much.' He starts to close the door.

'The market is really hot just now,' I continue glibly. 'Did you know, for example, that a house in this area, similar to yours, sold for over five hundred thousand pounds just last month?'

That's it. I've got him. I can see the glimmer of greed in his eyes.

'Five hundred thousand?' he says slowly. He hesitates only for a second. Then he stands back. 'You'd better come in.'

Entering the house is like disturbing the dank, dark underside of a rock. The curtains are drawn in the living room and it smells strongly of cigarette smoke, damp and something else, something pungent and foul – maybe cat pee. I'm guessing that no one has cleaned in here properly for a while. There's a thick layer of dust on everything and there are overflowing ashtrays and unwashed dishes and mugs strewn around the place. I fight a desperate urge to pull back the curtains and open a window to let in some air.

'How long have you lived here exactly?' I ask, looking around pretending to examine the fireplace and running my fingers over the grimy tiles.

He gives a loud hacking cough – the cough of a lifelong smoker. 'Oh, a long time. I moved here when I married. So about twenty-five years.'

I look around. There's no sign of anyone else. Everything about the place speaks of a drab, lonely existence. 'And your wife? Is she here today?'

His eyes cloud over. 'Nope. There was an accident. She's gone. Gone to a better place . . .' he tails off.

'I'm so sorry,' I say inadequately. How much bad luck can one family have?

He shrugs.

'This fireplace is really a nice feature,' I say, stooping over to move a dead plant out of the way. I wonder when his wife died. It's no surprise he seems so bitter. Who wouldn't be, having to deal with so much loss?

I wipe at some of the dirt. 'These tiles are gorgeous. Is there a reason why you've never moved?'

'Not really.' He sighs heavily. 'I suppose there are a lot of memories here. I've grown attached to the place.'

I inhale sharply, stifling a gasp, because at that moment, I notice a dusty photograph in a frame on the mantelpiece. It's of three children in the garden; two girls and a boy. The eldest, a boy of about nine or ten, is holding a football, while two small girls are in the paddling pool in their swimming costumes. It's the youngest, lying on her belly holding on to the edge of the paddling pool that catches my eye. She's smiling up at the camera. Her blonde hair is wet and sticking to her head. Two of her front teeth are missing. She looks shy and sweet.

Daisy Foster.

The photo must have been taken not long before she died – just before I killed her.

'My kids,' he says, following the direction of my gaze. His eyes glaze over. 'One of them died when she was just a baby, and I hardly ever see the other two. They grew up and they don't come and see me any more. Think they're too good for their old dad.'

I can't speak. I feel as if the room is folding in on itself, like a bad trip. I try to think of an appropriate response.

'I'm sorry,' I say inadequately.

'Yeah, well, that's life.'

'Mm,' I agree vaguely. 'How many bedrooms have you got?' I ask, trying to turn the conversation around. If he starts talking about Daisy, I'm not sure how I'll handle it. I'm not sure I'll be able to control myself. I might just throw myself at his feet and beg his forgiveness.

'Three,' he answers. 'Do you want to see them?'

'Sure.'

I follow him upstairs. I don't feel afraid of him any more. Just desperately sad and guilty. This man has every reason to hate me, but I'm almost certain he doesn't know who I am. And if he wanted to hurt me, he would have done something by now. Anyway, noticing his slight limp and the way he wheezes and coughs as he climbs the stairs, I'm sure if it came to it, I could take him in a fight.

The first bedroom is being used as a storage room and the small bunk bed is hidden under a pile of boxes. On the dresser there's a collection of semi-precious stones and shells, a shabby-looking dolls' house and an unopened box of Sylvanian Families. This must have been the bedroom Daisy shared with her sister. I close the door quickly. I don't want to look at the small, sad evidence of her short existence. The second room, I'm guessing, was the boy's bedroom. There are still faded posters of football players on the wall, their edges curled and yellowed. And by the bed, there's a lamp in the shape of a spaceship.

'This is the master bedroom,' Doug announces, opening the door to a room that doesn't really deserve the title 'master'. There's a small, unmade double bed with a fluffy grey cat lying on it. It stares at me with malignant yellow eyes but it doesn't move. On the bedside table there's another photo. It's of an attractive young woman on an ice-skating rink. Her hair is tied back tightly in a bun and she's wearing a leotard. One leg is lifted in the air, her arms outstretched, spinning on the ice.

'My wife,' he says proudly. 'She was the national champion two years in a row. Nearly made it to the Olympics. That was before the children were born.'

'Wow, really?' I pick up the photo and inspect it more closely, brushing off the dust.

'Those were her trophies.' He nods at a line of cups and medals arranged on the windowsill. 'I can't bring myself to throw them away.'

'No,' I say. I don't know what else to say.

He must be lonely here, all by himself, I think.

'And your children, do they live nearby?'

'Quite near –' he snorts – 'but you'd never guess from how often they visit their old man.'

'They've got busy lives, huh?'

'Something like that.'

I want to ask him more about his children, Daisy's siblings, but I don't know how without arousing his suspicion.

'So, how much do you think the house is worth?' he asks, as I follow him back downstairs.

'Well, it depends. It needs quite a lot of work,' I say, vaguely.

'Give me a ball-park figure.'

'About four hundred and fifty thousand,' I hazard.

'Really?' He looks pleased. 'Do you have a business card, so I can contact you if I decide to put it on the market?'

'Oh, yes.' I rummage in my handbag, pretending to look for them. 'Sorry, I think I'm all out of cards,' I say, at last. But you can always contact us through our website.'

He nods. 'Oh. Okay.'

'Well, thank you very much for your time,' I say, hurrying down the stairs. 'We'll be in touch.' I open the door before he has a chance to twig that there's something odd going on.

Outside, I turn my face to the sunlight. I gulp in the fresh air and try to shake off the gloom of Doug Foster's house, wrestling with a mixture of distaste and guilt.

I'm uncomfortably aware that he might be watching me through the window. So I head down the road, hoping that he'll assume my car is just parked around the corner. I'm sure he would think it was odd if I headed back across the field the way I came.

Taking the longer route back to the car through the village, I try to make sense of what I've learned.

Who killed Charlie? I run through possibilities in my head. It seems logical that Charlie's death was linked to Daisy's and that therefore Charlie's killer was someone related to Daisy.

Daisy's father? Probably not. Doug Foster has every reason to hate Charlie and me. But I find it hard to picture him as a murderer. Plus, it would have taken strength and energy to stab Charlie, and Doug Foster seems to have no strength or energy left. I got the impression of someone who has given up on life almost completely. Besides which, Charlie's killer knows who I am, and I'm almost sure Doug didn't recognise me – unless, of course, he's a brilliant actor.

Her mother? No, her mother is dead.

My thoughts turn to that photograph in the living room. Daisy with her older brother and sister. They must be in their mid-twenties by now. Besides Daisy's father, they are the people who have most reason to wish me ill. The more I consider it, the more I think it's entirely plausible that one of Daisy's siblings is behind both Charlie's death and the photos. I think about George from Wisconsin. Judging by his profile picture, he's too old to be Daisy's brother, and Doug said that his children lived nearby. Wisconsin isn't exactly nearby. But of course – George might not really live in Wisconsin. He could even have a fake identity. Anyone can create a fake account online, right?

Back in my car, I look at his profile again on my phone and scroll through his posts. There's almost nothing there; a photo of a house with an American flag outside and a couple of professional-looking shots of autumn scenes that I'm pretty sure have been downloaded from the net. He is almost certainly a catfish. He hasn't even gone to very much trouble to make his account look real.

'Who are you really, George?' I say out loud, peering at his photo. 'And what do you want from me?'

With a sigh, I start the engine and drive slowly back towards town in the gathering dark. My mind is only half on the road. I'm thinking furiously. *Plainly, George – whoever he is – wants the police to be suspicious of me, but he hasn't made a serious attempt to frame me. Perhaps he has other plans*, I think, with a chill. And a question forces its way into my head and lodges there.

If he killed Charlie, who wasn't even driving the car, what might he want to do to me?

Twenty-six

By the time I arrive home it's already late. The street lamp on the corner is broken and my house, swathed in darkness, seems unwelcoming and menacing. The ornate white lintel reminds me of bared teeth and the windows are like baleful eyes. I try to ignore the unsettling sense that someone is inside watching me. I've got an over-fertile imagination, I know – that's all it is – but even so, I wish I'd left a light on. All the lights are off in Eileen's house too. She must have gone to bed already. Right now, I'd be happy to see anyone, even Eileen.

When I enter the dark hallway, I'm assailed by a strong sense that something is wrong. For a start, I'm met by a gust of cold air as soon as I open the door. And when I pop the keys in the pot on the dresser, I get the distinct feeling that something is out of place. It takes me a few moments to work out what it is. It's the photo of Dylan in blue wellingtons. It's not where it should be. It should be on the other side, next to the bronze elephant statue that Theo bought in India. It's a small detail, but all the same it nags at me. Has someone moved it? Has Theo let himself in again? Damn him. I knew I should have changed the locks.

'Theo?' I call out tentatively, and my voice sounds small and timid in the darkness. I switch on the light, trying to control my nerves. I flood the house with light, looking in the living room and upstairs in the bedrooms, but there's no sign of Theo. And that's another thing: where's Delilah? Normally, she would be under my feet, reminding me with her silent, reproachful presence that it's way past her dinner time.

Delilah isn't in the kitchen, but I discover the source of the cold air. The French doors leading on to the garden are wide open. How? Why? I stare out into the darkness, feeling increasingly bemused and scared. Of course, I reassure myself, there's a simple explanation. I must have forgotten to close them. I was so preoccupied when I left the house. And Delilah will be fine. She's probably just wandered out into the garden.

I open a tin of dog food and empty the contents into her metal bowl, tapping it with a spoon. If Delilah doesn't hear this, she's sure to smell the meat and come running. I wait impatiently by the door for the sound of her nails clicking on the patio and the rattle of the ID tag on her collar, but she doesn't appear. Where the hell is she? I have to find her. I need to make sure she hasn't escaped from the house somehow and got lost. It's happened before. Once, when she was barely more than a puppy, she went missing for two days. We'd given her up for dead when she turned up again perfectly healthy and well. We never did find out where she'd been. But she was lucky to be unharmed. I can't risk that happening again. So, even though I'm feeling increasingly spooked, and all I really want to do is lock the door and barricade myself in, I switch on the flashlight on my phone and step out into the darkness.

'Delilah!' I call softly.

No answer.

'Where are you, Delilah? Bloody stupid dog,' I mutter. 'As if I haven't got enough to worry about.' I pick my way carefully down the garden path, shining the light into the flower beds and under the shrubbery. I look in her favourite spot under the hydrangeas. Maybe she's fallen asleep. Sometimes she likes to dig a little hollow in the earth and make a sort of nest for herself. But she's not there.

The wind hisses in the branches of the old oak tree and the garden seems alien in the torchlight, sapped of all colour. My legs grow heavy as I approach the shed and the darker area at the back of the garden, but I force myself on. On the patio around the shed I notice a couple of piles of grassy vomit and I almost step in a fresh pile of watery dog shit.

'Delilah, baby, where are you? Are you sick?' I say, peering in the gap between the fence and the shed.

And there she is.

For a few disorienting seconds, I think that she must be asleep. She's lying on her side, her legs outstretched, one ear splayed out over the ground, as if she's flying, the other flopping over her eye.

'Delilah, wake up.' I prod her gently.

Then I notice the quality of her stillness – the way she is not moving at all.

She's not breathing.

Twenty-seven

'Poison,' the vet pronounces grimly.

It's ten o'clock in the morning. At Pet Stop Veterinarian Clinic. As soon as I woke up this morning, I dragged Delilah out from behind the shed, wrapped her in a blanket and laid her on the back seat of the car. Then I drove her straight here. Now she's laid out unceremoniously on the cold, metal examination table, her tongue lolling, eyes glassy, her ear flopping over the edge of the table.

'We'd have to do a post-mortem to discover exactly what the poison was,' he adds. 'Did you leave any medications lying around? A surprising number of medications that are harmless to humans can be fatal to dogs.'

I think about the Xanax I took yesterday. *But I left the packet on the sink, didn't I? There's no way Delilah could have got to them and even if she had, how would she have got into the packet?*

'Yes, I know, but I don't think I left anything where she could reach it.' I voice a fear that's been preying on my mind ever since I found her. 'Do you think she could have been deliberately poisoned?'

He gives me an odd look. 'It's possible, but unlikely. More likely she ate something that someone had put down for another purpose. Rat poison, for example. People really should be more careful.'

I nod. I am thinking about the open patio door. The more I think about it, the more I'm sure I didn't leave it open. It's possible I might not have locked it, but I'm certain I wouldn't have left it wide open like that. A cold unease clutches me. What if the vet is wrong and someone broke into our house and poisoned Delilah?

'Are you all right, Mrs Bayntun?' The vet's voice comes from far away.

'Oh yes, sorry. What did you say?'

'It's quite all right. It can be very traumatic, the death of a beloved pet. I was just asking if you want me to do a post-mortem?'

'No.' I don't want to risk getting the police involved. They might ask all sorts of awkward questions.

'Okay, then. So, what do you want to do with her body?' he asks gently.

'Oh, I hadn't really thought about that.'

'Would you like her to be cremated, for example?'

'Er, yes, I suppose so.'

'Good. If you want, we can keep her here until someone from the pet crematorium can pick her up.'

'That would be good. Thank you.'

I feel bad leaving Delilah as if she's a piece of luggage to be stored, but it's one less thing to worry about and I'm not sure where I would put her if I took her home. So I kiss her on her soft, velvety head for the last time, say goodbye and pay the vet's receptionist a deposit.

It's only as I walk down the steps of the vet surgery that tears come. Big, fat tears rolling down my cheeks. They are tears of anger as well as grief. She was a good, sweet dog. What kind of person would do this to such a gentle, innocent creature? And how the hell am I going to break the news to Dylan?

I get home to an empty house and make myself a cup of tea. I start a packet of chocolate biscuits, but they taste like dust in my mouth and I throw the remainder of the packet in the bin. Then I wash up the breakfast things and sweep the floor. The rest of the day stretches out in front of me, empty and bleak.

I sit down in front of my laptop and try to write a few words of the *Embers* sequel, but nothing comes. Delilah is usually nearby, curled up in her basket next to me, and I miss her quiet, unobtrusive presence more than I would have expected. I keep thinking of Dylan too. He loves Delilah so much. He has grown up with her watching over him. She used to guard him from other dogs, growling when they came near his pram, and when he got older he would stumble after her on his little legs trying to grab her tail. She was always so patient. She never got angry or snapped at him. How am I going to tell him? I don't like the idea of lying to him, but perhaps it's kinder to make something up – the old cliché of the dog going to live on a farm. He's only five, after all. Isn't he too young to deal with the reality of life and death?

I'm washing out her feeding bowl and wondering what to do with it when Theo rings. He sounds chipper. It's a stark contrast to my mood. 'Hey, how are you doing?' he says.

'Not too good.' I'm trying not to cry.

'Oh, what's wrong? Is it the press? Are they bothering you again?'

'No, it's not that. I'll explain when I see you.'

'Okay.' Theo pauses. 'Well, I'm just ringing to say that you don't need to pick up Dylan from school. He felt ill this morning, so I didn't take him in.'

'He's ill?' Panic grips me. Everything is slipping out of my control. If they can get to Delilah, why not Dylan? 'Is he throwing up?' I ask, seized by a sudden panic that he's been poisoned too.

'Don't worry, he's fine. He's just got a touch of flu, that's all,' Theo reassures me.

'I want to see him. Can I come round?'

'Sure, of course you can.'

Twenty-eight

A few minutes later, I'm in Theo's flat trying to get Dylan to drink a glass of water. His cheeks are flushed and his forehead is hot, but to my relief, he seems okay and is sitting up in bed, playing games on his tablet.

'No more iPad,' I say firmly, taking it away. 'You should try to get to sleep.'

'All right,' he says, laying his head back down on the pillow, grabbing my hand tightly. 'Don't go.'

'I'll just be in the living room, sweetheart. Don't worry.' I gently release myself from his grip. 'I just need to go and talk to Daddy for a bit.'

'You see? I told you he was okay,' says Theo, as I enter the room.

Tears have welled up in my eyes.

'Hey, it's all right. What's wrong?'

I sit on the sofa and stare blankly at Harper's painting hanging above the TV. 'I just don't know how to tell him. It's going to break his heart.'

'Tell him what?'

'It's Delilah.' I rub my eyes and swallow back more tears. 'She's dead.'

Theo's jaw drops. 'What? Delilah? But . . . I don't understand. She was fine only the other day.'

'She was poisoned.'

Theo sits down opposite me clutching a cushion. His face pinches. 'Poisoned? How?'

'The vet said he thought she might have eaten rat poison.' I shake my head. 'But it makes no sense. She didn't leave the house yesterday. Where would she have found rat poison?'

Theo shakes his head disbelievingly. He looks stricken. Delilah was his dog too. He loved her. We picked her together from the dog shelter shortly after we first married, as a kind of trial run for having a kid. We chose her because, unlike the other dogs, who were leaping up at the bars, wagging their tails wildly, she was cowering at the back of the cage. It took months of TLC to transform her into the happy, trusting dog she became.

I take a deep breath. 'I think someone poisoned her. On purpose.'

Theo stares at me. 'Really? But who would want to hurt Delilah?' He breaks off, chewing his lip thoughtfully. 'Do you think it was Eileen? She was always complaining about the barking.'

I shake my head. 'Not Eileen. Someone else.' I take a deep breath. 'I think it was a kind of warning to me.'

Theo frowns. He looks confused. 'A warning? What do you mean by that?'

I slump in my chair, fighting back tears. I am so tired of bearing this by myself. I need to talk to someone, and despite everything, Theo is still my closest friend and the person I trust the most in the world. I take a deep breath. 'It's not just Delilah,' I say. 'There's something I haven't told you about Charlotte Holbrooke, the murder at Cecily House . . .'

He looks alarmed. I can see the cogs whirring in his brain. God knows what's going through his head. Maybe he expects me to confess to Charlie's murder.

'When I said I didn't know Charlotte Holbrooke, I was lying,' I say. 'She was an old school friend, but I hadn't seen her for years, not since we were eighteen.'

'I see,' Theo says slowly. 'But I don't understand. Why didn't you tell me the truth?'

I plough on. The words spew out. I want to tell him everything before I change my mind. 'The summer before we left for university, I went to an end-of-term party with Charlie. I drove because I was the only one who had a licence at the time. At the party we drank a lot. We were planning to sleep over but, well for complicated reasons, we ended up driving home in the early hours of the morning and we had an accident. A girl was killed.'

There's an appalled silence. Theo is staring at me open-mouthed. I close my eyes. I don't want to see the shock and disillusionment on his face.

'There was nothing we could do. We were on a lonely country road and she just appeared from nowhere – this little girl. I braked, but it was too late.'

As I'm speaking, I fight a wave of nausea so intense it feels as if I might throw up all my internal organs. I grip the chair and look down at the carpet, focusing on a small speck of dust, willing myself not to be sick.

When the nausea has passed, I raise my head and I'm relieved to see that Theo's not looking at me. He's staring at his hands instead, lacing and unlacing his fingers, a dark, brooding expression on his face.

'What happened then? Did you call an ambulance?' he asks quietly.

I stand up and move to the window, stare out at the road. 'No, what would have been the point? She was already dead.'

'What about the police?'

I shake my head. 'Charlie persuaded me not to. I'd been drinking. I'd have been charged with manslaughter. I'd have gone to prison. My life would've been ruined.' I turn and look at him pleadingly, begging him silently to understand. 'We made the decision to drive on and pretend it had never happened.'

'Oh my God, Cat.' Theo shakes his head in disbelief. 'And you never told anyone about this?'

'I know what we did was wrong, but we were so young, barely more than kids ourselves.'

There's a long silence. Eventually, he looks at me. His expression is hard to read. 'Jesus, Cat. I don't know what to say.'

'Do you hate me?' My voice is small, pathetic. I hate myself, I realise.

'No, I don't hate you. I could never hate you, but this is serious stuff. It's a hit and run. My God.' He rubs his hand through his hair so it's sticking up on end. 'You should have told someone.'

I see myself through his eyes, diminished in his estimation. I know he thought of me as a truthful person. It was a joke between us how bad I was at lying. It was one of the things he said he loved about me. My honesty.

'It wouldn't have done the little girl any good. Believe me, if I thought I could do something to make it right, I would.'

He stands up, paces the room, cracking his knuckles. It's what he does when he's stressed, a habit that used to drive me nuts.

'But I still don't see,' he says slowly. 'What has all this got to do with your friend's murder?'

'Don't you see? It's the only thing that explains everything – the murder, the photofit, the pictures.'

'Pictures?'

I explain about the photos in Dylan's book bag and the messages sent by George Wilkinson. 'I think he's a fake,' I say. 'That he's really someone related to the little girl who died. Her brother or her sister, maybe as a message or a warning.'

Theo looks doubtful. I know him well enough to read his thoughts. Right now, he's worried I'm losing my marbles. Women – scratch the surface and they're all emotionally unstable. I know that's what he thinks. Not because he's ever actually said that in so many words, but because of small throwaway comments he's made over the years.

'But how would they know it was you who killed her? No one knew, right?'

'I don't know how. I think Charlie must have told someone. Anyway, however they found out, they know and—'

'Let me get this straight.' Theo says. 'You think this person murdered Charlie and then tried to frame you for her murder?'

'Yes.'

'Do you know how nuts that sounds, Cat? Are you sure

246

that you're not reading too much into all this? I mean maybe it's because you feel so guilty about what happened—'

'Oh, spare me the amateur psychology.' I fish the last photo – the snapshot of the road – out of my handbag and thrust it under his nose. 'Look. It's just a nondescript stretch of road. There's nothing there. No reason why anybody would send it – apart from the fact it's where she died.'

Theo examines the picture carefully. He's thinking hard. 'I don't know,' he sighs at last. 'Perhaps you should take it to the police.'

'I can't. Don't you see? I would have to explain about the accident and then I'd go to jail.' I'm suddenly frightened, doubtful of my trust in him. 'Promise you won't tell anyone either. Just imagine what it would do to Dylan.'

There's a pause. Theo is a person who weighs every decision logically. I hold my breath. His loyalty is by no means a foregone conclusion. But Dylan is my trump card. Like me, Dylan is everything to him and I know he wants what's best for him.

'I won't go to the police,' he says at last. 'Not if you don't want me to.'

I've never known Theo make false promises, apart from the obvious breaking of our marriage vows, but I'm still not reassured. 'You can't tell anyone. Not even Harper. Especially not Harper.'

He sighs. 'There's not much chance of that. I won't be seeing her any more. We've separated.'

I stare at him. 'But it's just a temporary separation, right?'

He shakes his head. 'No, it's official this time. She's moved out. She's taken all her stuff.'

I absorb this, trying to work out how I feel about it.

'But you could get back together.'

'Nope. Not possible,' he says firmly.

'Why not?'

He looks at me directly with eloquent brown eyes. 'Because I'm still in love with someone else. Always have been. I can't help it.'

How many times have I fantasised about him saying exactly those words? Sometimes in my fantasies, after he's confessed his undying love, we fall into each other's arms and walk off into the sunset. Other times, I say something cutting and leave him to mull over his mistakes – to rue the day he treated me so badly. Right now, though, confronted with the reality, I don't do either of those things. I am too tired and overwhelmed. Instead, I decide to completely ignore it and pretend I don't understand what he means.

'What do you think I should do about Delilah?' I ask.

He sighs. 'I really don't know. Short of going to the police I don't know what you can do. I'd put money on Delilah's death being an accident. And as for the photos, if you're right and they were sent by someone related to this girl who died, maybe they've made their point. Maybe they'll leave you alone from now on.'

Theo's wrong, I think as I drive home with Dylan in the back seat. I know this in my bones. But then Theo doesn't really believe me about the photos. He thinks it's in my imagination. Dylan falls asleep in the car and he's a dead weight as I carry him in through the door and up the stairs. Still, I do feel better for talking to Theo – and maybe he's right about Delilah (she was always eating crap). Even so, I double-check I've locked every door and window and I put Dylan to sleep in my bed where I can keep an eye on him. I'm not taking any chances, not where Dylan is concerned.

Twenty-nine

It rains solidly for days, a steady, dismal rain, and the temperature drops dramatically, heralding the arrival of autumn. Even though Dylan is better, I keep him off school for a couple more days and we barely leave the house. I put on the heating and we sit by the radiator, eating biscuits, doing jigsaw puzzles and watching old black and white clips of Laurel and Hardy on YouTube.

In the end I decide to tell Dylan the truth about Delilah, not the poison part, but the fact that she's dead, and he takes it much better than I expected. He cries a little, but he seems to cheer up when I give him a packet of cheese and onion crisps and take him to the ballpark to play.

'But won't she be lonely without us?' he asks, tucking into a burger in the café next door.

'She has lots of doggie friends in dog heaven,' I tell him.

'What's dog heaven?' he asks, round-eyed.

'There are bones and dog biscuits everywhere and lots of cats to chase, I expect.'

'And everything smells like poo,' he chuckles, wiping away tears and snot.

'Oh yuck, trust you to think of that,' I laugh.

For a few days it feels as if Dylan and I are living in a safe, little bubble and I barely think about Charlie or the photofit. Fake it 'til you make it. That's what they say, isn't it? Well, I spend so much time pretending to Dylan that everything is okay that I start to believe it too. I almost convince myself that Delilah's death was just a sad accident and that Charlie's killer has forgotten about me.

But once Dylan is back at school and I'm alone in the house again, reality comes crashing back. Whatever I've tried to tell myself, I know that it's not realistic to hope that this will just blow over, that this person tormenting me is going to just give up and go away. I need to know who is doing this and to find that out I need to identify Daisy's brother and sister, because even if one of them didn't kill Charlie, they most likely know who did. Doug Foster told me that they live nearby, so I'm guessing it's quite possible they still live in Cirencester. With that in mind, on the first morning Dylan is back in school, I scour the online BT phone directory for people with the surname Foster. There are only two in the area and I phone them both pretending to be conducting a survey, but neither of them is a likely candidate to be Daisy's sibling. One is a lonely old woman in her eighties who wants to tell me at length about her family who have all emigrated to Australia and the other are a couple in their forties with three teenage children and no time to talk. They are the wrong age and have never heard of Daisy or Doug Foster.

Disappointed and frustrated, I decide to go back to Cecily House to talk to Adam again. He's the key, I think. He must know something. If Charlie confided in anyone, it would have been him. I'm just about to leave the house when Littlewood pulls up outside in her panda car and trots briskly down the garden path. 'Can I come in?' she asks.

'Okay,' I say. 'I was just going out but—'

'This'll only take a minute.' She seems friendlier than before, maybe even a little contrite.

'You'll be pleased to know that Luke Martin has changed his statement,' she informs me, sitting on my sofa, sipping the sugary tea I have made her. 'He didn't admit before to staying the night with you because he was worried that his wife would find out. We did assure him that everything he said would be confidential, but I suppose he didn't trust us.'

'So, what brought on this change of heart?' I ask disingenuously.

'He just said he'd thought about it and didn't want an innocent person to get in trouble for something they didn't do.'

'I see. So, I'm no longer a suspect?'

She sips the tea again and gives me a smile that's almost warm. 'I never believed that you killed Charlotte, but we have to follow up all leads, you understand. It was nothing personal.'

My relief is mixed with anger. For weeks now, I've been living under this cloud of suspicion, all because the police have mishandled this case so badly.

'What about the person who gave you the photofit? Don't you think there's something dodgy about that?'

She frowns. 'We're looking into that. Along with some other leads. We've got the DNA results back from the crime scene too.'

'Did you find any matches?'

Again, there's that smile. Would you believe DI Littlewood has dimples when she smiles? 'I'm afraid I can't tell you that,' she says. 'But I can tell you that we didn't find a match to the sample we took from you.' She stands up and heads for the door.

As she's leaving, she pauses in the doorway and frowns.

'If there's anything else you know, Catherine – anything you're not telling us – then please let us know. Whoever killed Charlie is dangerous. The sooner we catch them the better.'

'Of course, but like I said before, I don't know anything. I haven't seen Charlie for more than seventeen years.'

Thirty

The rain has stopped but the pavement is still slick and damp. The air, rinsed clean, feels cold but fresh and the sun is just nudging out from behind ragged clouds. I feel a surge of optimism as I skirt the high wall and yew hedge surrounding the Bathurst estate and turn up the river pathway towards Dylan's school.

It's been a couple of weeks since Delilah died, and I am in the clear. I decided not to go and talk to Adam in the end. There's no need now I'm no longer a suspect in Charlie's murder. There have been no more blue envelopes in Dylan's book bag and I'm beginning to think this all might blow over. I'm trying to look to the future and forget about the past.

Last night Theo phoned me and told me he's bought tickets to an open-air performance of *As You Like It* in the park.

Theo hates Shakespeare, so I know that he bought them especially for me and I can't help feeling touched. I said no, of course. But I'm considering saying yes next time. I know, I know. Trust me, I don't want to be that woman – the one who stands by her man, no matter what. The Hillary Clinton to her Bill. But Theo and I have so much history – eight years of living in each other's pockets. We share private jokes, we finish each other's sentences and, most importantly, we share a love of Dylan. It seems a shame to throw all that away without at least an attempt at reconciliation. I don't know whether it will lead anywhere but I'm looking forward to making him sweat.

For the first time in a while, it seems as though everything might actually turn out okay. The river by the path is full, water flowing rapidly after the recent rain. A heron flaps away as I get closer and I stop to pet a white horse. It's all very Disney princess and I'm surprised that I don't burst into song.

I've arrived deliberately late to avoid meeting Georgia or any of the other parents and there are only a couple of children left in the classroom, sitting on the carpet waiting, their bags on their backs, fingers on lips. Mrs Bailey is off sick and the elderly supply teacher that has replaced her seems confused when I ask for Dylan.

'Dylan?' she looks at her register, running a hand through her tousled grey hair. 'Erm. I think he's in the toilet. Ah, here he is,' she says, as a little ginger-haired boy comes running over, his trousers bunched up around his waist.

I grit my teeth in annoyance. 'That's Dylan Ward. I'm looking for Dylan Bayntun,' I say.

'Oh,' she looks more flustered. 'Um—'

'Where's Ms Hamlyn?' I interrupt. Lizzie Hamlyn will know.

'She's taken the afternoon-club kids to the hall. She'll be back in a minute.'

I'm not overly worried. It's not like the time Dylan went missing in the park when he was two and I instantly panicked. The school is a safe environment; everything is fenced off, so no one can get out or in. He's probably in another classroom, or he may be out in the small, wooded area at the back of the classrooms. It's happened before. According to Georgia, a boy fell asleep in the playhouse once.

'Do you mind if I check out the back?' I say, pushing past her, not waiting for a reply.

The wooded space at the back is empty. A couple of pigeons are pecking at an empty packet of crisps and fly away as I approach. There are a few buckets and spades strewn around and the sandpit is uncovered. But no sign of any children. The door to the playhouse is closed. I open it and peer in. Nothing. The play area is surrounded by a high fence, and beyond that is the field with the horses. No five-year-old could get over that fence. And I can't imagine Dylan even trying. Why would he? He's a good boy. A rule follower. He gets a bellyache if there's a hint that he's in trouble. *So, where is he?* I think. Anxiety is scratching at the back of my mind. I quash it. *He'll be in one of the other class-rooms, or in the toilets.*

I head back to the classroom. All the children have left now and to the obvious relief of the supply teacher, Ms Hamlyn has returned bringing with her an air of efficiency and the sense that everything is under control.

'Oh yes,' she says, vaguely scratching her head. 'Dylan left with Harry – Harry Martin. Have you forgotten? You told us his mum was picking him up today for a playdate.'

Of course, Dylan is safe. He's with Georgia. My relief mingles with slight annoyance at Ms Hamlyn's patronising tone. For a start, she's wrong.

'No, I said she was picking him up tomorrow,' I say firmly.

'Oh,' she looks confused. 'I was sure you said today.'

It's not worth arguing about. 'Well, never mind, at least we know where he is,' I mutter grudgingly. Ms Hamlyn is seriously taking a nosedive in my estimation.

'Here – he forgot this,' the supply teacher says, handing me Dylan's book bag as I'm leaving. 'I'm sorry about the mix-up.'

'No worries. Perhaps I did give the wrong day. I've been a bit hassled lately.'

Outside, in the school playground, I sit on a bench and call Georgia.

There's no answer.

It's annoying, that's all. She's probably driving, or maybe she's left her phone at home. I'll try again later. I'm about to stand up and head out of the gate when it occurs to me that she might have left a note for me inside Dylan's book bag. I peel back the Velcro and rummage inside, then empty the contents on to the bench. A book and a few pieces of paper randomly stuck together with glue fall out. Then I catch a glimpse of blue paper right at the bottom of the bag and my breath snags in my throat. A blue envelope – nothing written on it.

Not again. You've made your point. Now leave me alone, I think. I don't feel scared any more. I feel angry. Ready for a fight. I tear open the envelope. Whatever it is, I'm prepared.

But nothing could prepare me for this.

I'm drowning in the air around me. The words on the paper buzz in front of my eyes like a swarm of vicious insects, the letters, block-printed in blue biro. This is worse than anything I'd ever expected or imagined:

I HAVE YOUR SON. DON'T GO TO THE POLICE OR TELL ANYONE ELSE IF YOU WANT TO SEE HIM ALIVE AGAIN.

Thirty-one

This can't be real, I think. *They're just trying to scare me, that's all. Dylan is safe. He's with Georgia. Ms Hamlyn said so.*

I fumble with my phone and ring Georgia again, but there's still no answer and the bench I'm sitting on seems to be swaying, lurching from side to side like a boat. I grip the armrest, trying to hold on. *This isn't happening*, I tell myself. It's a nightmare. I'll wake up in a minute. I shake the phone vigorously as if I can make it respond. 'Georgia, pick up, for Christ's sake.'

'Are you all right?' A teacher heading to his car with a stack of books has paused and is looking at me oddly. I realise I must have spoken aloud.

'I'm fine,' I say, trying to smile. The air feels like gravel in my throat and I try to breathe, thick, desperate gasps.

'Are you sure?'

'Yes, I'm sure,' I say through gritted teeth.

'Okay then . . .' He hesitates, then shrugs and unlocks his car with a beep and loads the books he is carrying in his boot.

I watch him blankly as he gets in the car and drives out of the gate. *Dylan's safe*, I repeat inside my head. *He's with Georgia.* I stuff the envelope back in the book bag and lurch to my feet. Then I walk home in a daze, my feet moving themselves as if they're not attached to me. They feel numb, like the rest of my body. The only part of me I can still feel is my heart, which seems to have expanded and feels like it's going to burst out of my chest. Awful, horrific possibilities clamour in my mind. I picture Dylan scared, alone. Dylan hurt. Dylan . . . But my mind can't go there. That thought is too appalling.

Calm down. Calm down, I tell myself. If they wanted to hurt him, they wouldn't have sent a note. This is just another way to punish me.

They couldn't have chosen a better way.

At home, I pace the living room, trying to reassure myself. *Ms Hamlyn said that Dylan was picked up by Georgia, didn't she?* I think. *So – he's with Georgia. He's safe.*

I'm fumbling with the phone as I try her number again. I'm not really expecting her to reply, but this time she picks up immediately.

'Hi, Cat,' she says breezily, and her tone is such a contrast to the spiralling vortex of my thoughts that it feels like plunging into cold water.

'Where's Dylan?' I blurt. 'Is he with you? Is he okay?'

She sounds mildly alarmed. 'What? No, Dylan isn't here. Why?'

A black hole is opening. I'm standing on the edge, trying not to get sucked in.

'But I don't understand. You picked him up from school today, right?'

There's a short pause. 'No, we agreed on a playdate tomorrow. I've got it written on my calendar. Hang on a second,' I can hear her breath and the sound of her flip-flops on her parquet floor. 'Ah, yes, here it is. Tomorrow. Friday. Pick up Dylan. Did I write down the wrong day?'

Am I going mad? 'But Ms Hamlyn said Dylan went home with Harry.'

'Did she?' Georgia sounds confused. 'I didn't pick Harry up today,' she says. 'Luke did. He had a day off work. He was going to take him to the park. But I can't think why he would've taken Dylan too. I'll . . .'

Fuck. Fuck. Fuck. Luke. Of course. It makes a weird kind of sense.

Georgia is still talking, an anodyne background burble.

'Which park?' I interrupt.

'What?'

'Which park did they go to?' I repeat. I'm nearly shouting now.

'The park in Watermoor, I think – you know, the one with the crazy golf? But Cat—'

I hang up, and ignoring the call from Georgia, who is trying to ring me back, I pick up my keys and run down the path to my car. My heart is pounding as I press my foot on the accelerator and speed down the road.

Luke has Dylan. Luke.

Did he write that note? And if so, why? Is it his way of threatening me – to make sure I don't tell Georgia about what happened between us? Or . . . and my stomach clenches at a much worse thought. Much, much worse. Could Luke be Daisy's brother? He's about the right age. I try to remember the photo on the mantelpiece in Doug Foster's dingy living room. The three siblings. The skinny, dark-haired boy with the football. What would he look like as an adult? It's not inconceivable that he would resemble Luke. Maybe the night we met wasn't an accident. Maybe I was set up. He would have gone on letting the police believe I didn't have an alibi if I hadn't caught him out and threatened to tell his wife.

I don't have time to analyse these possibilities because I've reached the park and I skid to a halt outside. Without bothering to park the car properly, I fly out and hurtle through the park gates.

'Have you seen a man with two little boys?' I ask the elderly man in the kiosk where they rent out golf clubs and sell ice creams.

'Well now,' he says, ponderously, standing up with glacial slowness and scratching his head. 'I'm not sure—'

'Never mind,' I snap impatiently, and I rush on past the empty crazy-golf course towards the wooded play area. There's no one there, apart from a woman with a pram, keeping a watchful eye on a little girl on the swings and a couple of older children balancing on the wooden stumps that have been made into a sort of assault course.

Of course, Luke's not here. He's not that stupid. He would have known I'd speak to Georgia. He wouldn't have told her where he was really going. Even so, I scan the wide grass lawns just to make sure. I can see most of the park from this vantage point. There are a few teenagers sitting in a huddled circle at the far end. Otherwise, it's empty. The only other place he could be is the tennis court. It's surrounded by a high hedge and hidden from view. I know it's a long shot, but I run across the field and rattle the metal gate, peering in. No luck. It's locked and there's no one there.

Tears of rage, fear and frustration roll down my cheeks as I head back to the car. It's hopeless. Dylan could be anywhere. He's in danger and I'm his mother. It's my job to protect him. I need to do something. But what? What's the best course of action? I am tormented by the thought that every second counts, and every moment I dither or make the wrong move I am failing Dylan.

I take my phone out of my bag, unlock the screen with my fingerprint and bring up the phone number pad. The threat in the note couldn't be much clearer: *don't go to the police if you want to see him alive again.* But how would Luke find out if I called the police? He would have no way of knowing. And even if he did, what are the chances that he really means what he says – that he'd really hurt Dylan?

Sod it, you bastard, I think. *I'm going to call your bluff.* I start dialling 999, but as soon as I hear the ringtone, I drop the phone as if it's on fire. I stand and stare at it for a few seconds. Then I stoop to pick it up, pressing the red end-call icon, my heart slamming against my chest. What am I thinking? If Luke's crazy enough to take Dylan in the first place, not to mention crazy enough to kill Charlie, then he's crazy enough for anything.

I can't risk talking to the police.

Outside the park gates, a couple of cars are stuck behind mine, hooting irritably. A florid-faced middle-aged man swears at me. I stare at him blankly. The hooting seems muffled and far away, unimportant, like the buzzing of flies, and the man's anger leaves me completely unmoved. I am in a different world to them – a world of horror where snarled-up traffic means nothing. I start up the engine automatically and slot into a parking space up ahead. Then I sit there, in the driving seat, trying to breathe and thinking furiously. *It's all my fault. How could I have brought Luke Martin into our lives? I should have recognised the danger as soon as I met him, but I was blinded by lust and flattery.* The more I think about it, the more likely it seems that Luke is Daisy's brother and that he killed Charlie.

But then I am brought up short because that makes no sense. Luke was with me the night Charlie died, so he couldn't have killed her. He is my alibi. Therefore, I am his. He can't be Charlie's killer.

So why has he taken Dylan? My brain is in a whirl. Nothing makes sense. I want to scream but I can't. This is too serious for hysterics. I need to speak to someone to reassure myself that I'm not going crazy. Maybe I should call Theo. I pick up my phone and notice there are five missed calls, all from Georgia. I call her back.

'Cat,' she says, sounding a little breathless. 'Are you okay? Have you found Dylan?'

'Not yet,' I say abruptly. 'Can you give me Luke's number?'

'He hasn't got Dylan. I phoned him about ten minutes ago.'

I supress a scream. 'Could you give me his number anyway? I just want to speak to him. Find out if he saw who did take Dylan,' I say, attempting to sound calm.

'Er, sure. I'll text you it and let me know if you need anything else—'

'Thanks,' I interrupt and hang up.

A couple of seconds later my phone pings and I see that Georgia has sent me the number.

I call it immediately and to my surprise Luke answers after a couple of rings.

'Hello?' He sounds like he's outside. I can hear children laughing, shrieking in the background.

'Where are you? Where's Dylan? Is he okay?' I say. My voice is shaking with anger and fear. If he hurts Dylan, I'll kill him. I know that with bone-deep certainty.

'Cat,' he sighs. 'How did you get my number?'

'That doesn't matter. Just tell me where Dylan is.'

'I think you've got the wrong end of the stick,' he says with exaggerated patience. 'Georgia rang me earlier. She said you had the idea that I picked him up from school, but I didn't.'

Is he playing games with me? How fucking dare he? I'm filled with impotent rage, and I want to scream and shout at him, but I mustn't make him angry. That could be dangerous for Dylan. I must try to sound calm, conciliatory.

'What do you want from me?' I say. 'If you want me to go to the police and tell them what happened to Daisy, I will. I'll do anything you want, only please don't hurt him.'

He speaks slowly and deliberately, as if he's trying to

pacify someone dangerously unstable. 'I have no idea what you're talking about. I haven't got Dylan and I don't know who Daisy is. Look, Catherine, I kept my side of the bargain. Now you need to keep yours and leave me alone.'

He ends the call abruptly. But before he hangs up, I hear the deep, resonant chime of the church bell marking the hour. The sound is loud and close.

Church bells, children playing. I know exactly where he is.

The Abbey Grounds park is full of children, but I spot Luke straight away, sitting on a bench with his legs spread out straight in front of him, fiddling with a phone. I can see Harry too, climbing to the top of the climbing frame. But there's no sign of Dylan.

'What the . . .?' Luke exclaims as I stride up to him. His hand flies to his collarbone and his eyes widen. 'What are you doing here?'

'I told you. I'm looking for my son.'

He looks around to check that no one is watching us. 'Well, I told *you*, I haven't got him.' He lowers his voice before continuing. 'Look, I don't know what you want from me exactly, but you need to leave me alone. This is bordering on harassment.'

'Where have you hidden him?'

He stares at me. 'Hidden who? Your son? You're not right

in the head, you know that?' He taps the side of his temple to emphasise his point.

'Look at me, Dad!' Harry shouts. He has climbed to the bottom of the climbing frame and is running towards the swings. *If Luke won't tell me*, I think, *maybe Harry will.* So, not caring if I seem insane, I run after him and grab him by the arm.

'Hi Harry, remember me?' I say, breathlessly. 'I'm Dylan's mum.'

He nods wide eyed.

'Have you seen Dylan?' I ask.

Harry looks bewildered and a little alarmed. 'What?'

I try to speak less intently. There's no point in scaring him. 'Did Dylan leave school with you?'

Harry looks at his dad, who is striding up behind me.

'Um, no,' he says.

'Did you see who he left with?' I entreat desperately.

'No, you're hurting me. Let go.'

I look down and notice that I'm still grasping him tightly, my fingers digging into his arm.

'Get your hands off my son,' Luke growls, pulling me roughly away. 'Look, I don't know what's happened to Dylan. He's probably gone home with one of the other kids in the class or with your ex. All I know is, we haven't got him.'

He takes Harry's hand and stalks away, leaving me

standing alone in the middle of the playpark. A couple of women are staring at me. Maybe I look deranged. I certainly feel it.

Does Luke have a point? Should I ring Theo? I take out my phone. There's just an outside chance that he has Dylan. Perhaps Ms Hamlyn was mistaken. She could have confused Dylan with another child or just got confused in general. It can be chaotic at pick-up. On the other hand, what about the note? It's too much to hope that that note is just a hoax and arrived coincidentally on the same day that Dylan goes missing. Besides, I'm not sure telling Theo is a good idea. What if he decides to go to the police?

I'm slotting the phone back in my pocket when it beeps, and I see that I have a message from George Wilkinson. I open it quickly.

And my heart stops.

There's a photo of Dylan in his school uniform. He's leaning against a blank white wall, his hands behind his back. His expression is blank, but physically he looks well. There are no signs of bruises or marks to indicate that he has been hurt. I read the message underneath, bile rising in my throat.

Dylan is safe for now. He will stay that way if you go to the police and tell them the truth about Daisy.

270

I stagger backwards and sink on to a bench, trying to breathe. This is really happening.

Fingers shaking, I download the photo and gaze at his dear little face feeling heartsick. If only I could reach into the photo and pull him out. I just want to hold him close and keep him safe. *Where are you, Dylan?* I scour the image for clues but there's nothing to give away his location. Just a blank white wall and a standard light switch by his head. He could be anywhere.

For Dylan's sake, I would go to prison a thousand times over and I don't hesitate in typing my answer.

I will talk to the police. I will do whatever you want, but first I need to see Dylan.

I wait a minute, holding the phone in my hand as if it's a bomb that might go off. But there's no reply.

Please. Where are you? Who are you? Give me your number at least, so I can speak to him.

No response.

Thirty-two

One thing is certain. Luke didn't take Dylan. That's obvious now. He was here when I got the message. I could see him all the time sitting by the lake with Harry and he didn't have a phone in his hand, so he couldn't have sent it. But I need to make sure Luke thinks Dylan is safe now. I can't risk the kidnapper finding out that I've told someone.

I shove the phone back in my pocket and head over to the lakeside where Luke and Harry are sitting on a bench. Harry is eating some sandwiches from his lunch box.

'You're kidding, right?' Luke glares at me as I approach.

'This will be quick. I've just come to apologise,' I mutter. 'I made a mistake. I've just received a message from my friend. She picked Dylan up. Apparently, we arranged it weeks ago. Crossed wires.' I try a little laugh. It comes out as a strange, strangled wail.

He nods and grunts. 'Well, you can't just go around accusing people like that.' Then he pulls me aside and says in a lower voice so that Harry can't hear. 'This has got to stop. There's nothing between us. Do you understand?'

He meets my eyes directly. His green eyes are cold with anger. He doesn't believe that Dylan was ever really missing, I realise. He thinks this was just a ruse to get his attention. He's so egotistical. And how crazy does he think I am – to use my son in this way just to get close to him?

'No, you're right. I'm sorry,' I say. I don't want to argue with him. It's not important. Nothing is important except Dylan. Finding Dylan.

I am back to square one. I still have no idea where Dylan is or who he's with. My stomach is twisted in knots as I walk briskly back to the car. I can't afford to waste any more time. I need to think calmly and rationally. But working out who took Dylan seems impossible. Anyone could walk into the school at pick-up time. Who would notice a stranger among the crowd of parents? Then again, Dylan is a cautious child, mistrustful of people he doesn't know. I'm almost certain he wouldn't have willingly gone anywhere with a stranger. It stands to reason that he was picked up with one of his classmates, as Luke suggested. But who? I should speak to the teachers again to find out what they can remember. I swallow a hard kernel of anger at their sheer incompetence and negligence. Once all this is done, I'm going to kick up a stink about it. But as I'm driving, I realise with a kind of sinking hopelessness that I can't speak to the teachers. If they're aware that Dylan's missing, they'll insist on calling the police.

Temporarily defeated, I'm on my way home when, stopping at traffic lights in town, I notice the small, unobtrusive camera swivelling on the edge of an office building, its red light blinking. *That's it, they're everywhere*, I think, with a flash of inspiration. The school must have CCTV.

With a new sense of purpose, I turn the car around and head back to school.

Thank God, reception is still open and the secretary, plump, rosy-cheeked Nicky Ewens, is there. She's involved in an animated phone conversation, and when I enter the room, she cups a hand over the receiver, mouths hello and gestures for me to take a seat.

I perch on the edge of a chair, my knee jiggling with nervous tension. I still it with my hand and breathe slowly. I need to appear calm and collected.

'Hi,' she says, when she finally puts down the phone. 'Sorry about that. Can I help you?'

I take a deep breath. 'Hi, yes, I'm Catherine Bayntun, Dylan Bayntun's mother—'

'Oh, little Dylan! He's such a little sweetheart,' she beams. 'Where is he?'

'Um, he's with his dad,' I say, thinking fast. 'Anyway, the thing is, I've mislaid my handbag and I think I might have put it down somewhere here when I came to pick up Dylan. I was wondering if I could check the security footage to see if I was carrying it when I left the school.'

She frowns, 'Oh no. I'm sorry, I don't think I'm allowed to do that, but you can check lost property if you want. You'd be surprised the stuff we find in there. Last year we found a diamond ring in the pocket of a cardigan. It turned out it was one of the parents' engagement rings,' Nicky continues chatting in her easy, friendly way as I follow her into another office, and she hauls out a large cardboard box from under a desk. 'There you go,' she says. 'Be my guest.'

I rummage through the box, pretending to look for my bag. It's mostly full of old school cardigans and bizarrely a single shoe. How can someone lose one shoe?

'No luck?' she says when I emerge after a suitable length of time.

I shake my head. 'I'm afraid not. Are you sure you can't show me the CCTV footage?'

She bites her lip and gazes at me, head on one side. I can see she's weakening.

'Please. That handbag has everything in it . . . my whole life!' I beg.

She grins and lowers her voice conspiratorially, even though there's no one around to hear her. 'Oh, all right, then, as it's you. But don't tell anyone or muggins here'll be in trouble.'

Sitting at her desk, she clicks on a camera icon on her desktop and after a few moments, a split-screen live stream of various parts of the school appears on the monitor. There's the front gate, a car whizzing past, part of the empty playground, nothing but a few fallen leaves drifting in the wind and another section of the playground with climbing apparatus. Nearby, a cleaner is tipping a dustpan into the bin, but otherwise, there's not a soul about.

'About what time and where do you want to look?' Nicky asks.

'Can you look at just Butterflies classroom? Outside. From about four to five o'clock?'

She scrolls down, obligingly. 'I'm quite enjoying this. I feel like a detective,' she says laughing, and I smile wanly.

I watch the screen, my heart in my mouth, as the first parents arrive at four o'clock in dribs and drabs and until there are a crowd of them some with prams, some chatting, some just standing waiting. Then at four o'clock, the doors fly open and the children begin pouring out. I catch my breath and peer closely at the monitor until Luke arrives. I watch Harry run up to him, trailing what looks like a kite made of paper and string. *Now . . . where's Dylan?* But Luke shoves the kite into Harry's backpack, grabs Harry's hand and they walk away out of shot. There is no sign of Dylan.

Who took him? I can only think that it must have been someone in that crowd. I watch the footage like a hawk until most of the children have been picked up and I see myself arrive. But all that time Dylan never appears on the screen. I sit back, disappointment twisting in my belly.

'There you are, look,' Nicky exclaims suddenly, pointing with excitement at the monitor. 'You had your handbag when you arrived.'

It's an odd feeling, like an out-of-body experience, watching myself enter the classroom and emerge again a few minutes later without Dylan. I look relaxed, unhurried, as if I've got all the time in the world. I feel sorry for that oblivious woman, a stranger to me now. *In a few seconds*, I think, *your world is going to come crashing down around you.*

'You still had your handbag when you left,' Nicky says, triumphantly. She sits back as if she's solved a great mystery. 'You didn't leave it in the classroom.'

Thankfully, she's so focused on the missing handbag that she hasn't noticed the glaringly obvious absence of Dylan. 'Are you sure it hasn't fallen under the seat of the car?' she continues. 'I know that's happened to me before.'

'You're probably right,' I say, swallowing a sudden wave of hopelessness. I was so sure that I would see who had taken Dylan. 'I'll check the car again. Thank you.'

Dylan must have left through the back entrance to the classroom because he didn't come out the of the front. I want to ask Nicky if there are cameras at the back but can't think of a legitimate reason why I would want to see the CCTV footage of the back of the classroom when we've just established that I still had my bag when I left.

'You're very welcome, love,' Nicky smiles. 'I hope you find it.' And she turns away, back to her computer.

There must be something else I can do. Someone from the class must know where he is. I'm about to leave when I pause in the doorway. 'While I'm here, I don't suppose you have a list of contact numbers for Dylan's class?'

She shakes her head and presses her lips together. 'I'm afraid I can't give you that. Data protection. Sorry, I don't make the rules. What do you want them for?'

'Oh, it's just that he's having a birthday party next week. And I don't want to miss anyone out.'

She sighs. 'Well, I can give you a list of the children's names in the class without the phone numbers. Will that do?'

I suppose it's better than nothing. 'Thank you,' I say.

While she's printing out the list, grumbling about all the rules and regulations she has to follow, I glance at the various notices and photos on the wall. There are a few different timetables and a collage of pictures of children on a school trip and of various sports teams. And at the far end of the room, there's a large board with individual head shots of all the members of staff, accompanied by quotes from each of them in speech bubbles. One picture in particular catches my eye and I draw in my breath sharply. What's he doing here? Floppy blond hair, intense blue eyes and a smile of perfect white teeth.

'Life would b flat without music,' says his speech bubble.

I had no idea that he was a teacher. It can't be a coincidence, can it?

'I know Adam,' I say, trying to keep my voice light and conversational. 'But I didn't know he worked here.'

'What?' Nicky looks up from her computer. 'Oh, Adam Holbrooke, yes, he comes in sometimes to help out with extra music lessons. He plays the ukulele. He taught the year threes this term. The kids love him.'

'Was he here today?'

'Um, as a matter of fact, he was.'

'Wait, don't you want your class list?' Nicky waves a sheet of paper at me as I dive towards the door.

'Yes, sure, thank you,' I say, snatching it from her hand. 'Sorry, I just remembered something really important.'

'Well, good luck with finding your bag.'

'Thanks. I expect it's in the car like you said.'

In my car, I check my phone to see if I have any more messages. But there's nothing, just a message from Georgia apologising for the mix-up and asking if I'm okay. I wonder what Luke has told her about me. Still, I don't have time to worry about Luke and Georgia. I need to follow my gut – and my gut is leading me to Adam and Cecily House. I drive home quickly, drag out my photo album and select a photo. Then I hop back in the car and drive to Cecily Hill.

Thirty-three

Adam seems taken aback that I'm here, outside his house again.

'Catherine, hi,' he says warily over the intercom. 'We didn't have an appointment, did we?'

'No, but I need to speak to you. Can I come in?'

'Um, well, now isn't a good time,' he says.

I take a deep breath and try to remain calm. I'm not going to make the same mistake I made with Luke. I mustn't accuse him of anything or show how agitated I am until I'm sure he has Dylan.

'It's important. It's about Charlie,' I say.

There's a long pause. 'All right,' he agrees at last and he buzzes me through into the dimly lit foyer. As my eyes adjust, I see that he's already standing at the door to his flat, ready to greet me.

He looks sleepy-eyed, ready for a quiet night in, wearing grey jogging bottoms and an old, worn Rolling Stones t-shirt. The pungent smell of curry spice wafts out from his kitchen and the TV is burbling away in the background. He steps back and ushers me in. 'It's a bit of a mess, I'm afraid.'

He's not wrong about the mess. There are boxes and piles of clothes and books and crockery everywhere on every surface.

'I'm moving out soon,' he explains. 'It's amazing how much stuff you accumulate. Even though we were only here a few years.' He turns off the TV and gestures for me to sit. 'Most of it is Charlie's,' he sighs. 'I don't know what to do with it. You can have look through and take what you want. I'm sure she would have wanted you to have something.'

'Er, thanks.' I remove a pile of clothes and perch on the edge of the sofa. My heart is racing. Has he got Dylan? If so, where is he hiding him?

'You said you had something to tell me about Charlie,' he says.

'Er, yes, a photo.' I rummage in my bag and hand him the photo. It's a picture of me and Charlie on a school trip in France. We're on the beach. Mont St Michel in the background. We look so young. Charlie is wearing a beret and pretending to smoke a cheroot. We were going through a phase of trying to emulate the bohemians of the 1950s.

Charlie looks beautiful, slender and elegant. By her side, I look fat and frumpy.

Adam's eyes well up as he looks at the picture and he fingers it delicately, as if it might fall apart in his hands.

'Can I keep it?' he adds. 'I could make a copy and give it back to you.'

'Yes, sure,' I say, distractedly. I'm scanning the apartment for places Dylan could be. The doors to the bedrooms and the bathrooms are all closed, I notice. But how can I look inside without arousing his suspicion?

'So, you're moving?' I say, trying to sound politely casual.

He nods. 'Yes, I thought it best to have a complete break, a fresh start. There are too many memories here . . .' he tails off.

'Have you rented the apartment?'

He shrugs. 'No, not yet. I haven't had much interest. People are superstitious. You know – they don't want to live in a place where there's been a murder. I suppose I can't really blame them.'

'I might be interested,' I say, sensing an opportunity.

'Really?' he stares at me surprised.

'Yes, my place is a bit too big for just me and my son, now my husband has moved out. I was thinking of downsizing.' I'm already moving towards the closest door. 'Do you mind if I have a look around?' I don't give him time to answer before I push open the door and barge into the master bedroom. Inside, I inhale sharply. The room smells

283

slightly stale. There are a couple of black plastic bags full of clothes on the double bed. Drawers and wardrobe have been flung open as if someone has ransacked the place. There's no sign of Dylan though, and no obvious hiding places. I peer under the bed, just in case. Just as Adam comes into the room behind me. He gives me an odd look but doesn't say anything.

'There are two bedrooms?' I say, talking loudly, so that if Dylan is here, he'll hear me.

'Er, yes,' Adam's arms are hanging loosely by his sides. He's broad-shouldered and powerful-looking, but I'm not afraid. I'm too worried about Dylan to be afraid of anything. I will do anything, face any danger to get him back. I brush past Adam and open a door to another smaller bedroom and then finally the bathroom with Adam following, watching my every move.

'How much is the rent?' I ask, swallowing my disappointment as I realise that the apartment is empty, and that Dylan isn't here.

'Actually, I was thinking of selling it.'

'The whole place?' I ask, surprised, 'or just this flat?'

He sighs. 'Just this place. Charlie made me promise never to sell the house. She was dying of cancer, you see, and she was worried about what would happen to Ben and Meg after her death.'

'She was very generous to them.'

He bites his lip. 'Yes, maybe too generous. I'm not sure she was in her right mind the last few months. I don't know, but after her diagnosis she just seemed to go crazy.'

'Crazy how?' I'm only half listening. My mind is working overtime. Maybe Adam has taken Dylan somewhere else. Maybe Dylan is already dead. But I won't allow myself to think that. Dylan is alive and he needs me to hold it together. I try to focus on what Adam's saying. He's talking about Charlie.

'Well, for starters she gave away over half her money to charity and then she let the upstairs flat to Ben for free. I mean it wasn't exactly the soundest move from a business perspective. We argued about it a lot. But it's hard to win an argument with someone who's dying, and she was adamant. She had some crazy idea that she had sinned and needed to make amends.'

The hairs on the back of my neck stand up. 'Sinned? What did she mean?'

Was Theo right? Did she tell Adam about the accident? And if she did, what exactly did she say about me?

'I don't know,' he says, after thinking a while. 'I'm not sure she knew herself. I think she felt bad that she abandoned her religion. She was brought up a Baptist. Her family were religious. I suppose you know that?'

I nod impatiently.

'But then after her mother died, she stopped going to

church, stopped believing in God. It wasn't until she found out she had cancer that she discovered God again. She used to go and pray with Meg, next door.'

'With Meg?'

'Yes, Meg was fantastic when Charlie got her diagnosis. She helped her come to terms with dying and helped her keep a positive outlook right up until the end. Charlie said that if Meg could stay positive despite everything she had gone through, then so could she.' His eyes well up again. 'She was very brave, my Charlie.'

'Yes,' I agree absent-mindedly. I stand up. I'm trying to work out how to wind the conversation up so that I can move on. Dylan clearly isn't here, and this is a waste of precious time.

But Adam seems eager to talk now he's started. 'She's an amazing woman, Meg,' he's saying. 'I mean, imagine what it would be like to be a world-class athlete one day and in a wheelchair the next. But she's always upbeat. She never complains.'

'An athlete?' I stop by the door, my hand frozen on the knob. 'What kind of athlete?'

'She was an ice-skater, believe it or not. She won the British ice-skating championship.' He frowns, trying to remember. 'Something like that, anyway. She doesn't like talking about it, but Sophia, her care worker, told me once.'

There is a buzzing in my ears that's getting steadily

286

louder. I'm back in Doug Foster's dingy bedroom, the photograph of his wife, dressed in a frilled leotard, spinning on the ice.

I'd assumed she was dead, but had he actually said that? I try to remember his exact words. 'She's gone. Gone to a better place,' is what he said. Perhaps he didn't mean she had died but that she had literally gone to a better place – a place set up for someone with a disability, a flat which Charlie had had converted specifically for her. And if Meg is Doug Foster's wife . . .

'Thank you very much for the tea. I'll let you know about the flat,' I say hurriedly, heading for the door.

Dr Blake says I'm lucky. Ha! What does she know? She's young and strong and goes running every morning. I know that because I heard her talking to one of the nurses about how she ran her personal best only the other day. She didn't mean me to hear. She's not that insensitive. But I heard her all the same. So how can she know what it's like? She hasn't a clue how it feels to be trapped in this useless body, day after day. She can't imagine what it's like to have to rely on other people for simple tasks that you used to take for granted: getting dressed, washing, even going to the toilet. She doesn't know what it's like to dream that you're dancing and to wake up unable to move out of bed – to be left alone with your bitter thoughts and memories and only daytime TV to distract you. People are full of advice on topics they know nothing about, aren't they? My mother, for instance, is always telling me I should forgive and forget. 'Let bygones be bygones,' she says. The past is the past. She doesn't know that the past bleeds into the present and that I will never be able to forget and I will never be able to forgive . . .

Thirty-four

The door to Meg's flat is ajar and I can hear the low hum of the hoover from inside. I push my way through the narrow hallway without bothering to knock and burst into the living room. Meg is sitting by herself in her chair by the window, gazing out at the road. She has her back to me, her neatly bobbed grey hair curling at the nape of her long, stringy neck. She doesn't turn the chair. Maybe she's asleep. But something about the angle of her head tells me she's not.

'Where's my son?' I demand loudly.

The chair turns slowly until she's facing me, and she regards me steadily with pale blue eyes. Her expression is hard to read.

'What have you done with my son?' I repeat.

I wait impatiently as her eyes flick over the monitor.

'Catherine, hi. I'm sorry, I don't know what you're talking about,' says the friendly, robotic American voice.

'My son, Dylan. Where is he? I know you've got him.' I clench my fists, digging my nails into my palms. I'm tempted to grab her by her scrawny neck and strangle it out of her. It would be so easy, I realise. What could she do? She is completely defenceless.

There's a long silence and then the machine speaks again.

'I have no idea. I don't know your son.'

'Yes, you fucking do. Don't lie to me!' My voice rises, rage and fear choking me. I'm shouting now so that Sophia hears me in the other room, switches off the vacuum cleaner and comes rushing in.

'What the hell?' She glares at me, bristling like a guard dog. 'How did you get in?'

I ignore her, stepping closer to Meg. 'Where's Dylan?' I say.

Sophia grabs me by the arm. 'What the hell do you think you're doing? Do you want her to go, Meg? I can kick her out, if you like.'

I turn on Sophia. I'm hysterical now, gibbering like a mad woman. 'You don't understand. She's got my son. She took him from school. She's going to kill him.'

Sophia looks startled. Then concerned, as if I might be a dangerous lunatic.

'You need to calm down,' she says, taking a deep breath.

'I'm sorry, if it's true that your son is missing, but you can't just barge in here like this and accuse Meg of God knows what. You must realise you're being ridiculous. How do you think Meg could have taken him, for Chrissake? Think about it. Look at her. She's paralysed.'

I hear the words and I know they make sense, but I'm too far gone now and besides, I know that Meg is involved. She's Daisy's mother. I know that for sure.

I slip out of Sophia's grasp and fumble in my pocket for the note. Hands shaking with agitation, I thrust it in Meg's face.

'You wrote this, didn't you?'

Meg doesn't answer. Did I imagine it or is there a flicker of something, maybe alarm, in her eyes?

'What's that?' Sophia snatches the note from me and reads it with a look of increasing disbelief.

I HAVE YOUR SON. DON'T GO TO THE POLICE OR TELL ANYONE ELSE IF YOU WANT TO SEE HIM ALIVE AGAIN.

'Where did you get this?' she asks me.

'Ask her.' I gesture towards Meg who is slumped in her chair. She seems to have shrunk in the last few moments. I try to snatch the note back from Sophia, but she pulls it out of my reach.

'Do you realise how crazy you sound?' she fumes. 'This is handwritten, for a start. How do you think she wrote it? She can't move her arms.'

'I don't know,' I admit. 'Maybe you wrote it for her.'

She snorts with outrage. Her face red with fury. 'You're insane,' she says. 'I wouldn't be surprised if you wrote that yourself. I'm going to call the police if you don't get out of here in the next ten seconds.'

She starts counting. 'One, two, three—'

'Wait,' says Meg's machine voice loudly. She seems to have turned up the volume somehow.

We both turn and stare at her.

'Don't call the police, Sophia,' she says. 'I didn't write that,' she says. 'But I know who did.'

Sophia looks completely bewildered. 'What are you—?' she begins.

'We're out of milk,' Meg interrupts. 'Why don't you go out and buy some? And get me some cigarettes while you're there. I feel like I'm going to need them.'

'But you don't smoke. You gave up.'

'Just do what I ask please, for once.' The machine voice is perky as ever, but I guess Sophia senses the serious intent. She hovers uncertainly in the doorway, casting a sharp, suspicious look my way. 'Are you sure?'

'Perfectly. I need to speak to Catherine alone. Don't worry, I'll be all right.'

Sophia shakes her head. 'Okay then – if you insist. You're the boss.' She turns on me and hisses, 'If you so much as lay a finger on her, you'll have me to answer to.'

I wait until I hear the click of the outer door closing and the clack of her heels on the pavement outside. Then I say bitterly, 'I know who you are. Your real surname is Foster.'

'It was Foster,' she agrees. 'I changed back to my maiden name, Darley, when we got divorced. My husband couldn't cope with my disability.'

I ignore her. I'm not interested in the break-up of their marriage.

'You were married to Doug Foster,' I continue. 'I saw your photo at his house. Daisy Foster was your daughter.'

She doesn't answer.

I breathe in sharply. 'And you know who I am, don't you?'

There's a flicker of hatred, swift but unmistakable, in those expressive eyes, and finally she speaks. 'Yes. You're Catherine Bayntun. You killed my daughter.'

There it is, after all this time. This had been building like magma underground. The pressure has been so intense lately, it's almost a relief to hear the words spoken out loud.

'How do you know?' I ask. There's no point in denying it. We've gone beyond that.

'Charlie told me,' she says. 'A few months ago, she told me everything. She wanted me to know what you both had done before she died. She told me it was the reason she sought me out and offered me this flat in the first place. As a kind of compensation.' Meg makes a gurgling noise in her throat. 'As if anything could compensate for what we lost.'

Tears well up in her eyes and trickle silently down her cheeks.

I harden my heart against an instinctive feeling of pity. She's mourning an old loss. My loss is fresh and urgent. 'I know you must hate me, and I don't blame you,' I say. 'But it was an accident. We were young.'

'You're wrong,' she says. 'I don't hate you because you killed her. Accidents happen. People make mistakes. I could forgive that. What I can't forgive is the fact that you decided not to take responsibility for those mistakes. You could have called an ambulance and you didn't. Daisy was still alive when the ambulance arrived. She would have lived, if they'd arrived sooner.'

I stare at her appalled. 'No, that can't be right. We took her pulse. She was already dead.' Everything is slipping. Blackness curling at the edge of my mind. I want to throw myself down on the floor at her feet and howl.

Somehow, I claw myself back to reality, to here and now. What happened, what we did was terrible – worse than I even knew. But that's all in the past and Dylan is in danger right now. I must do everything in my power to persuade this woman not to hurt him and to return him to me unharmed.

'I'm sorry. I'm really so sorry. But all that happened, it had nothing to do with Dylan,' I continue shakily. 'Dylan is just a child. He's innocent. Punish me if you like, but not him . . .' My voice cracks and I can't speak any more for all the fear and anxiety threatening to overwhelm me.

'I don't know where your son is. I haven't got him.'

I'm confused. 'You must have. You gave the police the photofit of me. You sent me those photos, you killed Charlie.' But even as I say the words, I know that they're impossible.

'I gave the police the description of you. But nothing else is true. Look at me,' she says. 'How could I have killed Charlie?'

'You got someone else to do it for you, then. Sophia?' I hazard.

'No. Sophia knows nothing about any of this.'

'Who then? You know who. I know you do. Please, I'm begging you. My son is in danger.'

There's a long pause. I can see from her eyes, which are flickering wildly, that she's struggling with some inner conflict. Finally, she appears to come to a decision. 'You're right,' she says. 'She's gone too far this time. It was my daughter – Daisy's sister, Beth.'

'Beth?' I repeat, holding my breath.

Meg seems almost to be talking to herself. 'I never should have told her what Charlie told me, but at the time, I thought she had a right to know and I suppose I thought it might help her gain a kind of closure. But it had the opposite effect. As soon as she found out about you, she

295

became obsessed with tracking you down. And it didn't take her long. We're all easily traceable nowadays, if we have an online presence.'

'Where is she?' I demand. 'Where does she live?'

'She was always a difficult child.' Meg ignores my question. 'Even before Daisy died. She could be so kind and loving one minute, then if she lost her temper, she was a terror. I used to call her my girl with the little curl. You know the rhyme. "When she was bad, she was horrid".' She pauses. 'But it was serious, and it got worse as she got older. She could be violent. It was frightening sometimes. Daisy was the only one who could calm her down. She adored her little sister.'

'Where is she now? Has she got Dylan?' I demand impatiently.

'We tried to ignore it,' she continues. 'We hoped that she would grow out of it. But then after Daisy died, she became worse. She blamed Doug and me for what happened. And she was right. We were to blame. We had a party that night, the night Daisy died. It went on into the early hours of the morning. We let the kids stay up and nobody noticed when Daisy wandered off.'

'And your son. What about your son?' I ask, remembering the photo in Doug Foster's house.

'My son blamed us too. He left when he was sixteen. We haven't seen him for years. After he left, I had a huge fight with Beth.' There's a pause. 'That's how I ended up in this chair.'

'What?' I say, stunned and appalled. 'She did that to you. How?'

'It was an accident. We were screaming at each other. We tussled and I fell down the stairs. We covered up for her, of course, and told everyone that I tripped.'

'Is that why you gave my description to the police? To cover up for her?'

She moves her head slightly. 'It was her idea. She showed me a photo of you online – your author page – and told me to tell the police I'd seen you that night. I didn't want to at first, but then I thought there was a certain poetic justice to it. You escaped without punishment for one murder. I thought it made sense for you to take the blame for another.'

'And the man you said you saw visiting Charlie – you made that up?' I say, thinking aloud.

'Yes, that was to deflect attention away from Beth. It was all to protect her. You'll do anything for your children.'

It's true. I'll do anything to get Dylan back unharmed. I would rip out my own heart or strangle this helpless old woman in front of me if I thought it would help.

'Has she got Dylan?' I repeat. I'm even more terrified that he's in danger now I've heard Meg's story. If Daisy's sister was capable of injuring her mother so seriously, what else is she capable of?

'Will she hurt him?' I ask. My voice cracks.

There's a pause. 'No, I don't think so. She's not a bad person. Not really. Whatever you might think. What happened to me was an accident. She didn't mean to hurt me.'

Not a bad person? How can Meg be so deluded? What about what she did to Charlie?' But I don't have time to argue.

'Where is he?' I entreat. 'You must tell me.'

'I'm sorry, I honestly don't know, but I'll phone her. I can talk her round. She must know she's gone too far.'

'No, don't. Please don't. Promise me,' I blurt. I don't want Meg warning her that I know – alerting her to the fact that I'm coming. 'Just tell me where she lives, please.'

Meg seems to consider, then to my relief, she agrees. 'This is only to help your son,' she says. 'I don't care about you.' She gives me a local address in an estate on the other side of town and I scribble it down on the back of a receipt.

'Wait. You won't hurt her, will you?' Meg calls anxiously after me as I move towards the door. 'Tell her I want to talk to her. Tell her to phone me. I can persuade her to hand over Dylan. There's no need for any violence.'

Thirty-five

Ever since the accident, I've been a careful driver. Theo always used to complain about how slowly I drive and would make fun of me for getting stuck at junctions because I would always give way. He wouldn't recognise my driving now as I roar up the hill to the edge of town and veer around the corner into Elm Grove estate, screeching to a halt outside a normal, modern, cookie-cutter house.

It's surrounded by a plain, trimmed green lawn. There's nothing to distinguish it from its neighbours and nothing separating it, except for a low wall, which stretches out a couple of metres.

There's no car in the driveway, but the garage is closed, so there could be someone at home. A black cat runs up to me as I rush up the path. It meows plaintively and rubs its cheek against my leg when I ring the doorbell. I push it away and press the bell again – a long, insistent 'dring'. No answer. No one stirs. There's no one home.

I sigh. Meg must have phoned her daughter and warned her I was coming. I shouldn't have trusted her.

Unless Beth is hiding inside right now, watching me. What if Dylan is with her? The thought ambushes me, winding me and choking me with fear.

I cup my hand over my eyes, press my face against the window and peer into the living room, but it's dark inside and I start with surprise when the front door flies open and a young man with a towel around his waist peers out.

'Hello?' he says.

He's solid-looking with a pleasant gnome-like face, a thick, wet brown beard and tattoos running up his arms and over his chest. 'Sorry I took so long to answer,' he says. 'I was in the shower.'

Did Meg give me the wrong address? I think. *Did she set me on the wrong track deliberately? Or could this be Beth's partner or husband?*

'Um, is Beth Darley here?' I hazard.

'She's not here right now,' he says politely. 'Can I take a message?'

I repress the urge to scream. Is he covering for her? Does he know what she's done? On the whole, I doubt it – his manner seems too natural and relaxed. It seems like he genuinely has no idea what's going on.

'Actually, it's kind of urgent,' I say in a tight voice. 'Can you tell me where she is? I need to speak to her and she's not answering her phone.'

He frowns. 'I'm sorry, who are you exactly?'

I think quickly. 'I'm Catherine. I'm a care worker,' I improvise. 'I'm standing in for Sophia. It's about your mother-in-law, Margaret Darley. She's had a stroke. She's gone into hospital.'

'Oh my God,' he claps his hand over his mouth. 'She's going to be okay though, right?'

'Yes, she'll be okay. But can you tell me where your wife is? I need to contact her asap.'

'She's still at work,' he says. 'But I'll give her a call.' He disappears inside and reappears with a phone.

'Where does she work?' I demand.

'Um . . . At the school.' He's distracted, swiping agitatedly at his phone.

My breathing becomes shallower.

'Which school?

'Green Park Primary, but wait—'

Too late. I'm already getting back into my car.

Thirty-six

Ten minutes later, I pull up outside the school gates and veer into the staff car park, ignoring the 'Staff Only' signs. There are three cars still there. One, a silver Mazda I don't recognise – maybe it's Nicky's. One is the head teacher's old Mercedes and the third is Lizzie Hamlyn's distinctive red and white Mini with the eyelashes on the headlights.

Lizzie. Lizzie . . . Beth. Elizabeth.

I stand and stare at that car, bile rising in my throat.

Of course. I should have known. It makes a horrible kind of sense. Beth's maiden name was Darley, but if she's married to the guy I just met at her house, she could have easily changed her name to Hamlyn. Lizzie Hamlyn and Daisy's sister, Beth Darley, are the same person.

I trusted her, I think furiously as I rush across the playground and round the back of the old Victorian building to Dylan's classroom. I'd thought the school would keep my son safe. How could I have been so blind? I was taken in by her innocent appearance and the fact that she was in a position of trust. It seems incredible. But the more I think about it, the more certain I become. Lizzie Hamlyn is the right age to be Daisy's sister and, if she lied, it explains how easily Dylan could have disappeared at pick-up. Other things, small incidents, come back to me and take on a new significance in the light of this new insight: the way she seemed to single out Dylan for special attention; the fact that she had a job she was so blatantly overqualified for.

The classroom is empty and the door is locked. I rattle the handle in frustration and call for help. But there's no one around. The place is deserted. There are just a couple of forlorn lunch boxes lying around and PE bags hanging on the pegs, the empty water tray and plastic pots scattered over the floor. I peer in the other classrooms, in the toilets and then head to the office.

'Have you seen Ms Hamlyn?' I ask Nicky, who is still there but packing her bag, ready to go home.

'You're back,' she says cheerily. 'Any luck with the handbag?'

'Yes,' I say impatiently. 'That's all sorted now. I'm looking for Ms Hamlyn.'

'I thought she'd already left,' she says surprised. 'Why—?'

I don't wait to hear the rest of her question. I just dash back out into the playground.

Why didn't I see it before? It wasn't a mistake when Lizzie Hamlyn told me Dylan had left with Harry. Of course it wasn't. I should have known she was lying. But how did she get him out of the school without anyone noticing?

The answer, when it comes to me, is so simple, so obvious I'm amazed I didn't think of it before. *Of course, she didn't. She didn't have to. He was here all along, even when I came to pick him up.* The thought makes my stomach turn. But where was he exactly? I try to recall what the supply teacher said. Something about afternoon club. What if Lizzie Hamlyn had taken him there? Hidden him in plain sight. It would be easy to pass off as a simple mistake if anyone queried his presence.

I look at my watch. It's already seven o'clock. Afternoon club will have finished long ago. But Lizzie, Beth – whatever her name is – is still here. Where?

I'm heading back towards the front of the school and the assembly hall when I bump into Ms Gregory, the head teacher.

'Oh, hello,' she says, mildly surprised to see a parent on school premises so late. 'Can I help you?'

'Do you know where Ms Hamlyn is?' I ask breathlessly.

'Um, you just missed them. Lizzie and Dylan left just a couple of minutes ago. That girl is a treasure. She works so hard. She's often the last to leave. You might be able to catch them if you're quick.'

'Thank you,' I blurt, speeding towards the car park.

'Are you okay?' she calls after me. 'Lizzie said you had a hospital appointment?'

I reach the gate just in time to see Lizzie Hamlyn bundling something into the boot of her Mini.

In the back seat I can just make out the shape of a child. He's just a shadow, a black silhouette. I can't see properly, the low sun is glaring, bouncing off the window into my face. I hold up my hand to shield my eyes. But I know instinctively that it's him. It's Dylan.

My heart leaps with hope and fear. 'Dylan!' I call out, running towards the car.

He doesn't hear me, but Lizzie Hamlyn turns and stares at me, her pale face jerking upwards, grim determination stamped all over it.

'Wait! Stop!' I shout desperately, but she completely blanks me, and she walks quickly but calmly round to the driver's door and ducks inside.

'Dylan!' I scream – a primal sound of outrage and terror that comes from deep in my guts. 'Dylan!' I break into a sprint as she starts up the engine.

I arrive in the car park just as she approaches the exit and I throw myself in front of the car, trying to block her way. But she just speeds up and swerves around me, missing me by a hair's breadth. She's so close I get caught in the slip-stream and am nearly pushed over by the force of the air. I recover my balance and watch with helpless rage as the car roars past me out of the gate. As it turns, I catch a glimpse of Dylan looking out at me through the rear window, his pale face frozen in surprise and alarm.

Fuck fuck fuck. This can't be happening. Please God let this not be happening. There's no time to think. I tear across the car park to my car and leap inside. All I know is that Lizzie Hamlyn is unstable, Dylan is in danger and I can't afford to let them out of my sight. My heart is thumping, adrenaline coursing through my body. I start up the engine and screech out of the school gates, just in time to see her turn left on to Cotswold Street. I veer left after her, nar-rowly missing the SUV parked on the corner and we bump down the narrow, cobbled road. Then she swerves left on to the high street and I follow, close on her tail, determined not to lose her.

Where are you taking him, you crazy bitch?

On the high street she runs a red light, ignoring the cars from the other direction hooting and screeching to a halt. Then she heads out on the ring road towards Swindon. The road is straight and nearly empty. I stamp my foot flat on the accelerator, the speedometer approaching 80 miles an hour, then 90, then 100, 120. I've never driven so fast. This car is not made for speed. It rattles along the highway as if it will fall apart at any second, hurtling along, hedgerows whizzing past, but I'm gaining, and slowly but steadily the distance between us decreases.

Then suddenly, Lizzie swerves off the main road and on to another smaller road.

'What the . . .?' I mutter to myself as I brake sharply and screech round the corner after her. We're on a narrow country lane now, bumping over potholes. There's a tractor up ahead, crawling along at a snail's pace. Lizzie speeds up and overtakes. I start to try to pass too, but a car hurtles towards me in the other direction and I tuck back behind the tractor just in time.

My God, that was a near miss, I think, my heart hammering in my throat, but I can't afford to lose them. As soon as the other car has passed, I roar past the tractor just in time to see the red and white mini, far up ahead, racing round a bend. I press my foot flat to the floor. I'm absolutely determined not to let them out of my sight.

My phone is ringing loudly in my bag.

I'm rooting around in my bag, glancing down to see who's calling, when out of nowhere, a truck looms out of a side road.

I stamp on the brakes and wrench the steering wheel, but it's too late. It's rushing towards me. I don't have time to think. Everything is instinctive. I'm going to die. Please don't let me die, I pray. And I think of Dylan. I can't leave him. Not now. Not yet. He's too young. He needs his mother. Dylan is the last thought in my head, filling my mind so I can't think of anything else. Then I hear a crack and with a violent jolt I'm thrown up into the air and somehow I'm flying. Then there's another violent thump and searing pain as I'm slammed against hard concrete.

The last thing I hear is the screech of tyres and a door slamming.

Thirty-seven

Am I dreaming? Am I dead?

The sun is setting behind those trees, casting golden streaks of light up into the blue sky. It's beautiful and serene and I am not in any pain. In fact, I could be floating on a cloud. It must be the shock. Or maybe I'm in heaven. But when I raise my head, I see to my horror that there is a shard of glass poking out of my thigh. I move my arm experimentally and try to pull it out, but it is stuck there, wedged deep in my flesh. And I realise I'm not on a cloud. Instead, I am lying on hard, unforgiving concrete and there are pieces of broken glass all around me. I'm in the middle of the road. The impact must have thrown me from the car.

'Oh my God. I'm so, so sorry. Are you okay? Can you speak?' A man's face comes into focus, middle-aged, panic-stricken. He takes my hand, 'Just hold on, love. I'm going to go and get help.'

I don't want him to leave me and I try to grasp his hand, but he lets go gently and stands up. I hear him talking urgently to someone nearby but just out of my line of vision.

'Can you stay here with her, just until I get back?' he's saying.

A young woman's voice answers. She sounds calm and capable, just the kind of person you want around in an emergency. 'No problem,' she says. 'I'm first-aid trained. Don't worry. I know what to do.'

'What about your son? Will he be all right?' the man asks.

'He'll be okay. I've locked him in the car for now. I think it's for the best. I don't want him to see this.'

'Okay, well, I'll just be a few minutes. I'll be as fast as I can. Don't try to move her, okay?'

Then I hear the man's footsteps receding and I feel a flicker of fear. I sit up and try to struggle to my feet, but my legs won't co-operate, and I feel a wave of dizziness wash over me. I lie back down, fighting to stay conscious. The woman crouches beside me, her long legs folding under her.

'Not so nice, is it, being left to die?' she says, and I look up into a smooth, pretty face and a pair of dewy, brown eyes.

'Lizzie . . .' I try to say, but it comes out as a sort of gargle.

'I could kill you now if I wanted,' she continues conversationally. 'It would be pretty easy. I could smother you. Everyone would think it happened in the accident, or I could run you over. But I'm not going to kill you. That would be too quick.'

'Dylan . . .' I choke out. 'Dylan . . .'

'My sister, Daisy, was the same age as Dylan. Did you know that?'

Again, I try to move. I heave myself up by the arms and try to drag myself towards the red and white mini I can see parked just a few metres away. Lizzie walks along beside me, gazing down at me dispassionately.

'Dylan,' I say, collapsing again after I've hauled myself not more than a few feet.

'I was supposed to be watching her the night you killed her.' Lizzie crouches down beside me again. 'My parents left an eight-year-old in charge of a five-year-old. For a long time, I thought I was to blame, but then I realised. I was only eight years old. I should never have been left with that responsibility.'

I know it's very important that I stay awake – that my life and Dylan's could depend on it – but I keep drifting in and out of consciousness and Lizzie's voice keeps getting louder and quieter, as if someone is fiddling with the volume control.

'Then I was angry with my parents. It wasn't until I was seventeen or eighteen that I realised I was blaming all the wrong people . . . that I should have been blaming the one person who was really responsible – the person driving the car. But of course, I didn't know who that was. Until Charlotte came along. Do you believe in God, Catherine?'

I don't answer. Tears are rolling down my cheeks.

'I don't know if I do,' Lizzie continues. 'But it certainly seemed as though some higher power brought Charlie to us. She confessed to everything. She thought she could make up for what happened to Daisy by giving Mum that flat,' she snorts, scornfully. 'As if money could make up for what we lost.'

I try to raise my head. 'So, you killed her,' I choke out.

She shrugs. 'She would have died anyway. Killing Charlie was a kindness. It was you I wanted, not Charlie. I only killed her to get to you. I knew I could persuade my mother to tell the police that she'd seen you. It was only what you deserved. Okay, you didn't kill Charlie, but you are guilty of murder and you have never paid for it.'

I feel her hatred as if it's a physical force, and a wave of despair and hopelessness washes over me. Because she's right. I am guilty, if not of murder than at least of manslaughter.

'As soon as she told us about you,' Lizzie says, 'I started digging up all I could about you. It didn't take me long to find out you were Ophelia Black, the writer.' She practically spits out the words. 'I read your book – a pile of trash. You even had the nerve to write about a girl killed in a car accident. You *used* Daisy's death for your own gain.'

I want to explain that if I did use Daisy, it wasn't for any financial gain – that it was a way to exorcise my own demons. But she continues before I can speak.

'That made me so angry. I wanted you to feel afraid. That's when I started sending you messages on your writer page.'

'You're George Wilkinson.' I realise this with a flash of insight.

'Why yes, little lady,' she drawls, mimicking an American accent. And I realise with a sinking feeling that she's completely unhinged.

She carries on dreamily, almost as if she's talking to herself. 'Of course, I knew your real name from Charlie and with that, it was easy enough to find out your address. So I visited your house and watched you playing with your son. You know you leave your curtains open a lot.'

I feel sick at the thought of this gross invasion of our privacy.

'I guessed that you would enrol Dylan at Green Park Primary School. You were in the right catchment area. So I decided to apply for a job there. I didn't really have a plan at that point, I just thought it might come in useful. And, you see, it did.'

Dylan. I can feel blackness creeping at the edge of my mind. 'Dylan,' I gasp. 'Don't . . .'

But I can hear the sound of another car approaching and Lizzie leaps to her feet and runs back to her car. I hear her engine starting and the car turning. Then nothing.

Thirty-eight

I dream I am running, running through a corn field with Charlie. The sun is shining, and we're happy and free. We're running for no reason, like excited puppies. I'm young and strong, and I feel as if I could run for ever. But suddenly the scene changes as sometimes happens in dreams. I am at the edge of a fast-flowing river and dark storm clouds are gathering, swallowing the sun. Charlie is still there but she looks worried and a little embarrassed and she points down at my legs.

'Er, Cat, there's something wrong,' she says.

And when I look down, I see that a crocodile is gnawing on my knees, blood gushing out of the stumps, staining the river red.

I wake with a start in hospital to the groans of other patients and the clatter of the nurses. Feeling disoriented,

I open my eyes and look around. I'm in bed with a blue curtain partially drawn so I can see part of the ward. There's an elderly woman in the bed opposite mine; she's doing a crossword, reading out the clues loudly to her husband, who is looking bored and munching chocolates.

And Theo is here. He's sitting by my bedside holding my hand.

What's going on? I am confused and a little scared. What's going on? Am I still dreaming?

'You're awake,' Theo smiles at me. 'You drifted off for a while. But you're back now.' I can feel his hand in mine. It's warm and real. His brown eyes are kind and full of something that looks unnervingly like pity.

'Look, I brought you a packet of fudge. It's homemade. I bought it at the craft fair. He unties the ribbon and opens the bag and I get a whiff of sugar and vanilla. 'If you don't eat it, I will,' he says.

I turn my head away. I feel sick. Everything is flooding back. Charlie, Daisy. Lizzie. The accident. I was in a car accident. Dylan . . .

'Dylan?' I exclaim, panicked. I try to sit up, to swing my legs out of the bed but nothing happens. No movement. No feeling. 'Where is he?'

'Shh, relax, he's okay. He's with your mother,' says Theo.

I reach down tentatively with my hands and touch the

316

cool, flabby flesh of my thighs. My legs are still there but there's no feeling in them.

'But Lizzie Hamlyn . . . is Dylan hurt?' I stammer out the words.

'Meg Darley phoned the police. They arrested Elizabeth Hamlyn on the Swindon Road. She gave him up without a struggle. Dylan's okay. He's traumatised by the whole experience, obviously, but the doctor says that with time he'll be just fine.'

Tired tears of relief roll down my cheeks. If Dylan is alive and well, then the world is still on its axis and I can face anything.

'I want to see him,' I say.

'He'll be here tomorrow. He came this earlier this morning, but you were asleep.'

I try not to think about how frightening it must have been for him to see me in hospital like this.

Tentatively, I reach down under the covers and touch the tops of my thighs again. At least I think they're my legs. They feel waxy and soft and there's stubble growing where I've shaved. I take a piece of flesh between my thumb and forefinger and pinch hard. Nothing. They might as well be a stranger's limbs in the bed with me. It's strange, and very frightening.

'I can't feel my legs,' I say, fighting back a wave of alarm.

Theo nods and his brow furrows. He has that panicked

look he gets when I'm upset. He looks around over his shoulder as if he wants to escape. 'Yes, you had a car accident. The impact damaged your spine.'

I feel a heavy weight dropping in my chest. Spinal injuries are never good, and I can tell from the way Theo is avoiding my eyes that this is bad.

'Am I paralysed?' I whisper. I don't really believe that I could be, but I'm a worst-case-scenario kind of person. The flawed logic being if you think of the worst, then it can't possibly come true. It's worked for me many times before, but I suppose simple statistics mean the worst-case scenario will happen eventually, even if you try to pre-empt it.

Theo meets my eyes for a second, then looks away.

'Perhaps it's better if the doctors explain it to you.'

Coward.

'I want you to explain it. Am I paralysed?' The fact that he hasn't outright denied it is making me nervous and my voice is rising in alarm. I try moving again, nothing happens. I feel a cold chill run through me.

He brushes his hand through his hair. 'Um, I'm not sure I really understood what the doctors told me. There may be a temporary paralysis.'

'Don't lie to me please. People don't recover from spinal injuries.'

'There are some exercises you can do. We'll get through this, Cat. We'll fight this together.'

We? Together? 'You, me and Harper, you mean?' I say bitterly.

'Harper's out of the picture. You know that. I want us to get back together. I want to take care of you. I want to take care of Dylan.'

I stare out of the window, at the clouds sailing past in the blue sky. I don't like the way he says he wants to take care of me – the implication being that I'm not going to be able to take care of myself. And I'm still desperately worried about Dylan. Is he really safe? Could Lizzie try to take him again?

'What about Lizzie Hamlyn?' I ask.

'I told you, she's been arrested and charged. The police are doing a psychological evaluation.'

'You don't understand. She's really dangerous. She killed Charlie Holbrooke.'

'Yes, I know. The police know too.'

'They do?' I digest this information with mixed feelings. 'What I don't get,' I say, 'is how she did it. How did she get Charlie to let her in, in the middle of the night?'

Theo shrugs. Apparently, she knocked on Charlie's door and pretended that Meg had fallen and needed bandages.'

Hence the ransacked medicine box out on Charlies kitchen table, I think. *It was nothing to do with Ben.*

'And she's in custody? Because I don't want her anywhere

319

near Dylan,' I say, trying to sit up again, alarmed at the thought that Lizzie might be free to roam around.

'Shh, don't worry,' he says soothingly. 'She can't hurt Dylan now.'

I sink back on to the pillow feeling dizzy and only a little reassured.

'What about Delilah? Was it Lizzie who poisoned her?'

Theo nods grimly. 'Yes, she confessed. According to the police, you left the back door open and she let herself in.'

I think about Delilah and shudder. How much must Lizzie Hamlyn hate me to do something like that to such a sweet, innocent creature just to hurt me?

My voice lowers to a whisper. 'Did she tell the police about the hit and run? About Daisy? Do they know?'

He frowns and nods slowly. 'The police will come to speak to you later when you're better. But you shouldn't worry about that for now. You need to concentrate on getting better.'

Clouds sail past my window, shape-shifting as they go, and I pass the time by trying to work out what they resemble. That one, with the hint of grey at the edge, looks like a crab claw; another is like an embryo or a mermaid – I can't decide which. I wish I could defy gravity and float up there with them. It seems blissful, the idea of resting my head on a cloud. But I know that in reality a cloud would just be damp and cold, like fog.

I notice things like clouds now. I notice a lot that I never noticed before – for example, the way the leaves on the bush outside my window shiver in the wind and the spider's web that's tangled in its branches. There's no sign of the spider, but I can see a fly caught in the deceptively delicate thread. It isn't moving but that doesn't necessarily mean that it's dead.

I know how that fly feels. I know what it feels like to be trapped – how quickly anger and frustration can turn to despair, and despair to resignation. I know that prisoners try to find ways to keep their sanity – that they jealously store memories and feed off them slowly, rationing them so there will be enough to last. And that when they run out of memories their imaginations expand to fill the void.

Thirty-nine

Dr Blake tells me I'm lucky. Ha! Ha! According to her, I'm lucky that the damage to my spinal cord was in my back and not my neck because that means I still have full use of my upper body. Lucky, lucky me!

'I'll be straight with you,' she said as she sat opposite me this morning, her frank blue eyes unflinching. 'It's not likely you will heal completely from a spinal-cord injury, but you can maybe regain some motor function if you exercise regularly.'

I'm lucky. Well, everything is relative, I suppose.

After Dr Blake leaves, the physiotherapist arrives in a waft of positivity, badgering me to exercise, bending my legs, moving me around like a slab of meat. Then she leaves me alone again to sit and stare at the white walls and listen to Mary snoring in the bed next to mine. I must have drifted off to sleep because when I wake up, it's visiting time. And here is my mother, marching in like she owns the place, with Dylan clinging to her hand, grinning.

'Ah, thank goodness you're awake this time, Catherine,' she says in her usual disapproving tone, as if I've been deliberately unconscious, just to inconvenience her. 'How are you feeling, darling?'

'I've been better.'

She pulls up a chair and starts unloading her bag on to my bed. 'Now, I've brought you some books and some grapes. And Dylan's done you a drawing, haven't you, Dylan?'

Dylan nods bashfully and unfolds a piece of paper with an indecipherable scribble on it. He has written in a shaky hand: to Mummy love Dylan.

'That's beautiful, sweetheart,' I say. 'Thank you.'

He's looking wide-eyed at the wheelchair next to my bed.

'That's my new chair,' I tell him, trying to sound enthusiastic. 'Pretty cool, don't you think?'

'Can I sit in it?'

'I don't see why not.'

Dylan clambers into the wheelchair and sits there, legs swinging, while Mum gives me the rundown on things that have been happening at the WI and on her street.

'And Theo's been helping with fixing the fence,' she says. 'He's such a treasure, that man. You know, he's been here to the hospital every day. He slept here the night of the accident. He's so devoted to you.'

'Hmph,' I say. I don't want to say too much in front of Dylan, but she gets what I mean.

'You need to forgive him, Catherine. You know, "Forgiveness is the attribute of the strong". I think Gandhi said that.'

Perhaps my mother is right. Maybe I should forgive Theo. If he can forgive me for what I've done, then shouldn't I forget about Harper and give him another chance? There is no point in holding on to anger. It only festers and corrodes. I know that. But forgiving isn't always so easy. I'm not sure I can ever excuse Theo. And forgiving myself is even harder. What is it they had in South Africa? A truth and reconciliation commission. It was a good idea. Before you can even begin to forgive you have to start with the truth, not a vague semblance of it, but the whole truth and nothing but the truth – like in a court of law. I'm not so bad at the 'nothing-but-the-truth' part, but the whole truth? Now that's a different matter. And if I'm completely honest, there are a few things I've left out – that I've found hard to admit even to myself.

There's one thing in particular. A small detail. But the devil is in the detail, as they say.

2002

'Shit, shit. Is she dead?' Charlie appeared beside me. She looked like the Joker, mascara-blackened tears rolling down her cheeks. She tugged at her hair, as if she wanted to pull it out at the roots.

'Yes. I think so.' I tried to gather my wits. 'I suppose we need to call an ambulance,' I said. 'Have you got a phone?'

Charlie stared at me, her features frozen in horror. 'I left it at Nessa's.'

'It's okay. Mine's in my handbag.' I stood up and walked to the car in a dream and fumbled for my phone. My fingers were wet with the rain and the phone was slippery in my hands as I held it. I switched it on with shaking fingers and started to dial.

But my finger froze, poised over the last nine. I was suddenly paralysed. I couldn't bring myself to touch it. If I called an ambulance now, I'd be in big, big trouble and what good would it do? The little girl was already dead. It wouldn't make any difference to her. I looked over at Charlie who was crouching by the side of the road with her head in her hands. No one need ever know, I thought. And quickly, before I could change my mind, I pressed the button on the side, turning off the phone and I shoved it in the side pocket of the driver's seat.

'Shit,' I called out to Charlie.

'Did you get hold of them?' Charlie asked, as I got closer. She was shivering, whether from cold or shock I couldn't tell. I felt completely numb, as if I was in a dream, but at the same time all my senses were alert, like I was superhuman. It was the shock, I suppose.

'No,' I said through the rain. 'I couldn't. My phone's run out of battery.'

Acknowledgements

I owe a big debt of thanks to my brilliant, tactful and patient new editor, Florence Hare, to Anne Newman, whose thorough approach was very helpful in establishing an accurate timeline and to the whole team at Quercus, who have helped make this book a reality. I also want to thank Toby and Max for putting up with me talking endlessly about plots and characters and for never failing to make me laugh. Finally, as always, I would like to thank my partner, Jim, for more than I can express in words.